I0619483

Silent Partner

Book 9 in the By the Numbers series

Featuring Carly Turnquist, forensic accountant

By Leeann Betts

(c) 2018

ISBN13: 978-1-943688-50-0

Cover Design by Donna Schlachter

Published by PLS Bookworks, Denver, CO

Where Publishing Dreams Become Reality

Acknowledgements

First and foremost, to the Glory of God the Father,
His Son Jesus Christ, and the Holy Spirit—
without the One True God,
no story is worth telling.

Special thanks to Barbara Ann Dawson for the use of her name—
you are a special person for trusting me!

To Bill and Belle, Dave and Dewey—so good to meet you on the cruise,
and thanks for letting me use your alliterated names.
I couldn't have come up with anything better!

To James Walker of CruiseLaw.com – thanks for the
insight into Cruise Ship Law prior to 2010.
Your information fell right into line with the story!

To Eric Olson of PureTech Systems – thanks for the
information about Man Overboard Technology –
Exactly what I needed.

And, as always, to my precious husband Patrick.
Without you, these stories would never have come alive.

The grand life of luxury cruise
ships is stuck
in the 1800's, complete with
tuxedoed waiters,
brass spittoons, and
round-the-world tours.

Carly Turnquist, forensic
accountant,
is stuck in 2005,
right where she belongs.

Chapter 1

Carly Turnquist, forensic accountant, shifted her weight from one foot to the other. Would the line never move? Ahead and behind, all she saw were heads. To her left, a panoramic wall displayed the planning and construction for the current event on their sightseeing tour: the Space Needle.

The sepia photographs and illustrations, intended to depict the creation of the iconic structure in 1962, were easy on the eyes, but not exactly the stuff adventures were made of. In fact, if she had her way, she'd be over there chatting with the man decked out with an ear bud, hand gun, and Taser instead of standing in line. But husband Mike's mathematical mind wanted to check out the mechanical and structural systems of the landmark up close and personal.

She dragged him along to enough of her own points of interest. The least she could do was humor him. But just this once.

She'd talk to security later. Ask what happened if there was an earthquake. What safety precautions were in place to assure their arrival in one piece to the top and then back to the bottom of the structure? Maybe get him to open up about whether there'd ever been a murder in this place.

She glanced to the tower above and grinned. It would be the perfect setting for one of those scare-the-pants-off-you movies where the power went out and the actors were stranded at the top with a homicidal killer on the loose.

A man near the end of the line behind called out. "Line is moving, lady. You might have all day, but we don't."

Carly tossed the man the most insincere smile she could muster—actually half sneer, half snarl. There was something so satisfying about the fact he was at least six people back. "So-o-o-o-rry." She shuffled forward the fourteen inches left vacant by the person in front of her then leaned toward Mike on her right. "Some people's children."

Mike rolled his eyes. "Be nice. Maybe he worked all night and has to go back on the assembly line in a few hours."

Now it was her turn to roll her own orbits. "Right. He lives here, can see the tower any time he wants, and decided he had to visit today, in between shifts. Unlikely."

Her husband smiled which warmed her heart—and her attitude—immensely. "Could happen. Just sayin'."

She shook her head at his use—yet again—of his favorite new phrase. Seemed he looked for opportunities to toss out the words as an explanation for every outlandish comment. "Seriously, Mike. He's probably on a whirlwind tour of the country because he's got terminal cancer and is going to pop off in two weeks."

Mike bent so his breath tickled her ear. "If he was, would you let him take your spot in line?"

She adopted her most shocked look—eyes wide, brows raised. "Why? If he's going to be dead in a couple of weeks? He can't take his memories with him." She peered up at the underside of the tower again. "And I doubt this place would be on anybody's bucket list. Great Wall of China, North Pole, Australia. Now there's a bucket list. Not the Space Needle."

Mike shook his head. "Be nice."

"I am. If I wasn't, I'd have told him to back off and not crowd my personal space. This is America, after all. We expect at least three feet of room all around us. Not like we're in Africa or something."

"I don't know if that applies in lines or rock concerts."

She snorted. "Apparently not."

Mike turned back to reading the interpretation board about how deep the foundation was set for the Needle while Carly returned to watching the crowd. That really was her favorite pastime—people watching. Over there, just beginning their shuffle trek up the ramp-like walkway, a young mother with a toddler in a stroller and an infant in one of those front-worn packs.

Boy, she has her hands full.

Which reminded her of her own grandchildren, older than these by several years. She clasped Mike's arm. "I miss the grands."

"We've only been gone two days."

"Doesn't mean I can't miss them. I think it's knowing they're three thousand miles away."

"You'll see them in a week's time. After the cruise."

Yes, the cruise. The real reason they were in Seattle to begin with. A gift from her best friend Gloria Markham to thank Carly for saving her from a shyster who tried to get her to change her will to his benefit. A gift delayed over a year because of scheduling conflicts and prior commitments.

A gift she was determined to enjoy. Seven days of sailing the Pacific on a luxury liner with two thousand strangers she'd never see again.

Well, the sailing part was good—the two thousand people were simply part of the bargain. As a dyed-in-the-wool introvert—although Mike always argued the point when she made claim to that personality trait—meeting new people was a chore that left her exhausted. Still, she'd make the best of it on the ship, be nice to folks, and then return home and be happy to cocoon for a month. At least.

She tucked her arm through his and pulled him close. "I can't wait to get onboard."

He nodded. "Me, too. And even though this won't be a working vacation for either of us, I'm sure you'll find enough trouble to keep both of us busy."

She pinched his arm. "Mike Turnquist, what a terrible thing to say. Anybody listening would think I purposely—"

He held up his free hand in surrender. "Fine. You don't go looking for trouble. But you must admit, bodies and killers are drawn to you like metal shavings to a magnet."

"Just because I—"

"Just because you can't go anywhere without getting involved in something—usually law enforcement-related—doesn't make you a magnet. I know. I've heard it all before." He turned to her and gripped her by the shoulders. "But you must admit, somehow trouble follows you."

"We've been here two days and nothing's happened." She had to make him see she'd turned over a new leaf. "And standing in line has been uneventful."

"So far."

She gestured to the check-in desk about twenty feet ahead, then waved her hand at the fifty or so people still in line behind. "None of these look like hardened criminals." The man behind glared at her, and she lowered her voice. "'Cept maybe him."

"Be nice."

Someone brushed past her, and Mike gripped her arm to keep her from losing her balance. She stared after him. "Excuse me!"

The person, wearing a hoodie fastened tight beneath his chin, along with oversized aviator sunglasses, turned and stared at her, his mouth in a straight line.

Carly shivered and clung to Mike. "That's just plain rude."

"Maybe he can't see because of the dark glasses."

"Or he doesn't have any manners. Did you see the way he stared at me?"

"Let it be. We're on vacation."

But Carly couldn't ignore the young man's behavior. The spring sunshine warmed the ramp area, and with the added bodies, the air was warm. Much too warm to be bundled up in a fleece jacket. Seattle, mild at this time of year, had enjoyed uncharacteristically summer-like weather for the past few days.

Anybody who dressed—and acted—that way was suspicious. At least in her books.

She kept her gaze fixed on him. He wove in and out of the line, bumping an overweight man ahead of them before easing away. When he turned around again, she jutted out her chin and made eye contact with him, resisting the urge to point to her eyes then to him in the universal code for 'I'm watching you'. Instead, she returned his stare, narrowing her eyes when he glared at her. The man turned, glanced from side to side, then blended into the crowd.

She shrugged the tension from her shoulders. "Good, he's gone."

Mike looked up from reading yet another factoid about the Needle. "Who's gone?"

"The guy who bumped into me."

Mike scanned the crowd. "Oh, him."

She patted her back pocket where her cell phone resided. Still there. But something about the man's behavior seemed out of place. Why did he find it necessary to insert himself into the line of folks waiting to enter the elevator to ride up the tower? If he had a ticket, he should wait his turn like everybody else. If he didn't—her ticket. Where was her ticket? She checked the other pocket. Not there. Front pocket? No, too small. She shoved her hands into her jacket pockets. Empty except for a candy wrapper and a tissue. "Mike, do you have the tickets?"

He nodded.

"Can you show them to me?"

He sighed. "Why?"

"That guy. He was acting strange."

Another sigh. "You're the one acting weird. You're looking for a mystery where there is none. The guy was drunk or high on something. He twisted an ankle. He was looking for a friend. Thought you were his mother, maybe."

"Mike, the tickets."

Her husband pulled their admission to the tower from his inside jacket pocket. "Satisfied?"

She mumbled insincere thanks. So much for that idea. Maybe Mike was right. She had too much crime on the brain.

A shout from ahead caught her attention. "My wallet. It's gone."

She smiled up at her husband. "That's the man that strange dude accidentally bumped into." She created air quotes with her fingers. "Only not so accidentally, it seems." When Mike opened his mouth to speak, she laid a finger across his lips. "Hold my place."

She hurried up the remaining distance to the man, whose wide eyes and tinge of perspiration on his face communicated his concern. By this time, a small crowd encircled the victim, including Mr. Security Man.

Oh, good, maybe now I can ask him some questions. After we catch that kid.

The officer mumbled into a microphone clipped to his collar. "BOLO pick pocket. No description."

Carly stepped forward. "I know what he looks like."

Officer Ramzan, identified by his name tag, stepped forward. "You do? How do you know this?"

His swarthy skin, dark hair, and accent indicated his ethnicity hailed him from India or Pakistan, perhaps. Which fascinated Carly. Why would a man travel so far to a strange land to take on a job as a security guard at a tourist attraction?

But that was a question for another time and place.

"The same guy bumped into me back there." She pointed to where Mike stood. He raised a hand and waved at her. "He didn't get anything because we don't keep our billfolds in our back pocket." She glanced at the victim. "Carly Turnquist. I noticed him because of the hoodie and sunglasses."

The large man nodded. "John Porter. I usually do that, too, but these crazy sweatpants don't have front pockets." His brow drew down and he glared at the woman standing beside him. "Told you I didn't like them. Now I know why." He wrung his hands together. "I've gotta get my wallet back. It has all our vacation cash, my ID, credit cards, everything."

Carly pointed to the last place she saw the man. "He went that way."

Officer Ramzan nodded. "Would you recognize him again?"

"Yes. So long as the mustache wasn't fake and he hasn't changed clothes, that is." She headed toward the exit, the guard in tow. "Of course, if it was me, I'd have a fake 'stache. And a reversible hoodie. Ditch the sunglasses."

"Do you usually go around telling law enforcement how you would commit a crime?"

She slowed and he trod on her heels before stopping behind her. "No. But I think about it a lot. My husband says I draw criminals like vultures to a carcass."

"You sound almost proud of the fact."

"Not really. But he's right." She spotted her quarry through the gift store window. "He's in there."

"Where?"

"Near the book display. No sunglasses. Hood down. Red fleece jacket. And mustache." She pushed through the door. "I'll go around and—"

The guard slowed her by gripping her forearm. "Thank you for your help, but we'll take over from here."

"Oh, sure, let me find the guy and you make the collar."

"Please, ma'am, stand aside and let us do our job."

"Fine." She folded her arms over her chest and let him pass her. He pulled the door open and entered the shop while she stepped back out of the way. "But I don't have to like it."

As she watched, the young man—for now that his face was exposed she could see he was barely out of his teens—pressed in behind a slightly stooped older lady, bumping into her and knocking her handbag to the floor of the shop. She lost her balance and careened into a display of stuffed animals before sinking to the floor in a heap. Her attacker apologized and bent to pick up the purse, made as if to return it, then deked left before tucking the bag under his jacket and heading for the door.

The security guard, intent on talking into his microphone and directing two other officers to move through the crowded shop, continued on his way while the new victim struggled to get to her feet with the aid of several onlookers.

Once upright, the woman called out. "Oh, no. He stole my purse. Help."

All three officers converged on her while the thief made his getaway.

Straight into Carly's path.

She stepped away from the wall and jammed her foot against the bottom of the door as he pushed through. When it didn't open, he tried pulling it toward him. He glanced over his shoulder at the security officers who, by now, realized their quarry was escaping, then back at her.

She waggled a finger at him then did what she wanted to do earlier but hadn't as Officer Ramzan's hand gripped the kid's shoulder.

Two fingers in a V-shape pointed to her eyes and then to him.

I'm watching you.

He glared at her then mouthed words for her benefit only: And I'm going to find you.

Chapter 2

The next afternoon, Carly strolled down the long hallway leading from the aft of the ship toward the bank of elevators that would carry her to the Exploration Deck Four. Mike was already on the observation deck listening to a talk by the onboard naturalist about wildlife they might view along the way, his camera at the ready. Which meant she had plenty of time for her own appointment: a book club discussion led by a famous mystery author, Barbara Ann Dawson.

While she enjoyed the light mysteries swaddled in romance, she always figured out the killer by the middle of the book, although the motive usually left her confused. Somehow, the reason for the crime never seemed quite strong enough. Murderers she knew of personally—and there were several over the years, including a close friend, a man she didn't like, and a mobster—had fairly straightforward reasons for doing what they did. Maybe she was missing something. After all, the write-up in the daily itinerary heralded her as 'the new Agatha Christie'.

Carly snorted. Not hardly. Nobody could compete with Dame Agatha. At least in Carly's books. She chuckled. If she ever felt an urge to pen a book, hers would be limited to the credit and debit, accounting type. No, siree. She'd have nothing important or exciting to say in a book.

She nodded to their room steward, Samuel, who told them to call him *Sam the Man* or *Sam I Am*. "Thanks, Sam the Man, for the warm welcome."

He half-bowed. "My pleasure, madam."

She rounded the corner then turned right for the brass elevators. While she waited, she studied the frosted sea dollar-shaped light fixture and the warm cherrywood paneling enveloping the elevators. Elegant burgundy and black carpeting muffled footsteps and delicate sconce lighting on the walls created a gas-lamp ambiance.

The doors of the elevator furthest from her—wasn't that always the way?—swished open, and she stepped inside. An older couple eyed her up and down then sidled closer together in the corner of the car.

At her destination, she stepped out and held the door for her co-travelers, but they remained huddled in the corner as though afraid to exit. She tossed them a smile, turned a corner, and paused to read the small marquis sign that told her where to go.

She snorted. Mike liked to tell her where to go. Maybe in his next life, he'd be a sign.

Stifling a chuckle, she headed forward to the library where the meeting was due to start in a couple of minutes. When she entered, the sight of the shelves lined with books gave her a momentary longing for the library back in Bear Cove. But only for a second. She could spend her entire cruise in this one room, so long as somebody brought her food and drink.

But then her husband's voice screamed in her head. Why would they pay for a cruise so she could read her way from Seattle to Juneau and back? They could have stayed home and saved all that money...

Except this was a gift from a dear friend. One they couldn't turn down. Gloria even made certain to load their onboard account with enough spending money that they wouldn't run out in a month of Sundays. In fact, her lavishness knew no bounds. Included in the gift were two days in Seattle and a rental car so they could see that part of the country before their embarkation.

Hence the trip to the Space Needle yesterday.

She sighed. If nothing else exciting happened on this cruise, she'd gotten her money's worth—proverbially speaking—already.

So if she chose to stay in this room for the entire cruise, he wouldn't be able to complain.

Well, he could, but it wouldn't matter.

She checked the almost-full room. Only one seat left. In the front row. She groaned. Mike's insistence that nobody in their right mind would go on a cruise and spend the first hour at a mystery book club talk, turned out to be wrong.

She'd take great delight in telling him so.

She sidled and crab-walked her way to the lone empty chair and sank onto the hard folding plastic seat. Thankfully it was more upholstered than her derriere as she wriggled into position. A young man sat to her left, and a mid-to-late-thirties woman to her right. She nodded to both.

Her compatriot to the left offered his hand, which she shook. "Edward Byrne. I can't believe I'm going to meet Ms. Dawson."

She smiled. Fan club president, no doubt. "Yes, it's very exciting."

"I've read all her books. Several times. In chronological order. How about you?"

"Just once. In order."

He blinked from behind round wire-rimmed glasses. "Surely you own them?"

"Um, no. Library."

Several more blinks. "Oh. Not a *true* fan, then. Simply a reader."

Not only fan club president, but probably the only member of his local chapter. "I always figure out the solution before the main character does."

This time he seemed to shrink back from her, whether in mock horror or real she wasn't certain. "Really? I find her plotting to be so intricate and deep that I'm never quite certain of the outcome. Even after she explains it, I am still baffled by her brilliance."

Carly pondered her response. *Baffled by her brilliance* wasn't exactly how she'd sum up the often convoluted and unsubstantiated reasoning used to explain the outcome. While she did enjoy the stories, she found the author placed more emphasis on the romance than the mystery. Which was fine. But character development far outweighed plotting. At least, in her opinion. Still, the man seemed genuine in his assessment, if a little juvenile in his hero worship.

She eased back in her chair. "I'm looking forward to gaining insight into her writing process. How she comes up with the ideas. The characters. She has a real knack for titles with a twist."

A couple more myopic blinks, then he turned to the person on his left and struck up a conversation.

She shrugged and turned to the woman on her right. Perhaps she'd have better luck with someone of her own species. "Hello."

"Monica Maguire. Librarian from Riverside, California." The woman, her dark hair accented with highlights, nodded. "Good day." She leaned closer, and Carly caught a whiff of an old-fashioned cologne like lily of the valley mixed with something else—nervousness? "I see you've met the national fan club president, Teddy Bear, already." She grinned. "That's what we call him. Behind his back, of course."

The name was so appropriate. Carly nodded. "I suspected he was president. He's very passionate about the author and her writing."

"Most of us in this room chose this cruise because she was lecturing on it. How about you?"

Carly shook her head. "Didn't know a thing until we boarded. Saw the announcement in the schedule. Is she speaking more than once?"

"Oh, yes. Every day. Same time, same place. Different topic."

"Goodness, that is a bonus. I hope it doesn't conflict with anything else we want to do."

"Do?" Apparently the blinking affectation was a mandatory skill for membership in the club. "Most here book all other events around this. We simply cannot do it any other way."

Carly nodded noncommittally. Fanatics always creeped her out. No telling what they might expect of others. "Do you think—"

Monica stopped her with a shushing sound. "Here she comes." She stood, joining the majority of the other attendees, and clapped boisterously for several seconds before the entire group—or at least those in the know—broke into a well-rehearsed chorus of "Barbara Ann", an old Beach Boys song. After resuming her seat, Monica whispered to Carly. "She's my hero."

A tall, lanky woman who looked more suited to walking across meadows or making her own goat cheese than sitting behind a typewriter—or a computer—writing romantic mysteries, strode across the front of the room and plopped a notebook and bottle of water on the lectern. She adjusted her glasses and then the microphone before peering at the group assembled before her.

An old line trickled across Carly's memory, paraphrased for the occasion: *Miss Dawson, I presume?*

After much rustling of papers and settling of behinds from the audience, the author spoke. "Thanks so much for stopping by today. Since this is the first day of our week-long adventure, I'll give you some of my background, and then a mini-agenda of what we'll discuss in the coming days. At the end of each talk, you'll have the opportunity to purchase books and I'll be happy to sign them for you. Please, don't ask me to sign anything you bought somewhere else. And no stories about how you picked up the book at a thrift store for a quarter."

Ms. Dawson paused then tossed the group a half-smile. "I really had that happen to me at a conference one time." She waited while a quiet chuckle circulated the group before continuing. "And the funny thing was, this woman was so serious about her joy over purchasing a book and then asking me to sign it for her. I mean, she was stealing my bread and butter, so to speak, since authors don't earn royalties on re-sales."

Teddy Bear—Edward—called out. "Did you sign it for her?"

"I didn't have the heart to say no. I mean, she was so—so innocent, you know?"

Another laugh. Carly cringed inside. That would be exactly the kind of thing she might do. Revealing her cheap—frugal—side to Teddy Bear might make her the butt of jokes in the future. She could hear the comments now. *Imagine. She doesn't even buy books. Gets them from the library. Next she'll be scouring yard sales and used book stores.*

She sighed. Oh, well. Unlikely she'd ever have the opportunity to take another cruise, so she'd never know what these kind of people thought about others not like them.

These kind of people.

She turned a few degrees in her seat to study the twenty or so others in the room. And exactly what kind of people were they? If she met them on the street, she'd think them ordinary, run-of-the-mill people. Well, perhaps not Teddy Bear. With his gauche eyeglasses highlighted with little sparkly stones at the corners, and his not-quite-punk hairstyle, he'd stand out in a crowd—no matter how large.

Even the author. She'd pass her on the street and not take second notice of. Or would she? There was something in the set of the woman's chin, in the piercing way she looked at people that might draw her attention.

A couple of middle-aged women in the back row chattered on about their winnings in the casino on a previous cruise. Carly snorted to herself. Unlikely. The slot machines were intended to make money for the cruise line, not for the gambler. In fact, the only machine she knew about where she was guaranteed to receive a hundred percent return was the ATM at Guest Services.

Miss Dawson cleared her throat softly. "Thank you so much for coming to our little book club discussion today. I want to thank several of you for making this possible." She went on to mention Edward as well as two or three others who waved or half-stood when their names were mentioned. "Without the encouragement and assistance of my loyal fans, we'd all be shopping at the onboard stores or losing just as much money at the one-armed bandits."

She paused while chuckles rippled around the room. "Today we'll delve into my latest novel, *Deadly Encounters*, and then we'll talk a little about writing mysteries and how to use book clubs to your advantage, whether you're a reader or a writer. And the best part is, it won't matter whether you've read my book or not." Another pause for yet another round of laughter. "So, let's begin."

As it happened, Carly recently completed this particular book and so was able to follow the discussion without getting lost too many times. Teddy Bear and Monica tended to hog the spotlight by answering questions, some of which seemed repetitive. What made Arial choose Spenser for her partner in the scavenger hunt? Why did Spenser think he was better than everybody else? And what event in the killer's past propelled him onto the path of crime?

Carly listened with an ear for details she might have overlooked in the mystery part of the story, because honestly, she figured out who the killer was by eliminating the other suspects early on, but she never quite knew the why. Apart from the inciting event of the victim angering the killer by cutting in front of him at a coffee shop, there seemed no other good reason for the murder. In fact, most of the discussion—and indeed the book—focused on the on-again, off-again relationship between the two love interests.

As the time drew near the end, Carly raised her hand. Miss Dawson peered over her bifocals and nodded in her direction, so Carly asked her question. "I know that Spenser felt slighted by his father and so had a lot of anger issues, which Arial exasperated by stepping in front of him in the line, but really, that seems like a poor reason to kill her. Had they met before? Did he date someone who always did this? Was she simply an archetype in his life? A bullying mother or sibling, perhaps?"

A collective gasp circled the room, and Carly sensed that everybody wanted to know the answer to this question but were afraid to ask.

Or perhaps they were simply afraid.

Miss Dawson tapped a manicured fingernail on the lectern several times before answering. She cleared her throat in a most genteel way and sighed then pasted on a smile that didn't quite meet her eyes. "Well, fans, what do you think?"

Teddy Bear shot to his feet and faced Carly, peering down at her. "I think your question is most inappropriate."

Monica raised her eyebrows and offered a half-smile. "Really, dear, we don't concern ourselves with the why. Only the who. And Miss Dawson does that most splendidly, don't you think?"

The rest of the group erupted in applause and nods, while Carly seethed inside. In fact, Miss Dawson didn't do the mystery most splendidly. The whodunit portion of the plot always felt tacked on, like a paper tail on a children's game. There for looks only. Perhaps to fill a few more pages. To give the love interests something to do other than sip coffee, hold hands, and stare dreamily into each other's eyes.

She glared up at Edward until he resumed his seat. "Thank you for your insightful answers."

Inside, she transported back to the time when she was four and the bully on the street pushed her off her tricycle and stole her bike.

Only, in that case, after she asked her father for help and he told her to get her own bike back, she marched over, gave that kid a shove, and regained her property.

If she could figure out how to do that now, she'd do it.

As it was, she remained silent for politeness' sake. Mike often said her sharp tongue could gut a whale in three strokes.

No point cutting a strip off somebody on her first day at sea. She had to live with these people for the next week.

Chapter 3

Butterflies danced in Carly's stomach, and thankfully they had nothing to do with the gentle rocking of the cruise ship in response to the increased wave activity as they left landfall behind and headed for the open sea.

No, this excitement focused entirely on the activity she enjoyed best next to sleuthing and listening in on other people's conversations—eating.

Mike stood beside her, looking dapper indeed in his black polo shirt and pants, topped by a herringbone-patterned sports jacket. While this wasn't one of the more formal gala night dinners, she insisted on making a good impression. After all, this wasn't the Lanai Buffet line—this was the Captain's Table Restaurant. Not only linen napkins, but tablecloths instead of the woven placemats, and servers wearing ties and waist-length black jackets.

The hostess smiled broadly. "Your name, please?" After Mike introduced them, Emehlia, a charming olive-skinned beauty from Indonesia identified by her name tag, checked the seating chart. "Do you mind sharing a table?"

Before Carly could reply, Mike answered for them. "Not at all." He turned to her. "We love meeting new people, don't we?"

She groaned inside. All thoughts of a quiet dinner where she could eat every morsel, including licking her fingers if she liked, and not feel like some svelte model-type was counting her mouthfuls slipped away. She pasted on a smile. "Yes, dear."

His brow drew down a moment before he turned back to Emehlia when she gestured to another server waiting to lead them to their table. "Please follow Ari."

Carly gritted her teeth behind her smile and followed her husband and the young man to a table for four in a corner.

Ari, also from Indonesia, pulled out a chair for her. Well, she could get used to this really quick. She sat, then he attended to Mike, seating him beside her, before returning to her. The young man opened her plumed napkin and placed it in her lap. She grinned. Had he also heard she was a messy eater at times?

After preparing Mike to eat—seemed it was the thing they did and had no bearing on previously-acquired information—Ari folded his hands. "Shall I send the sommelier?"

Pleased she knew he was asking about the wine steward and not a soup—a mistake she made one time before in a fancy restaurant, much to her embarrassment and tickling Mike's funny bone—she kept quiet while Mike answered. "Not for us, thanks."

He nodded and left them to ponder the menu, a delightful collection of tasty tidbits. Well, she hoped more than tidbits. Included in the cost of the cruise, this was the way to live. No cooking. No cleaning. No making her bed. No grocery shopping. No living out of a suitcase while she experienced something different every day.

She returned the menu to the table and settled back in her seat. The dining room was semi-full. Apparently they weren't the only passengers who liked to eat dinner sooner rather than later.

Mike set his menu aside and reached for her hand. "Isn't this romantic?"

She smiled. "Sure. Dinner with two strangers and a hundred of our closest friends."

"Not too much for you, is it?"

"Nope." She squeezed his fingers. "I made a promise to myself to relax and enjoy the trip. Meet people. Have fun."

"And not get involved in a mystery?"

"No mystery. I mean, what could happen on a cruise ship?"

He groaned. "I asked myself the same thing when we went to the Space Needle, and look what happened."

"I couldn't very well just let that kid get away with stealing the poor man's vacation, could I? Or knocking that old woman down and taking her purse?"

He shook his head. "It's never your fault, is it?"

Despite his downturned brow and stern words, the smile tickling at the corners of his mouth took the sting out.

She tapped the menu. "What are you having for dinner?"

"I thought the shrimp cocktail, house salad, and beef. What about you?"

"More importantly, what about dessert?"

He chuckled. "Strawberry cheesecake, of course."

"And I'm having—"

He held up his free hand. "Let me guess. Escargots. Beet Salad. Spinach ravioli. And skip dessert."

She wrinkled her nose. "You are incorrigible. You know all that stuff tastes like—"

"I know." He laughed. "Like dirt." He shrugged. "I've never met anybody who says that about food."

"Well, I have." She opened the small book in front of her that touted the restaurant's offerings. "Shrimp cocktail. Italian Wedding Soup. The duck. And chocolate torte."

"I knew that."

She looked up as Ari returned to their table, a couple following in his wake. He repeated the process of pulling out a chair for each of them and placing the napkins before asking about the wine steward.

The gentleman nodded. "Yes, please." After Ari left, he turned to Mike and offered his hand. "Hi. I'm Bill, and this is Belle."

Mike returned the gesture. "Good to meet you. Mike and Carly."

Carly smiled at Belle. "That's a beautiful necklace."

Belle's hand went to her neck. "A gift from Bill."

"Anniversary?"

The woman's cheeks colored. "We're not married. Partners for many years. I live in Illinois, and he lives in Florida."

Oops. Better not make assumptions.

Carly tossed her a half-grimace. "Sorry."

Belle smiled. "No worries. Happens all the time. I guess we've been together so many years, we act like an old married couple."

Ari reappeared and waited while the couple made their dinner selections, then the sommelier sidled up and set a previously-opened bottle of white wine on the table. Bill nodded, and the steward pulled a corkscrew from his vest pocket before opening and then pouring the wine.

Bill sipped the liquid. "We bring our own on board. Even with the cork charge, it's cheaper than buying it here." He gestured with his glass. "Would you like a glass?"

"No, thanks." Mike sipped his iced tea. "Are you retired?"

Bill pulled back a few inches. "Do I look old enough to be retired?" He patted his receding hairline. "Maybe I do need a toupee, Belle." When Mike's cheeks colored, he laughed. "Just trying to get your goat, old man. Of course I'm retired. Almost twenty years now. But I retired young. Used to be an engineer. You?"

"Computer programmer. Still working. Run my own business."

"Ah, can't hold down a real job, huh?" Another uncomfortable silence, then he guffawed, drawing the attention of diners at nearby tables. "Joking."

Mike's shoulders relaxed, and Carly breathed easier. What looked like the birth of a disaster now appeared to turn the corner. Mike addressed Belle. "How do you put up with this man?"

Belle giggled and nudged her partner with her shoulder. "Turn off my hearing aid."

Carly laughed. She liked this woman already. "Did you have a career?"

"Secretary. It was about the only choice in those days. Or a nurse. And I can't stand the sight of blood. Women today have it so much easier, don't you think?"

"Well, I think more career options are available, if that's what you mean."

Belle leaned forward and reached across the table as though thinking of grasping her hand. To nip that notion in the bud, Carly picked up her water glass and sipped.

Belle lowered her voice as though sharing a confidence. "That's true, dear. And women are so bright these days. Not like when I was just starting out. Our men didn't expect us to be able to out-think or out-talk them in anything other than changing diapers or doing laundry." She paused and glanced out toward the ocean, her eyes filling, before turning back and completing her thought. "I wasn't very good at either of those tasks, or so my ex constantly told me."

Carly smiled. "Did you hire out the laundry? And the diaper changing?"

A single tear slid down the woman's well-made-up cheek. "No children. We couldn't have them. One of the reasons we split." She leaned toward her. "He re-married and has six kids now. Serves him right."

Carly cringed at the implication of Belle's words. "I don't see children as a punishment."

"Sometimes they can be."

Determined to change the tone of the conversation, Carly persevered. "I, for one, am glad for changes in how men view women. Those were important years, as women stepped forward and insisted on being given equal treatment in the workplace. Equal pay. Equal education opportunities. To make a difference in the world."

The older woman patted the table. "You were but a child at the time, looking at it from the outside in. I lived it. I wanted to put my husband and children first. It was my chance to make a difference in my own little world." She exhaled loudly. "But it wasn't to be."

Carly glanced at the woman's left hand ring finger. Bare. "So how did that work for you?"

She tilted her head to one side. "Not so well, I guess. Until I met Bill. He has two daughters and eleven lovely grands. Who call me Gramma. Kind of makes up for the lost years, I guess. Fulfills me in a way I can't explain."

Any ire fermenting in Carly over her new friend's old-fashioned attitudes—at least, as far as Carly was concerned—slipped away like a vapor on the wind. In her own previous marriage, she didn't have the advantage of a stable relationship or secure finances. Her first husband, an abusive alcoholic, rarely held down a job for more than two paychecks, and she was forced to work. A succession of entry-level positions led to her current profession as an accountant. One thing she could thank him for.

If he were still alive.

Killed in an auto accident while coming home drunk one night, his death freed her to step out on her own and experience the world. And meet Mike, a recent widower, with two grown children who she now called her own.

Life was funny. From despair to joy in such a short time.

Maybe her daughter Denise was right. God did care. If Mike was one of those gifts Denise talked about, she surely was blessed.

Their appetizers arrived—everybody chose the shrimp cocktail—and conversation halted while they ate. The second course followed a few minutes later, then the main course. Sprinkled amidst murmurs of appreciation and offers amongst couples to share a tidbit from their plates were reminiscences of prior cruises, books they'd read recently, and favorite movies.

After dessert and coffee, Carly sat back in her chair. "Well, that was fun. And delicious." She eyed Belle's half-eaten bread pudding with vanilla bean ice cream. "Too full to finish?"

"Oh, dear, I need to keep my figure trim. Unlike you married gals, we single ladies must stay in shape."

Carly gritted her teeth. Belle reminded her of another friend who sometimes spoke her mind with a dash of vinegar. Thankfully, at least with Gloria, no harm was ever intended. She patted her tummy. "Well, I promised myself to have dessert only at special meals. This is our first semi-formal dinner, and I fully intend to enjoy myself."

"Well, whatever works for you. Me, I never finish anything on my plate. It's an old rule I established early on."

Time to change the subject.

"Is this your first cruise?"

Belle nodded. "Yes. I won it in a supermarket drawing. How gauche, wouldn't you agree?"

Carly wasn't sure of woman's definition. "Our first, too. From a grateful client."

"How nice for you dear. But to have to work at your age." Belle patted Carly's hand. "Still, somebody has to, I guess."

Carly turned to Mike. "What shall we do next?"

He drained his coffee cup and pushed his empty dessert plate away. "I heard about a singer from one of those Broadway musicals. She's in the Explorer's Lounge in about twenty minutes." He smiled at Bill. "Want to join us?"

Bill and Belle exchanged a glance then he shook his head. "I think these old *retired* folks need to head for their bunks."

Belle giggled again. "Not to sleep, however. There is something about the rocking of a ship that ignites passion." She set her napkin on her plate. "It's been a blast. Maybe we'll see you another time."

Mike stood and pulled out Carly's chair. "Look forward to it. We've really enjoyed ourselves. Haven't we?"

Carly nodded. Despite her earlier desire to dine alone, the time passed quickly and the conversation was fun. "We have. Before we separate, let's share contact information so we can keep in touch."

Bill patted his pockets. "I have a business card here." He offered an ivory slip toward her. "There you go."

Carly glanced at it. "I thought you were retired. Says here you work for an oil and gas company."

"Consultant only. Geophysical engineer. That's me."

He offered his arm to Belle and two preceded them from the dining room. Carly and Mike followed in their wake, thanking the serving staff once again for a delightful meal. By the time they reached the bank of elevators, their new friends were gone.

Mike led the way past the Faberge display, the library, and through the shopping area. Carly hung back and enjoyed the sparkle and allure of necklaces and earrings.

Mike paused and pointed to a particularly pretty pendant. "Tanzanite, according to the sign."

She admired the sky-blue stone surrounded with diamonds. "Pretty. But where would I wear it?"

He chuckled. "Yeah, it would clash with your sweats."

She grasped his hand and pulled him along. "I'd rather have another cruise than a necklace like that. Two cruises, maybe, for that price."

The lounge was filling up fast, and the only empty seats were at the bar. Carly hiked her skirt up to give her enough room to sit on the stool, wishing her legs weren't quite so short. When the server came along, her tray balanced expertly in one hand, Carly shook her head. "Nothing right now. Thanks."

A mid-forties chanteuse, svelte in a sleeveless sequined sheath, stepped up behind the mic and smiled out at the audience, making eye contact around the room. "Thanks for coming, folks, on our first night out. My name is Penny Goodnight. And before you ask, yes, it is my real name." She waited while a ripple of laughter circulated the room. "Tonight I'll perform hits from the blues era, beginning with a song *a la* Benny Goodman." She pressed a button on a piece of electronic equipment on a stand beside her. "Forgive me for not bringing my band with me, but it's hard to travel with all that brass."

Mike nudged Carly. "This is nice."

"Yes, it is. We'd never go to a bar in Bear Cove and listen to a singer."

"If Bear Cove even had a bar, it would be a local band of the guys playing a wash board and a mouth harp." He glanced around. "Already feels like an adventure, doesn't it?"

She smiled at him. "You usually say simply being married to me is an adventure."

He rolled his eyes. "I mean a good adventure this time. No mysteries. No bodies. No law enforcement."

She shook her head. "It's only the first day of the cruise. Don't get your hopes up."

In reality, she looked forward to spending quality time with her husband. Time that wasn't pigeon-holed between unsatisfactory talks with recalcitrant police chiefs or detectives who snubbed her because she didn't carry a badge.

A nice, peaceful week of sleeping, eating, and experiencing new things.

The singer addressed the audience again. "Hope you'll enjoy this next song. It's one I wrote myself, about a broken heart and the bad boy responsible."

Miss Goodnight began with a soulful rendition reminiscent of *St. Louis Blues*. She was quite good, her voice matured by time and practice, and the emotion of the experience written all over her well-made-up face.

Carly settled in, her head resting against her husband's strong, sure shoulder.

Yes, indeedy. A week of living in a dream world.

What could go wrong?

$ $ $

Two hours later, Mike slipped his key card into the lock on their stateroom, then stepped back to allow Carly to precede him. At her squeal, he stepped in, his heart thudding.

Could the woman not go anywhere without encountering drama?

She stared at the bed. Then she laughed and pointed. "Oh, it's a puppy dog. With a bone in his mouth."

Mike peered over her shoulder. She was right. Bath and hand towels expertly formed a floppy-eared pup, complete with googly eyes. And beside the creation, two squares of dark chocolate. His favorite.

He chuckled. "Looks like our stewards have been busy."

"You're right. The bed is turned down, and—oh, chocolate."

He scooped them out of her reach. "Dark. You don't want it."

She snatched one from his grip. "Chocolate is chocolate. Although I hope tomorrow it's milk."

They perched on the bed, munched on their treat, and petted the dog for a minute.

Carly turned to him. "Penny was good, don't you think?"

He nodded. "And I thought her play on her name at the end was cute."

"Yeah. 'Now, folks, Penny Goodnight bids you a good night.'" She giggled. "I half-expected her to tweak her ear lobe or something."

"Like Carol Burnett used to do?"

She reached over and tugged on his ear. "Just like that. It was her way of saying she loved her grandmother."

Those were good days, watching the program with his family gathered around the floor model television. Laughing at the antics of the characters. Life was a lot simpler then.

Unlike life with Carly.

Not that he wanted the former without the latter.

He waggled his eyebrows at her, a motion that always brought a smile. "Ready for sleep?"

She pursed her lips. "I think I'd like a cup of decaf, a snack, and a few minutes to read."

He lifted the receiver and dialed for stateroom service, placed their order, then hung up. "Twenty minutes."

She stood. "Sounds good. Shower for me."

Another waggle. "We could save water."

She laughed. "Not a chance." She headed for the bathroom. "But we could talk while I'm in there."

He followed her as she shed her clothing and dropped the articles into the hanging clothes basket, then sat on the closed toilet lid when she disappeared behind the curtain and turned on the water. "What do you want to talk about?"

"I thought the story Penny told about being conned by someone close to her was really sad."

Mike recalled the tale. A trusted friend. Missing money. Placing blame on her. "I wondered if she ended up going to jail over that."

Carly gasped. "Hadn't thought of that. Maybe so. How terrible."

"Nothing worse than being blamed for something you didn't do."

"True."

Steam built up on the mirrors, and Mike flipped on the exhaust fan to clear the room. "Do you think it's why she sings the blues?"

"Maybe. She sure has that sultry voice for the genre though, doesn't she?"

That was true. "And she has a great range of vocals, too."

"Do you think there is any way she might still hold a grudge against that person?"

"Don't know." Mike studied the silhouette of his wife through the thin water-resistant material. "Would you?"

"Guess it depends on how serious it was. If I went to prison for somebody, maybe."

"Thinking as someone who loves a mystery, what do you think happened?"

"Embezzlement, maybe. Or maybe she was married to a cat burglar who went out on his own and left her holding the bag."

Mike laughed. She watched too many old movies, even incorporating the corny lingo into her own vocabulary. He tried on his best Brando impersonation. "Or maybe she went up against the Godfather."

Carly turned off the water and reached for a towel, retreating once again behind the curtain. "That's terrible."

"I thought I did a passable job on that one."

She slid the curtain aside and appeared, her skin pink and kissable-looking. He tossed her a grin and stepped forward, but she placed her hands against his shoulders and pressed him back to his temporary chair. "No way. Our snack will soon arrive, and the last thing we want is to keep Sam standing outside."

"Fine. But once we have our snack, and you're done reading, then I get to say what happens next."

She towel-dried and finger-combed her hair. "Back to Penny. Maybe the story is all part of her act. A way to explain why she sings the blues so well. Like a fake background or something."

"If it is, it's well-rehearsed. Her voice broke at the appropriate points, and I'm pretty sure I saw a tear slip down her cheek at one point."

Carly headed for the closet, her towel wrapped circumspectly around her then dressed. As she slid her feet into her slippers, a knock came at the door. "Oh, good, the food is here."

"Check the peephole first. Don't just open the —"

But he was too late. She yanked the door open. "Come in. We were just talking about you."

Their olive-skinned steward stepped in, carrying a tray loaded with a coffee service, a covered plate, two bowls of fruit and yogurt, and two personal-size bags of potato chips. He nodded to Carly. "Madam." Then to Mike. "Sir."

Carly stepped back and cleared a space on the table-desk combination near the wardrobe. "Set it right here." When he did, she lifted the lid from the plate. "Oh, yum, little sandwiches."

Sam, their steward, stepped toward the door. "Will there be anything else?"

Mike slipped him a tip. "No, that's it."

Sam bowed. "Please to set the tray in the hall when you're done."

Carly popped a grape in her mouth. "Thanks for the cute puppy. Do you do a different one each night?"

A wide smile split Sam's otherwise somber expression. "Yes."

"Good. We'll have a competition to see who figures out the creation."

"Very good."

Carly trailed him to the door. "I prefer milk chocolate. Can you bring one of each instead of two of the same?"

Mike laid a hand on his wife's arm. "I think we'll manage to live regardless of which kind he brings."

Sam nodded. "I will remember your preference, Madam."

"Thank you, Sam."

"Madam." He gestured toward the door. "And this is my assistant Shandra. He is also from Malaysia. If I am not available, he will be pleased to assist you."

A younger version of Sam stepped into the doorway and bowed to them then stepped back.

This is really nice, having two people at their beck and call.

The only downside was he'd best be careful, or Carly would expect this same kind of treatment all the time.

Chapter 4

The next morning, Carly awoke before the alarm. Mike snored softly in the bed beside her, and she relaxed for a few minutes, the gentle rolling motion of the ship and the thrumming of the engines reminding her of the exciting adventure she was on.

Her first cruise. To Alaska, the place more people said they wanted to go than she imagined possible. Everybody in Bear Cove was positively green with envy at her good fortune.

In fact, on this, their first full day on board, she wondered if she needed to pinch herself to make certain she wasn't dreaming.

She slipped out of bed and got ready for the day, pleased to see her husband able to relax enough to sleep in. She turned off the alarm and laced up her sneakers. Time for a walk. Signs on the deck above them informed passengers that three-and-a-half times around the deck equaled one mile.

She could do that.

Maybe twice as much.

She pushed through the double set of doors leading to the deck then toward the stairs leading to her destination: the Promenade deck, aptly named as it was the only one that went clear around the ship.

She arrived at the top of the stairs and followed the arrows directing her to walk to the right. A power-walker, arms pumping and hoodie hiding their identity, swooshed past. Carly fell into an easy rhythm and walked, glancing occasionally at the sea to her right. Far in the distance, close to the inland horizon, the land appeared as a blurry purple mass. She rounded the bow, passing several closed doors, then emerged on the starboard side which faced the open ocean.

Whitecaps dotted the waves, and the sun reflected off the water. She squinted. Was that a whale spout about half a mile away? Yes. Although she couldn't see the creature, just knowing that at least one was out there cheered her. Mike would be envious when she told him.

Deck chairs hugged the left-hand side of the deck, and a steward wheeled a cart of lounger pads out of a crew door and began preparing the chairs for the day. A number he equipped with a little slipcover that indicated RESERVED, a fact confirmed by signs which advised those specific chairs, about a dozen of the forty or so stationed on this side, were for the exclusive use of the passengers in the cabins in the vicinity.

She harrumphed. Wasn't this America? Hadn't the class system been abolished? She chuckled as she passed the chairs. Apparently not in cruise-land. Then again, if somebody wanted to pay more for their stateroom so they could have their own deck chair, that was capitalism at its best, wasn't it?

Lifeboats lined along the outer railing reminded her they were on a large ship, and she recalled reading in the itinerary last night about an emergency drill scheduled for later this morning. Which sent her mind retreating into history to the Titanic and its disastrous maiden voyage.

As she emerged from the stern area and back to the port side, she recalled the information in the in-room binder that showed this ship as compared to that Grand Dame of cruise ships. The boat she rode in was at least three times larger, but there were more passengers on the Titanic. Rooms were smaller, but there was no doubt the older ship was far more elegant and opulent.

The power walker pressed past again, muttering a brisk "make way" as he did. For there was no doubt it was a man.

How rude.

Why was he in such a rush? They were on a ship in the ocean, for crying out loud. There was nowhere to go except around.

The wind slapped at her cheeks, and she hunkered down into her fleece jacket. Reaching into her pockets, she found a pair of knitted mini-gloves that stretched to fit her hands. Maybe later today she'd buy herself a hat or a head warmer band. She clapped her hands on her ears as they chilled with the wind, then inhaled deeply. This far out, there wasn't any real smell to the air, unlike in Bear Cove where there was always a pervasive odor of seaweed, salt, and fish. She could get used to this. Perhaps be one of those ladies who retired and lived on a cruise ship—all services provided, and she could see the world.

She glanced at the choppy waves, felt the cold wind sneak down the back of her neck.

Then again, maybe not.

Once again she rounded the bow, where a door leading forward swung open on well-oiled hinges. She paused and peered through the opening. Apparently the real front of the ship was out there. She spotted a few chairs, a table or two, a railing, and a flagpole. Maybe she'd—

A crewman appeared in the doorway as she stepped over the bulkhead. "No entry, madam."

She peered over his shoulder. "I just wanted—"

He shook his head. "At glacier only."

She took a step back and exhaled. "Fine."

He nodded and closed the door. Strange. Why wouldn't they want passengers out there? What was the big deal anyway?"

She turned to resume her walk then glanced back. Two sets of wet footprints led to the door. Hers. And the crew member she just encountered? Which meant he was out there by himself.

So what was he doing?

She continued around, nodded to the stewards placing cushions on the chairs, and avoided the power walker by stepping aside when she detected his footsteps coming up on her left.

She slowed for the final half-turn. No point in getting all sweaty. A big believer in being granted a certain number of heartbeats for her lifetime and not wanting to waste any on exercise, she hated perspiring or being out of breath. Both made her neck and face break out in red blotches. Most unbecoming.

She descended the stairs and headed for the passageway leading to her stateroom. At the sound of raised voices, she paused. Few things in life more embarrassing than being overheard during a heated discussion.

Except maybe walking into the middle of somebody else's fight.

A woman and a man. She peeked around the corner. Penny Goodnight. The man she didn't recognize. He stood with his back to her.

The wind snatched at their words, making it difficult for her to hear, but she shrank against the lifeboat at her elbow and did her best.

"I don't know why you think that."

Penny.

"I don't have anything in common with them anymore."

The man.

"Why?"

"Because they are life-focused, and I am death-focused. They are looking to leave a heritage, and I am hoping to leave a legacy."

"That's a morbid way to think."

"It's the truth."

She folded her arms across her chest. "Well, I won't accept it."

"I know it isn't what you want to hear. But it's the way it is."

"We need to talk about this."

He shook his head. "We're done talking. You can't change my mind because the facts are what they are."

Penny's hands clenched at her sides. "You're wrong. You say you know me, but if you really believe that, you don't know me at all."

He raised his hands as if in surrender. "Fine. I don't know you. And I don't want to know you any longer. Leave me alone."

She reached for his arm but he pulled out of reach then walked past the singer and went through a crew passageway. She turned to stare after him as the slam of the door echoed across the deck.

Miss Penny Goodnight stood for a long moment, her fists clenching and unclenching, before she whirled about and strode toward Carly.

Straight toward her.

Carly shrank back, pressing against the railing, her breath trapped in her throat. Penny stomped up the stairs, her heels ringing on the metal in time with Carly's pounding heart. Her mouth, clamped into a straight line, and her eyes, squinting, looked frozen as a mask.

Whoever that was definitely stepped outside the singer's good graces with his proclamation.

Once Penny was out of sight, Carly exhaled and headed for the crew door on the bow. She pulled on the handle. Locked.

Rats.

But that wouldn't stop her from discovering what was going on.

Despite what Mike said, some mysteries were simply too delicious to ignore.

$ $ $

Carly checked her reflection in the mirror. That little tuft of hair near her right temple needed something. She glanced at her husband, who paced the short hallway as he waited. "I'll just be another second."

He checked his watch. "All the best tables will be gone."

She smiled. "The best tables are within view of the buffet. That's what counts."

He shook his head. "I want to look out over the water. Maybe I'll see a whale today."

After she shared about seeing the water spout, he took that as a challenge, one where she was in the lead. He was determined to see more whales—or evidence of the huge mammals—than she did, if he stayed up all night.

On her way to the bathroom to see what she could do about her 'do, she planted a kiss on his cheek. "Why don't you go on ahead? I'll be there in no time."

His brow pulled down. "You're not going to take a detour to the Observation Deck, are you?"

Touted on today's itinerary as The Place to see whales, the deck boasted lounge chairs, hot beverages, long-distance magnifiers, and loaner binoculars. She shook her head and made an X over her heart with a forefinger. "Cross my heart and hope to die. . . ."

He clamped a hand over her mouth. "Don't even say that. See you soon."

She waved him through the door then returned to the bathroom, where she soon set that recalcitrant lock in place then headed for the elevators. Simply thinking about Mike chowing down on breakfast made her stomach rumble.

But when she stepped off the elevator behind an elderly couple in matching track suits, she stopped short and looked around. This wasn't the Lanai Buffet. This was—she giggled. She forgot to press the button and instead spent her short ride studying a painting in the car. Although why a cruise ship would choose to display artwork of ships in storms and shipwrecks was beyond her.

Perhaps to remind the passengers that the upcoming emergency drill wasn't a joke?

She shrugged and turned back to the elevator to press the call button when a familiar voice caught her attention.

Miss Barbara Ann Dawson.

She pivoted. Set against the far wall was a small conversation pit, with a sofa and two armchairs pulled into an intimate circle. Miss Dawson sat on one end of the sofa, while a man she didn't recognize perched in a chair, his arms folded across his chest.

Carly stepped back into the shadows. This might prove interesting.

Miss Dawson leaned forward, a notebook and pen at the ready. "But Hamish, really, as cruise director, you know so much about how the ship works."

"As I told you, Miss Dawson, I am employed by the hotel side of the ship, not the ship itself. I don't know what the protocol would be."

The author tipped her head to one side. "Have you ever had anybody die of natural causes?"

His foot swung in a semi-circle. "No."

"What about anybody disappearing?"

His eyes widened and his foot froze. "You mean like go overboard?"

"Exactly. Or go missing? Maybe you found them stuffed in a locker later. Or hanging from a—" A hand waved toward the ceiling. "I don't know. Hanging from a yardarm."

His chuckle held a frosty note. "Modern cruise ships don't have yardarms. And no bodies of any kind. Missing or stuffed. Perhaps you should talk to Security."

She dismissed his suggestion with a shake of her head. "I already asked. They put me off by saying I needed to arrange that before sailing." She flipped a couple of pages. "If there was a body, who would have jurisdiction?"

He exhaled and his foot began its rotation again. "There is no international law regarding jurisdiction. The captain of each ship holds that authority."

"But what would they do if somebody was murdered?"

He shrugged. "Assign Security to investigate? I don't know."

"What if it was an American who died?"

"The captain could call ahead to our next port of call. Or our previous port. Or the FBI. I guess they could come to the ship in a helicopter. Or in a boat, depending on where we were."

"If it was an international passenger?"

"Same thing, I suppose." He stood. "I really must go. I have a presentation to make in about three minutes."

She huffed. "Well, I must say, you've been most unhelpful."

"As I said—"

Again she brushed his words aside. "Yes, I heard. You don't know."

He turned to leave but paused when she spoke again.

"Maybe I'll need to kill somebody to find out what really happens when a crime is committed."

$ $ $

Carly sipped her third coffee of the morning in the Lanai Buffet and beamed at Mike. "This is such good food."

He nodded as he forked another mouthful of personalized omelet into his mouth. "This is the best breakfast I've had since—"

She drew her brow down. "I make breakfast for you most days."

"That's what I was just about to say." He swiped at a spot of cheese on the front of his polo shirt with his white linen napkin. "Since the last time you made me breakfast."

"Good save, Turnquist." She nudged his foot with hers under the table. "But seriously, I didn't expect this much food. I mean, I've heard cruises are lavish, but this is almost unbelievable."

A suited man appeared at their table and bowed. "Is everything satisfactory?"

Carly glanced at his name tag. "Thank you, Tomas. Yes."

"Almost everything."

Tomas looked to Mike, the wrinkles in his brow telegraphing his concern. "Sir?"

"Do you serve food that contains no calories?"

"Sir?"

"We want to eat more, but don't want to gain weight."

The crewman relaxed his brow and smiled. "American humor."

Carly rolled her eyes. "Or an attempt at it." She read the small print on his identifier. "You're the dining room supervisor?"

"Yes, madam. Sometimes I serve at The Captain's Table. And sometimes I serve in The Crow's Nest."

She smiled. "We ate at The Captain's Table last night. But there's another dining room?"

"Yes. Our most formal." He studied his shoes. "It is not complimentary."

Now she giggled. "You mean it says unkind things?"

He blinked a couple of times before smiling. "Ah. American humor again. No, I mean you must pay for your meals at The Pinnacle."

Mike spoke up. "We'll stick with the free stuff."

"Of course, sir. Tonight is a gala night. Have you made a reservation?"

She shook her head. "Not yet. What would you recommend?"

"I will serve at The Captain's Table tonight. Very nice menu. I think you would like it."

"Oh, that would be fun."

He bowed again. "What is your stateroom number? I shall make a reservation for you. At what time?"

"Mike likes to eat early, so five?"

"Very well, madam. Five this evening. I shall see you then."

Mike leaned forward. "Before you leave, Tomas, where are you from?"

"Indonesia, sir."

"Married?"

"Yes, sir. With three children."

Carly hadn't thought about the crew's personal lives. "That must be hard. Being away from family so much. I have two grandchildren, and I miss them after only three days."

"Yes, madam."

They chatted with the man another few minutes, learning he was at sea for nine months at a time, with three months off between contracts. But apparently he loved his job, as he would soon renew his eighteenth contract with the same line. And when his wife went into labor the previous year with the birth of their third child, the cruise line allowed him to take time off to spend with his family. She was pregnant now with their fourth, due to deliver any day. He was hoping the company would grant him an early leave if necessary.

Carly pushed her plate away. "Sounds like they are good employers."

"Oh, yes, madam. Very. I shall look for you tonight."

He moved on to the next table while Mike drained his orange juice.

Carly leaned forward. "Wait until I tell you what I heard on the way here."

He rolled his eyes. "I can't leave you alone for five minutes, can I?"

His typical reaction whenever she prefaced a conversation with those words. She really needed to figure out a better introduction. One that didn't put him instantly on the alert.

But before she could assure him she hadn't gotten into any trouble— this time—the PA system crackled to life, and the background music faded.

"Good morning, fellow passengers. This is your captain, Graham Lycas, with your daily update. We're currently sailing north-northwest at a speed of nineteen knots, or about eighteen miles per hour. We have smooth seas ahead, and sunshine promised for the next couple of days. In a few minutes, you'll hear a single gong of our emergency system. If this were a real emergency, this would be your notice to listen for further instructions."

The resonant voice with a touch of a Scottish accent went on to tell them that in a real emergency, another alarm consisting of two long gongs would alert preliminary personnel to go to their stations. If that didn't resolve the issue and an abandon ship order was necessary, a series of continuing gongs would alert passengers to the necessity for them to return to their stateroom, obtain their life vests, then go immediately to their life stations.

The captain informed them this was a full emergency drill, and for them to follow the procedure by doing just that, proceeding to the life station identified on the placard on the inside of their stateroom door.

By the end of the message, Carly was mesmerized by the inflection and accent. "So what do we do?"

Mike shrugged. "Ignore the first gong, or pretend to. When the second sounds, head for the stateroom to get the vests. Wait there for further instructions."

She looked around. Most people seemed to be doing their best to ignore the announcement. "He sounded like Sean Connery, don't you think?"

"A little."

"I loved him in—" She paused when a single tone sounded. "Let's leave early. Avoid the rush and all that."

He nodded. "I'm done eating anyway."

They headed for the elevator that would carry them down to their second deck stateroom. And apparently they weren't the only passengers thinking about getting a head start, as the waiting area in the elevator banks already held about thirty people. While they waited, a second alarm sounded, two very civilized tones. The serving staff on the buffet pulled down the screens indicating those stations were closed, while supervisory staff—including Tomas—headed for a stairwell.

The trip down in the car went fast, and soon they were donning their vests.

Carly chuckled at her husband. "You look kinda silly."

He quirked his eyebrows at her. "Too bad they don't come in designer colors."

She opened the cabin door. "I don't want to miss the next

announcement."

She tried hard not to think about how terrifying this process would be if it weren't a drill, and thought back again to the Titanic. Not enough life vests. Not enough boats. Water pouring into steerage and cargo compartments. Freezing water and dark of night beyond the railings.

Would she have had the courage to leave the ship? Or would she have stayed with her husband? Could she have been as brave as the men who stayed? Or the band that continued playing right until the end?

She shivered. Thankfully, she didn't have to know the answers to those questions right now.

The third alarm, a steady ringing tone, insistent.

Mike gripped her hand. "Up we go."

Their life station was on the third deck, station twelve. When they arrived, a group of about twenty other passengers clustered together as Sam their steward, holding a clipboard, and the purser in his white uniform encouraged them to form four lines and crowd together to make room for other passengers making their way to their own stations.

Neil Williams held up his hand for silence. Carly continued holding Mike's hand. Even though she knew this was simply practice, she didn't want to become separated from him. He squeezed her fingers, reminding her she was safe with him.

The purser addressed them. "Ladies and gentlemen, thank you for your prompt response. In a real emergency, our goal is to be at this point within ninety seconds." He glanced at a stopwatch in his hand. "You did a little better. Eighty-four seconds. Next we'll scan your keycard for roll call."

Sam stepped forward with a card reader gun at the ready. He finished the task then showed the screen to Neil who scanned at the group. "Sometimes the card reader fails. We are missing three people from our electronic record. Mr. Johannson?"

A man at the end of the line to Carly's left raised his hand. "Present."

The purser nodded. "Thank you. Mrs. Adams?"

An older lady seated on a walker squeaked from the back row. "Here. Just like in school."

Several around her chuckled.

"Thank you. Miss Dawson. Is Miss Dawson here?"

Carly glanced around and didn't see the author but did catch a glimpse of Bill and Belle. She crooked two fingers at them in an air-wave motion. Belle smiled but Bill looked past her. Or pretended to. Strange. She turned back to the purser. "She's not here, sir."

"Are you certain?"

"Yes. I saw her earlier. I'd recognize her."

Of course, at that time, the author had been threatening murder.

Had she made good on her words?

Or was she simply holed up somewhere cranking out another book?

"We'll wait a few more minutes. We can't dismiss you until everybody is accounted for."

Mr. Johannson swore under his breath. "Is that really necessary?"

"In a real emergency, all passengers must be present, sir." Neil pasted on a tight smile. "I'm sure if you were the one asleep in your stateroom, you'd like to be awakened."

Another chuckle rippled through the group.

The purser nodded to Sam. "Call her room."

The steward dialed a number and waited then disconnected. "Not answering, sir."

"Then go knock."

A collective groan from a few of the more vocal passengers indicated their displeasure.

Bill spoke in a stage whisper to Belle. "That woman could drive me to murder."

Carly agreed with the general state of mind, although she wouldn't go so far as to kill anybody over it. This drill started out as an exciting adventure, but the thrill was just about gone, and she wanted to get on to other things. Funny how when somebody chose not to participate, it was ruined for everybody.

A few minutes passed, with their station group shuffling their feet, a few complaints, and Mike resting an arm over her shoulders. Sam returned and shook his head.

Neil checked his stopwatch again. "We are well past our three minutes total allotted time to prepare to enter the life rafts. I'll dismiss you, and thank you for your patience."

Mr. Johannson pushed his way through the group. "If I get my hands on her, I'll kill her. Some people think they're just too good to follow the rules."

The purser stepped in front of the angry man. "Please, sir, I understand you're angry. Frankly, her behavior insults all of us. But allow us to deal with this situation."

He stepped back, fists clenched at his side. "Oh, yeah? And what are you going to do about it?"

"That will be up to the captain once we investigate the situation. Perhaps she's ill. Or didn't hear the announcement and the alarm. I'm sure there's a good explanation."

"Always is for people like her, isn't there? More likely she's passed out somewhere. She is so full of herself. I don't know what my wife sees in her. If I had my way, people like her would be drowned at sea." Mr. Johannson stood on his toes to peer into Neil's face. "And people who defend people like her should be shot."

Neil's face lost its color, and Mr. Johannson strode away. Carly turned to Mike. "Did you hear that?"

He nodded, his jaw muscles working, a sure sign he struggled to retain his temper. "I did. And so did everybody else."

"Sounded like a threat to me." She glanced over her shoulder. Bill and Belle slipped through the group and walked away from them. She nodded in their direction. "And they weren't happy, either."

Mike pulled her toward the door leading back to the passageway. "More likely just a big guy with a short fuse. He didn't want to be here anymore than we did." He opened the door for her and she stepped inside. "As for our dinner companions, I'm sure it was just a figure of speech."

Carly nodded, holding back what she really thought.

If looks could kill. . .

Leeann Betts – Silent Partner

Chapter 5

Carly glanced at the nautically-themed clock near the bank of elevators in the Lanai Restaurant and sighed. "This is the life. My new definition of vacation."

Mike smiled across the table. "Is it the never-ending bounty of food that has you so infatuated with cruising?"

She spread her hands in an all-inclusive gesture. "How can it get any better? I unpack once. Visit many different places. Know where I'll sleep tonight. No worries about finding good food."

He waggled his eyebrows at her. "Not to mention a quiet stateroom that has seen far too little of us."

She rolled her eyes. If he could adopt his 'whatever' affectation, surely she could have one of her own. "You are incorrigible."

He chuckled. "Is that something your mother said to your father?"

"Sometimes."

"Surprised you didn't have more siblings."

A dull ache formed in her chest. She had no siblings. But if Mike was right, it wasn't for lack of trying on her father's part. And now both parents were gone, as were Mike's. Didn't quite seem fair. She knew folks in their seventies who still had at least one.

She tossed him a half-smile. All she could muster at the moment. "What's on the itinerary today?"

Mike clamped a hand on the side of his neck. "Ouch. Whiplash from that abrupt change of topic." With his free hand, he reached across the table. "Today is a free day. Meaning we are at sea. But hopefully not a-sea." When she didn't react to a second waggle, he continued. "This afternoon's movie is the one about a boy warlock. Or I might go to a digital workshop on managing email."

"I'm going to Miss Dawson's talk at two."

"Sounds like we could meet up in the stateroom before dinner."

His bushy eyebrows, which reminded her of a drunken caterpillar, rippled across his brow once more.

She giggled, the sound freezing in her throat at a familiar voice nearby. One that didn't sound very happy.

She shifted in her seat. Sure enough, not ten feet away, in another section separated by a half-wall topped with exotic blooms in ceramic planter boxes, sat the purser, Neil Williams, and Miss Barbara Ann Dawson.

And judging by her red face and the bulging veins in his forehead, neither appeared very happy.

She glanced at her husband, whose brow was now pulled down. She smiled brightly. "Isn't it time to head off to your workshop? If it ends a little early, you could make the movie, too."

He squinted over her shoulder then shook his head. "I don't know what you're up to, but it's something."

She jabbed a forefinger into her chest. "*Moi?*"

"And Miss Piggy ain't gonna get you out of this one." He stood and moved around the table, plunking himself into the empty seat beside her before imitating her previous movement. Thankfully, a mini palmetto blocked his view. "I don't see anything." He sighed. "Maybe I jumped to conclusions."

She planted a kiss on his cheek. "You've been hanging around me too long, I guess." Another smile then she gently pushed him. "Off you go. I'm going to enjoy another cup of java. Miss Dawson's talk doesn't start for another hour."

He returned her kiss, this one landing square on her lips, before he headed off to the elevator. He tasted of coffee and chocolate. She savored the combination a moment. Cutting back on dessert to gala nights was hard. And last night wasn't technically a formal night, but it was the first night of their cruise. So dessert was warranted. But maybe enjoying the treats vicariously through her husband's lips wasn't such a bad deal after all. And salad every day for lunch? What had she been thinking?

That she wanted to come off the ship as a passenger, not as cargo, that's what.

And if it took eating lettuce so she could enjoy her dinner, that's what she'd do.

But not Mike. Seemed very unfair he could eat what he liked. Then again, he wasn't already packing a few extra pounds. Insulation, she preferred to think of the weight as. Or, as the big orange cartoon cat would say, she wasn't overweight. Just undertall.

When Tomas paused at her table and asked if she'd like more coffee, she nodded. "Thank you."

"And heavy cream?"

"Just a little."

"I have some hidden in the refrigerator just for you." And sure enough, when he returned less than a minute later with a fresh cup of coffee and tiny pitcher of cream, a tag affixed to the china container read *Miss Carly*. "Enjoy."

"Any news of your wife?"

He shook his head. "No baby yet. She had the pains last week, but the doctor said it was false labor." He chuckled. "She said doctor was crazy. Pain was very real."

"Has your approval come through to leave early?"

His eyes saddened. "Not yet. Still hoping. And praying."

Another reference to faith. Seemed everybody had some. Except her. And Mike.

Which was silly, of course. Most people believed in something. Even if only themselves.

As for her, she wasn't certain where she stood. If pressed, she'd say there was nothing beyond what could be proven by the five senses.

But deep down, she really wished there was something—or

Somebody—out there she could turn to when she came to the end of herself.

As Tomas did now. Praying the company would allow him to leave his contract early to be present for the birth of his fourth child. His first son. Already named—Putu—as was traditional for Indonesians.

Tomas bowed and moved to the next table. Carly fixed her coffee and sipped, one ear tuned into the conversation going on behind her. Because whatever the topic, the discussion appeared to escalate.

"Neil, it's not fair. That's not what we agreed."

"Doesn't matter what you remember. I know what I said. And I'd never agree to a fifty-fifty split. There's nothing in it for me at that price. Seventy-thirty."

"That barely covers my airfare."

"But the bookstore is selling every book you brought with you. That's enough to make up the difference."

"I counted on that extra money. I made commitments."

"Not my fault."

"Ooh, I could just kill you right now."

Carly gasped and held her breath. She'd thought those words about another from time to time, but never spoke them aloud.

How would he react?

"Wouldn't that be like shooting the golden goose, dearie?"

Carly moved an inch to the right. Sure enough, the writer was still upset. Her mouth, taut as the spring in a mousetrap, created a scarlet slash across her now-pale face. Her lipstick and heavy eye shadow seemed overdone for this hour of the day, particularly in the informal atmosphere of the Lanai.

Then again, she was giving a presentation in—Carly checked the clock—about forty minutes.

The purser, his chin jutted out, slightly elevated, strained to project a cocky attitude, but his clenched jaw muscles belied his attempt.

Both were angry. Both ready to pop their corks.

And Carly was in perfect position to watch it unfold.

Still the purser wasn't done with his taunting. He quirked his chin toward the plate stacked high with desserts and sweets. "You always have to be in control."

She glared at him. "I don't care today. I wish one of us would drop dead. Preferably you."

Then Tomas, his grey suit and matching tie orderly and official, appeared at their table, his hands clasped at his waist, a tiny smile offsetting his knowing glance. "Good day, Miss Dawson. Mr. Williams. Can I assist in any way?"

Apparently the interruption achieved its required effect, because the purser shook his head and stood. "Thanks. I was just leaving."

Tomas nodded and turned to Miss Dawson. "And you, madam?"

She sat back in her seat, a trembling hand sloshing her coffee into its saucer. "Thank you, Tomas. Nothing right now."

A silent bow and the dining room supervisor drifted away.

A group of four or five simpering women blocked Carly's view as they passed. She peered between them, but saw nothing more than brightly-colored track suits, oversized sunglasses, and lithe bodies.

When they finally cleared away, so was her subject of interest.

Miss Dawson's table was empty, and a server cleared the dishes.

Carly turned back to her now-cold coffee. Rats. Cold java and unfinished business.

Totally unfair.

After all, despite what Mike said about most people not listening in on other's conversations, *this* enquiring mind wanted to know.

$ $ $

Carly pondered what she just saw and heard. Except for a pinched look that deepened the crow's feet around Miss Dawson's eyes, she might have convinced herself that the overheard conversation wasn't as serious as she thought.

Or wanted it to be, perhaps.

On her walk from the restaurant down to the meeting room two decks below, she almost convinced herself Mike was right. She tended to look for trouble where none existed. Maybe that was her Mid-Western upbringing. Or a result of her disastrous first marriage. And perhaps—just perhaps—he was correct when he said mysteries found her like iron to a magnet. Which she could blame on her training as a forensic accountant. After all, she didn't get a project unless the client thought there was a problem, and she didn't look good if she didn't find one.

But he was wrong in this one instance. She neither wanted, nor sought out, overhearing the purser and Miss Dawson arguing.

This time, she chose a folding chair in a corner, away from the spotlight, so to speak. She'd not garnered any popularity votes in the previous talk, so staying on the fringe seemed the wisest choice for now. Maybe she could talk to Miss Dawson later. Find out about the argument.

Teddy Bear and Monica sat in the front row again, separated by three other women Carly recognized from the prior session. The two chatted animatedly with those seated on both sides, with Teddy expansively describing a party he attended several years back where Miss Dawson thanked him *profusely* and *publicly* for his role as president of her fan club.

Of course, the way he described the event made it sound like he was the reason for her success, but let the man live in a dream world.

Everybody was entitled to at least one figment of their imagination.

Carly nodded to the middle-aged woman wearing too little clothing and too much perfume who sat beside her.

The blonde extended a hand garnished with overly long nails painted electric blue, which clashed with the fuschia short shorts and deeply plunging tank top that delved almost to her naval. Still, the colors showed off a great tan, albeit on skin the texture of leather. "Rene." She pronounced her name in one syllable. "From Wisconsin."

"Carly. Maine."

Rene lowered her voice as Miss Dawson rose from her seat to the left of Teddy and tottered toward the lectern. "I just love her stuff. Don't you?"

"She's good."

Apart from that, Carly would commit no more. Given the apparent dirge of mystery-writing skills needed to appease the masses, she wouldn't open her mouth to question or criticize the author's ability—or lack of—to hold her attention to the end of another heart-rending romance. She pulled out her notebook and pen, hoping this would cut off more conversation where she would surely get herself into trouble.

Rene took the hint, crossed one leg over the other, and turned to the front, her smile at the perfect angle to not mar her face with a single wrinkle.

Miss Dawson tapped the microphone. "Thank you so much for coming back, for those of you who were here last time." Her eyes roved the now-crowded room. "I see some familiar faces, and a few new ones."

While she shuffled her notes, Carly checked the other attendees. Mostly women, as many of these author events seemed to be. At least the ones by romance writers. Perhaps more men attended talks given by action and thriller writers. Since she didn't read that genre, she'd never know. And while she didn't completely agree with the majority opinion regarding Miss Dawson's abilities, this was a pleasant way to spend an hour.

And maybe she'd gain insight into characters and suspects that would assist her with her real-life work.

And her hobby.

Mysteries.

All around. Bubbling below the surface. She simply had to lift a rock and one popped out.

She focused back on Miss Dawson, who cleared her throat and began.

"Today we'll talk about how to develop characters and suspects. Many of you are not writers, but I guarantee that this session will help you even if all you do is read."

Carly harrumphed under her breath. The author made readers sound like a sub-human race or something. *Even if all you do is read.* Miss Dawson better hope there were folks out there who didn't read *and* write. Those would be her direct competition. True readers devoured books like Carly devoured two-bite brownies.

But apparently her response was louder than she thought. The woman sitting in front of her turned to toss a scathing glance over her shoulder.

She hunkered down and pretended to cough as she doodled on the page. When she raised her eyes, the woman had resumed her former position.

She'd best keep her opinions to herself.

Miss Dawson cleared her throat. "The best characters are believable. People you'd meet at a party, on the street, or in a movie theater."

Which really didn't make much sense. After all, how many parties could a person attend? And unless she was standing at a bus stop—which she never did—how would Carly meet somebody on the street? It wasn't like she could simply stop a person walking the other way and strike up a conversation. And a movie theater? Who talked during a movie? Apart from her husband, who enjoyed predicting the outcome of a scene, or expanding on the unreasonableness of a character's actions. Or the stilted dialogue. Or—oops, she was missing the next point.

"The trick is to make sure we portray folks as they really are, warts and all."

Well, Carly certainly knew some people with warts. Take the purser, for example. Trying to do Miss Dawson out of her share. Or maybe the author was to blame. Wanting to change their deal after the handshake, so to speak. And then there was that weird conversation between Penny Goodnight and the same Neil Williams. Seems he upset a lot of people.

What was it about some folks who seem to rub everybody the wrong way?

"So what makes a great character?" She pointed to Teddy, whose hand danced and waved. "The young man in the front row."

His hand dropped like he'd lost all strength, and his cheeks pinkened. "Give them a fault."

Strange she'd act as if she didn't know him. "Such as?"

"A fear."

"Example, dear?"

"Of the dark."

The author rubbed her hands together. "Ooh, and then lock him in a closet?"

"Or her. In a coffin, maybe."

Carly held her breath. Three heartbeats passed before Miss Dawson chuckled, releasing pent-up breaths around the room.

"Sounds like the makings of an interesting tale. Why does having a fault make a great character?"

"Makes them seem more real. Like the people we know and admire."

"Good answer. Seems you've been to a few of my talks before."

A chuckle rippled through the audience and Teddy's coloring darkened a shade.

"Another trait?"

Monica raised her hand, and responded when Miss Dawson nodded in her direction. "Give them a quirk. Like calling people pet names, or a stutter."

"Right. But we don't want to make it too common, or too irritating."

Rene raised a hand. "How do we write a stutter? I mean, it really bugs me when every word begins with two or three consonants. I mean, I get it. I hear it in my head, don't I? I don't need to see it on the page. It's like the author is trying to pad the word count or something."

A pained smile flew in Rene's direction. "First of all, a good author never pads her word count."

Teddy snorted then ducked his head between his shoulders, reminding Carly of a tortoise she once saw at the zoo. He stared at a paper in his hands while Miss Dawson bored holes through him with an oversized auger.

"And secondly, indicating a stutter doesn't increase word count. Hyphenated words, which is what a stutter is, are counted as one word." She glanced at her notes. "Those are some good examples of creating a believable character." She flipped a page. "Now, how do we write good suspects?"

Nobody moved, perhaps cowed by the author's condescending attitude toward those who previously responded. Carly shrugged. She had nothing to lose. She was already on Miss Dawson's Naughty List.

She waggled her fingers. Miss Dawson stared directly at her then moved her gaze around the room. Carly raised her hand, not waiting for an invitation to speak. After all, even though they might be officially in international waters, this ship still represented everything that was good about America. Including the right to freedom of speech. "A good suspect will have a crystal-clear motive."

Now the author seemed intent on putting her in her spot. "And how do we do that?"

"Overheard conversations. Background story. Opinions of other characters. Misdirection. Untrustworthy narrator."

"Goodness. Sounds like you've written a lot of mysteries." She peered at her. "How many have you penned?"

Carly swallowed hard. She should have kept her mouth shut. "None."

Miss Dawson cupped a hand around her ear and leaned forward. "What was that? None? Did I hear you right?"

Most everybody in the room swiveled in their seats to stare at her.

She nodded as heat rushed to her cheeks. She should have gone with Mike. Although she had no problem managing her email, she wished she were anywhere but here. Perhaps when the spotlight now blinding her was turned to some other hapless victim, she'd sneak out.

"Well, I can see why you think you're such an expert. None. Zero. Zilch. Nada." Miss Dawson touched her forefinger to her thumb, creating a circle. "Now, perhaps I can return to my outline." She licked a finger and turned the page. "Creating a good suspect involves many aspects, including giving them a reason to be suspected."

The author then went on to expand on Carly's cryptic list, albeit in a different order, using different words.

Carly bit her tongue.

Some people could be so infuriating.

Maybe Neil Williams wasn't the one who should die and put them all out of their misery.

And although she didn't know the man, she shifted mentally to his side of the boat.

If there was a problem between the purser and the author, Carly knew the cause.

And it wasn't Mr. Williams.

Chapter 6

Despite Carly's previous weak protests, she couldn't resist her husband's boyish good looks and waggling eyebrows. A short nap and a quick shower later, she sported the reversible skirt, plain jersey shirt, and black shawl planned for this first of two Gala Nights. Ahead of them at the elevators, three couples decked out in formal gowns and tuxedos chatted.

She squeezed Mike's hand. "Do you think this is dressy enough?"

He scanned her from head to toe. "Absolutely."

She patted the lapel of his single-breasted sports coat. "You look great."

He smiled down at her. "Don't make it sound like that's unusual."

"Well, your hair is sometimes a little crazy. And those eyebrows."

He chuckled. "I only keep them like that because they hypnotize you."

"Is that what you call it?" The doors swished open and they stepped inside. "Keep your voice down."

His laugh this time drew sidelong glances from their fellow passengers. "Deck Five, please."

An elderly man nodded and pressed the button. "Going to The Captain's Table?"

"Yes."

"Good food. We dine there for breakfast each day. Like to start out the day less formally."

Carly pressed forward from her spot. "And you?"

"The Crow's Nest."

Carly gulped. No wonder he thought The Captain's Table less formal. The ship's itinerary advised—or perhaps warned was more like it—that meals in The Crow's Nest would normally require three hours. Even the two hours for their choice seemed excessive. After all, it didn't take that long to prepare a meal, did it? "Do you eat dinner there every day?"

He blinked myopically at her a moment as though she spoke a foreign language before clearing his head and giving a brief nod.

"Then what do you do to make Gala Night special? Dress up?"

He looked down at his suit as though noticing it for the first time. "Dress up? This is every day wear for dinner. True dressing up is saved for the second Gala. White tie and tails." He sniffed as though she carried an unpleasant odor. "Much more formal than you'd prefer, I'm sure."

Carly opened her mouth to reply, but perhaps thankfully, the door opened and the man and his companions flooded out as though borne on a tidal wave. The fourth-deck Crow's Nest, where meals were never complimentary, resided on the bow, providing diners with an unobstructed view.

She and Mike rode in silence to the next deck and stepped out into a foyer full of milling passengers waiting for the doors to open. She checked the clock. One minute to go. An air of anticipation thrummed through the group. She made eye contact with several women dressed similarly.

Finally, she was among her own.

Not like she couldn't afford a long dress, or Mike a tuxedo. They simply chose a less formal lifestyle.

At least, that's what she kept telling herself.

When they stepped up to the lectern to give their stateroom number, they were quickly and efficiently handed over to a hostess who led them to their table. Having already indicated they were happy to share a table, she wasn't surprised when another couple joined them as they were being seated.

Ricardo, their host, pulled out Carly's chair first and then the other woman's, before seating the men. The chairs, on wheels, slid easily into position. Next, a linen napkin dropped casually into their lap, and then he asked if they wanted the wine steward. Dave and Dewey, pronounced Deway, indicated their choice when the same young man from the previous evening appeared. Carly and Mike stuck with water and iced tea.

While the previous night had been what Carly would call formal, tonight went a step beyond. Embossed menus at each place setting, crystal goblets, and a string quartet in the bay window overlooking the stern enhanced their dining experience.

Carly scanned her menu. "The shrimp cocktail sounds good again. Salad. Pork. And Baked Alaska."

Mike snapped his menu shut. "Agreed. Me, too."

Dave, a lanky man who appeared to be about their own age, nodded. "I think we can make that three."

Dewey, an exotic beauty from the Philippines, smiled. "Let's make it easy on our waiter. Me, too."

Ari, their server from the previous night, appeared. He nodded as Dave ordered four of each course—the only difference being he and Dewey preferred their dressing on the side—then hastened off.

The sommelier brought the wine for their new friends, and Carly relaxed. Dewey was an easy conversationalist, although her accent took some getting used to. Dave, it appeared, was an IT guy, so he and Mike soon were deep in discussions about bytes and boards and code.

Carly sipped her iced tea. "Are you celebrating an event?"

"Our twenty-fifth wedding anniversary."

"How exciting. Congratulations."

Dewey's downcast expression, however, did not communicate her enjoyment of what should have been a happy occasion.

Carly, one to pry—sometimes to her detriment, at least according to Mike—couldn't let this barn door-sized opportunity escape. "Is something wrong?" She glanced around the restaurant. While perhaps not convenient, perhaps she and Mike could be reseated to allow the couple time alone. "We could ask for another table if you prefer?"

Dewey shook her head and gripped Carly's hand. "No, I'm fine. Please don't leave."

"Okay."

Dying to know what the problem was, Carly held her tongue. She nodded toward the quartet. "They play quite well."

"Oh, yes. The cruise line hires nothing but the best. Most of the time."

Well, if that wasn't an invitation to ask questions.

She leaned forward. "What do you mean?"

Dewey's eyes widened. "Did I say that out loud?" Her mouth lifted in a half-smile. "Perhaps I need more wine."

Carly doubted that was her trouble. Usually people talked too much when they consumed alcohol. "Oh, look, here comes our appetizer."

Glad to be able to change the subject—at least for a few minutes—she savored the tender monster-sized shrimp and zesty cocktail sauce. She closed her eyes, enjoying the tomato, horseradish, and sweet and tart flavors.

When she opened her eyes again, she caught Dewey dabbing at her eyes with her napkin. She sighed. Another gold-lettered invite.

"Have you taken this cruise before?"

Dewey shook her head. "No, but we've been on a dozen or more ships. Always with this company. They're the best. All our friends cruise, too, and you should hear some of the horror stories." She took another bite of shrimp. "Then again, maybe you shouldn't. Might scare you off completely."

Carly waved off the suggestion. "Cruising is my new vacation. It's the first time I've been able to really relax. Mike says I'm a magnet for mysteries. Of course, he's exaggerating. But I haven't gotten involved in anything on the cruise yet."

"Mysteries?" Dewey sipped her wine. "What kind of mysteries?"

Carly lowered her voice. No point in Mike thinking she was on crime-solving alert again. "Well, I helped catch a purse snatcher in Seattle."

She wouldn't mention the killers she'd nabbed in the past, either. Or the time she almost ended up getting killed.

Times, rather.

More than once.

Dewey's countenance hardened and her eyes narrowed. "I think thieves should be hung." She practically spat out the words. "I mean, they don't just take your stuff. They steal your sense of security, don't they?"

Carly hadn't given it much thought before, but as she considered her new friend's words, she agreed she might be right. "I guess if I knew they rifled through my dresser, I'd want to replace everything."

Tears moistened Dewey's eyes. "You can't replace everything, though. Peace of mind. Retirement."

A story poised to be told, to be certain.

Carly touched Dewey's hand. "Want to talk about it?"

The sultry beauty exhaled. "Nothing to talk about. Financial downturn." She glanced at her husband then back to Carly. "At least, that's what we were told. Good thing this cruise was already paid for before that happened." A tiny sob escaped. "Might be our last cruise. Better enjoy it while we can."

Sounded to Carly like she was repeating words spoken by somebody else—her husband, perhaps?

"Did you make some unwise investment decisions?"

"Not me."

Uh-oh. Financial troubles between husband and wife are the leading cause of divorce, according to statistics. As a forensic accountant, Carly was often called in when one party felt the other was trying to hide assets.

"Dave seems too wise to—"

"Oh, not Dave. Wasn't his fault." A trembling hand gripped the stem of the wine glass as she took a deep draught before setting the empty goblet on the table. "We trusted him. And he stole from us. We just couldn't prove it. He walked on that thin line between fiduciary responsibility and fraud. And not just us. Others, too. Ruined them. One man killed himself over it, so we heard." She looked up and pasted on a smile. "But enough of that. Our salad has arrived."

And for the rest of the meal, Dewey seemed to cast off the cloud of despair that enveloped her early on, chatting about their children and grands. Sharing pictures. Laughing about stories from previous cruises. Listening with interest when Carly shared.

If she didn't know better, Carly'd say nothing was wrong.

But she knew what she saw and heard.

Something was very amiss in Dave and Dewey's world.

$ $ $

Carly perched on a wingback chair while waiting for Mike, who decided to make a quick trip to the restroom before they completed their evening adventure with a stroll around the Promenade deck. Despite her best investigative techniques, Dewey told her nothing else about their problems, and indeed, seemed to work diligently to change the topic whenever conversation drifted into the arena of financial matters.

Which only confirmed Carly's theory, rather than dispelling it.

She nodded to a couple who acknowledged her as they entered The Captain's Table. At almost half past seven, seemed late to just be starting a two-hour meal. Why, that meant they wouldn't finish until nearly ten. Then again, maybe they were night owls.

She yawned. Unlike her and Mike. While not exactly up with the birds—at least, not her—they tended to retire early and rise a little earlier than most self-employed folks they knew. Which weren't many. Even Dave and Dewey—who were older than they looked as they were retired— admitted to rarely seeing nine o'clock in the morning anymore.

A couple strode past her, the woman's hands clenched into fists. Carly looked up then turned quickly aside, hoping to hide her face in the shadows.

Teddy and Monica. Miss Dawson's biggest fans.

Teddy jabbed the UP button for the elevator. Monica hesitated a split second then pressed the disc for down.

Teddy snarled at her. "Your cabin is on the same deck as mine. You're just being contrary."

"You always do that. You deride my feelings and opinions. Well, I'm telling you he was wrong, and I'm going to get even, if it's the last thing I do. Right now, I don't want to be on the same planet as you."

"And I don't want to breathe the same air." He took a huge gulp and puffed out his cheeks, reminding Carly of a squirrel. But after a few seconds, he exhaled in a whoosh. "Well, that was pretty silly." He laid a hand on his companion's arm. "Can we make up? I'm sorry. I shouldn't have said what I did. What you feel is credible. I just think you over react. Surely there is another solution."

Carly shuddered. If this was a lover's quarrel, she'd never have picked two more unlikely candidates. He was years younger. And—well, not her type. Then again, Carly didn't have much experience with matters of the heart. A bad first marriage. One date in the intervening six years. Head-over-heels in love with Mike by their second date.

"No. I will have my revenge." Monica shrugged off his touch and stared at him. "Apology rejected. You've gone too far this time, *Teddy Bear*."

The nickname, derisive in tone as well as context, stung young Teddy. As intended, no doubt. He took a step back, inhaled sharply, then turned and headed for the stairs leading to the deck above.

Monica leaned against the wall and took several deep breaths while Carly begged Mike silently not to come out just yet.

But he didn't hear her, apparently, and came through the door to the restroom as though given a new lease on life. Carly sat back in the chair and closed her eyes, feigning sleep. Perhaps if Monica didn't know she'd just seen and heard the entire conversation, she wouldn't dislike her so much.

Although why Monica's approval was important, Carly wasn't certain.

Except she didn't want to be on the receiving end of dagger stares.

Too late.

"Sorry to be so long. What a line up. And then I got to chatting with a man from Boston. Not quite home, but close enough." Mike paused then shook her shoulder. "Did you fall asleep?"

Carly opened her eyes and stretched her arms over her head. "Goodness. Are you back already?" She met Monica's stare. "Oh, hi Monica." She stood and introduced her husband. "Monica is a great fan of Miss Dawson, aren't you?"

Instead of responding, Monica pivoted and went down the stairs.

Mike shrugged. "Not very friendly, is she?" He held out an arm. "Shall we walk?"

"Yes."

Carly linked her arm through his. She needed time to think. To ponder the situation. So many people. So many conversations.

So much tension.

Whatever happened to relaxing?

Seemed some folks hadn't gotten the memo.

$ $ $

Chlorinated water, wet towels, and the spicy smell of Mexican food permeated the air as Mike and Carly stepped into the Lido Pool area. A street-style cart of tacos and burritos stood next to a beverage cart at the far end, while lounge chairs and table-and-chair arrangements dotted the pool deck. Not overly busy at this time of the evening, couples chatted while children cavorted in the pool. Overhead, skylights opened onto the night sky. This far at sea, the moon shone bright in a velvety background of twinkling lights.

She headed for an empty table near the hot tub, with Mike close on her heels. "I'm so looking forward to some quiet time in the tub."

He quirked his chin toward their goal. "Only two other people. Should be fun."

She groaned. How could she have known that finding a place on a ship this size where she was the only person—okay, Mike was allowed sometimes—would be so difficult? She set her towel on a chair.

Breathe in. Out. Relax. You're on vacation. No worries.

A glance at the tub and she exhaled in a whoosh. Not only was somebody already occupying her not-to-be-private tub, but that person was none other than Miss Barbara Ann Dawson. Oh, well, might as well make the best of it.

She slipped off her flip-flops, tugged on the skirt of her bathing suit, and followed Mike to the tub. Holding the rail so she wouldn't slip— nothing more embarrassing in her book—she stepped into the water, enjoying the sensation of heat on her cooling skin.

Settling her back against a water jet, she smiled in Miss Dawson's direction. The author stared at her a long moment before turning to Mike—who sat on her right—and introducing herself.

How rude.

Mike shook the woman's hand and reached across to the other woman on the mystery writer's left. "Mike. From Maine. And this is my wife Carly."

"Athena. From Georgia." She made the state sound like Joe-Ja. "Nice to meet you, I'm sure."

Carly nodded then turned back to Miss Dawson. "I enjoyed your discussion about characters and suspects today."

Another long stare and then the cold shoulder again as the author engaged Mike in a discussion about current bestselling titles, of which Mike knew little to nothing. Carly could have contributed, but the woman's attitude and failure to include her in the conversation screamed as loud as if she'd used a bullhorn.

Carly was on the woman's No-Like List.

Athena tossed her a smile. "Do you read?"

"I do. I love mysteries. And yourself?"

"Afraid my tendencies flow toward treatises on the Colonial War." A mock frown marred an otherwise perfect complexion, and for a moment, Carly wondered if her new acquaintance undertook the services of a plastic surgeon. If she did, the medico did good work. "But there are mysteries everywhere, don't you think?"

"I do. In fact, my husband says—" Carly halted. Mike's claim that she was a magnet for crime or mystery was overstated to say the least. Why, there were entire days when she didn't get involved in anything more suspenseful than deciding what to throw in the crock pot for dinner. "Oh, look. They're bringing the drink trolley. What will you have, Athena?"

Miss Dawson stood, water dripping from her leopard-spotted suit. "I'll have an ice water. With three cubes." When the young man chunked a scoop of ice into a glass, she clucked her tongue. "Do we have a language barrier? I said three cubes because I meant exactly that."

The server's cheeks colored beneath his olive complexion. He murmured his apology, dumped out the ice, and began again. "One, two, three cubes, madam. And ice water." He handed the glass to Miss Dawson then turned to Carly. "And for you?"

"Cola, please. With lots of crushed ice if you have it."

He bowed. "Yes, madam."

In turn, he filled Athena's and Mike's requests then strolled away, pushing his cart before him.

Carly sipped her drink, savoring the chips of ice and sweetness on her tongue, before setting her glass aside and slipping into the water up to her neck. She leaned her head back on the edge of the tub. "This is delightful."

Miss Dawson sniffed. "This hot tub is neither as hot nor as large as the one I have at home. Twelve can fit in mine."

Carly smiled. "I'd hate to be anywhere with a dozen people crowded around me in a bathtub."

Another sniff. "Hot tub, not bathtub."

Mike nudged her with an elbow. "My wife, the introvert."

Carly opened one eye. "Nothing wrong with that. Just because you're a social butterfly doesn't make me weird."

Another sniff from the author. "I've never understood the mindset of people who think being around others is a trial. I, for one, revel in crowds, audiences, and fans."

Athena chimed in. "I think there's room in this world for both kinds of personalities, don't you? I like to be in groups, but then I find myself needing some alone time."

A fourth sniff. "I believe people needing alone time are simply selfish."

Carly sighed and pushed herself upright. "Well, I guess if we were all like you, how would we ever get the attention we wanted? It would be a competition to be sure."

"The best would always rise to the top, like cream."

Carly shifted closer to Mike and lowered her voice. "Or like pond scum."

Miss Dawson's brow drew down. "What did you say?"

Carly forced a smile. "Just reminding my husband we need to call home."

The author thunked her glass on the concrete deck, sloshing the remaining water and scattering the cubes. "Good night, Athena." She nodded at Mike. "Mark."

Mike's eyes widened. "That's Mike."

"Whatever."

Carly stifled a chuckle. His favorite phrase of the week, coming from the author, made no more sense than when he said it. Perhaps now he'd understand why she disliked it so much.

What she didn't comprehend was why the novelist disliked her so much.

Was it because of her comments at that first meeting?

Her questions at the second?

Or was there some other reason?

Chapter 7

Carly gripped the swim towel wrapped around her hips in one hand and waved to Mike with the other. "See you in a few minutes."

With her mother's warnings tumbling around the edges of her memory—wait an hour after eating before venturing into a pool—and her recent Internet research fresh in her mind—that's an old wives' tale—she stepped into the women's changing room.

Then froze.

A familiar voice echoed around the corner of the tile-floored area.

None other than Miss Barbara Ann Dawson, her voice raised as though speaking to someone hard of hearing. "So, Talia dear, where did you say you were from?"

A soft-spoken young woman, her lilting accent identifying her as from Indonesia or Malaysia, answered. "Perai, Malaysia, madam. It is a small town in Panang."

Carly chuckled as she shed her flip-flops and towel. Funny how some people speak louder when dealing with a person from another country. As though that made their words easier to understand.

"And how long have you worked for Holland America?"

"Three years, madam."

"Do you like it here?"

"In Alaska, madam?"

"No, no, no. I mean, in America. The United States."

"Oh, yes. Very much, madam."

"Do you have family back in Malaysia?"

"Excuse me. I must do my work."

"Certainly. I'll just tag along, if you don't mind."

"Not at all, madam."

Carly smiled again. The poor woman probably minded very much, but was too polite—or intimidated—to say different. She peeked around the corner. A slender olive-skinned woman, her hair tied back into a single braid down her back, polished a mirror over a sink, while Miss Dawson stood to one side, a notebook and sheaf of papers in hand.

The author scanned a page then nodded. "Yes. My next question, dear, is have any of the men ever bothered you?"

Carly's breath caught in her throat. That seemed a very personal question—and an impertinent one, at that.

The young woman shuffled to the next sink and sprayed cleaner on the glass. Even from this angle, Carly noted the color rise in her neck and face.

She was totally embarrassed.

Yet Miss Dawson seemed impervious to the housekeeper's discomfort. "Well, have they ever, you know, taken liberties?"

The woman paused, her cleaning cloth gripped between her hands like a lifeline. "Liberties, madam?"

A tiny smile lifted one side of her face.

Carly clapped a hand over her own mouth and stepped back.

You go, girl!

Miss Dawson was about to get a dose of her own medicine.

"Yes, you know, have they ever made a pass at you?"

"Pass, madam?" The younger woman shook her head and stepped back. "I sorry. I don't understand."

Carly recognized the woman's ploy. Dropping back into idiomatic English when moments before she had an excellent grasp on the language displayed her intelligence, not her ignorance.

Miss Barbara Ann Dawson would have to fight for every answer at this point.

And try the author did. Her tenor raised half an octave—along with the decibels—as she persisted. "Have you ever been molested?"

The housekeeper shook her head.

No, that's probably correct. Except by nosey passengers.

"Do you know of any instances where that has happened?"

"Madam, I agreed to answer questions for you as research for your book. I thought you wanted to know about my job. My life on board the ship. My friendships. That's what you said. Had I known you would be so impertinent as to interrogate me in this way, I would have declined your invitation. As I'm sure most of my co-workers would, also." Talia stepped forward, forcing the author to move away or invade her personal space. "I have a job to do. I do it well. I work here because I want to. I enjoy the people—most of the time. I am like any other employee."

Miss Dawson's eyebrows shot up, resembling upside-down precision-shaped crescents. "Well, I never—"

Talia turned to walk away then paused and pivoted on her heel to face the author again. "And that, madam, explains much."

Carly smothered another laugh that threatened to give away her eavesdropping activities before ducking around a locker as footsteps neared. Talia strode through the doorway, muttering to herself in a language Carly didn't understand, then through another door marked EMPLOYEES ONLY.

Giving a final tug on the skirt of her bathing outfit, Carly headed for the entrance to the pool area. Boy, would Mike be interested to hear about this.

$ $ $

Mike shook his head at his wife's words. "I can't believe that you would purposely stay there to listen in on their conversation."

"I didn't purposely—"

"Yes, you did." Using a Styrofoam board as a floatie, he paddled in a circle around her. "You could have left as soon as you realized they were engaged in a private conversation."

"I wanted to be sure she didn't need help."

He sighed. "If you're talking about this Talia, she sounds like she can hold her own. And I imagine she's been well-trained for dealing nicely with pesky passengers who ask personal questions." He slapped water in her direction. "And if you mean Miss Dawson, since when is she on your list of favorite people?"

Carly smacked water right back at him, which sent them both into a spate of antics that left him gasping for air and her doubled over with laughter.

Good thing they were in the shallow end.

Carly dog-paddled to the side of the pool and sipped her sparking water. "Miss Dawson isn't on my list of faves, as you call them."

"So it really was nosiness. Why don't you just admit it?"

She held up her hands in surrender. "Okay. Fine. I wanted to know what Miss Dawson wanted to know. She writes romantic mysteries. She's good on the romance, but not on the mystery. I think she was trying to dig up a story idea. Maybe something about a woman being attacked on a ship." She glanced around and shuddered. "I guess I felt like I was living in a dream here. I didn't think about that kind of thing happening. Not on a nice ship like this one. Not with nice people like Sam and Shandra. And Tomas."

He kicked over to float on his back beside her, staring up at the cloudless sky through the open skylights. "I know. I don't want to think about it. But we have to remember, we're living in a town of two thousand strangers for a week. People are the same everywhere. It doesn't mean we have to be frightened, just careful."

She nodded. "A good but sobering reminder that if bad things can happen in Bear Cove then they can happen here."

He knelt on the bottom, the water just below his chin. "The only difference here is that you don't need to get involved if it occurs on this ship. Or in one of the towns we visit. Or in the airport on the way home. Or at any time on our vacation. You've already had your mystery."

She patted his arm. "No worries. I have no intention of getting involved in anything else."

He groaned.

Where had he heard those words before?

$ $ $

Carly and Mike stood along the railing as their ship docked in Ketchikan. She gripped the barrier, not from nerves, but from excitement.

Her first time in Alaska. Her first cruise. And now—a second shore excursion.

Three stories below, crew scurried over the main deck, lowering anchors and tossing ropes as big around as her arm—and some as small around as a sausage—to dock workers who fastened them to the iron stanchions. To their right, another cruise ship that preceded them into the bay discharged its passengers, while off to their left, a third ship chugged into harbor.

Today would be a busy one for the town.

And for her and Mike.

Just this morning they decided to visit the town's world-famous Lumberjack Show, touted as a piece of historical interest with family-friendly entertainment.

She gripped Mike's arm. "Let's go."

His eyes never left the beehive of activity below as the ramp was unfolded and maneuvered into place at the same time a docking door below them opened and a forklift pulled up, a pallet of goods ready to load on the ship. "Go? Where?"

"Ashore."

"Not yet." He leaned over the rail for a better look. "Amazing how much stuff we've consumed in just two days."

She shook him. "Not just us. The other two thousand people did their part, too. Let's go."

"They haven't made the announcement yet. Remember? The itinerary said Hamish would tell us when to go to A Deck."

She glanced around. Several couples strolled past, arm-in-arm or hand-in-hand, and an insistent walker who bumped into her the previous day—rudely, as it happened, and never even slowed to apologize—stomped past, knees high and arms pumping. "There aren't many passengers out here. Maybe he already made the announcement and we couldn't hear it."

"What time is it?"

She checked her watch. "Ten after ten."

"Show doesn't start for another hour and twenty minutes. We have tickets. They'll let us in."

"Maybe I want to do some shopping first."

He turned to face her, arms folded over his chest. "Would you rather wait to hear the announcement, go to A Deck and leave in an orderly fashion, or do you prefer to go down early, stand in line, and get herded out like cattle?"

She sighed. After all these years of marriage, didn't he understand she'd rather be fifteen minutes early than five minutes late? "But if we go early, we'll be at the beginning of the line. So we won't be like cattle. We'll be like the pace car at a race. Or the lead dog in a dogsled race."

"Because you think nobody else had that same idea?" He shook his head. "Fine. They're done loading. I've seen what I want to see. Let's go."

Invigorated by a good breakfast, a swim, and her near-encounter with Miss Dawson in the changing room, Carly led the way, Mike following in her wake. She had a full morning ahead of her, and she didn't want to miss a single thing.

But, as usual, Mike was right. She hated when that happened—which it did, most of the time. When they arrived at the departure deck, about twenty people formed a line. But within minutes, they shuffled forward at a snail's pace, like penguins migrating across Antarctica, one baby step at a time.

Fourteen minutes later—she knew because Mike kept track—they stepped off the gangway and onto solid ground, which still felt shifty beneath her feet.

She giggled and gripped his arm. "Feels like I'm still on the ship."

"Yeah, that's what they mean when they say 'getting your ship legs'."

She unfolded the town map thoughtfully provided by the ship and scanned the streets. "Okay, looks like if we go this way, we can take in the three diamond merchants I want to visit, and still make it to the show on time." But when she stepped forward, his hand in hers, his failure to walk beside her tugged her back. She turned to face him. "What?"

"Three diamond merchants?"

"For the freebies. In the first one, I just have to try on something. In the second, we simply tell them Hamish sent us. And at the third, we turn in our coupon and get our gift."

"And they are?"

"A charm bracelet and charms."

He held out one hand. "Which will look so cute on me."

She playfully slapped his arm. "Silly. One for Denise, one for Sarah."

"Right. I knew that."

She turned to walk again and stopped when he stood still. "Now what?"

"No buying anything. You know they'll want you to buy."

With an index finger, she made an X over her heart. "I don't want their diamonds. I got the one I want." She held up her left hand. "Don't worry."

He rolled his eyes. "Somehow those two words bring a chill to my heart." He shrugged. "But let's forge on."

After standing in three separate lines to claim their free gifts, they were finally on their way to the show. When they arrived at the ticket booth, another line faced them.

Carly surveyed its occupants. Nobody she recognized. Nobody she could pretend was holding their spot for them. She exhaled. "How about you stand in line while I go to the restroom, then I'll come back and you can go."

"Sounds like a plan."

He headed one way while she went the other. Scanning for signs and finding none, she paused to ask for directions from an older woman behind a cash register in the gift store.

Her skin like leather, wrinkles almost obscuring her eyes, the woman looked like a hippy who refused to grow up, complete with a tie-dyed shirt, bell bottom jeans, and grizzled hair that hung to her waist. Still, she knew the way and pointed, her talon-like nails decorated with sparkling flowers. "Through that doorway, around to the left, second door on the right."

"Through the door, to the left, second on right." Carly nodded. "Got it."

She headed that way, pausing when a mother with three children in tow blocked her path. Then a cookbook caught her attention. Mike was always saying he wished she cooked more. Tried new recipes. More variety in their diet. Maybe she should—she replaced the book on the display.

Vegetarian. No way.

Through the door, she paused. Was that left then left? Or left then right? Or the other way around?

Probably no matter which way she went, she'd end up eventually in the right place. Left then left it was.

Except that took her between two buildings. The sun, blotted out by the dark wooden structures on either side, only dimly lit a little-traveled and even less-maintained alley. A startled cat darted out of a collection of trash bins, screeching its displeasure at her presence.

She paused. Should she turn around? Or keep going? She glanced over her shoulder then ahead. Might as well keep going. She could retrace her steps any time. It wasn't like she was out in a forest and might get lost.

At the end of the alley, another running perpendicular. If she went left again, that would take her back where she started, where there were no bathrooms.

Right it was.

Except in this direction, the alley ended at a brick wall. So she turned right this time, certain that was a direction in the original set of instructions. Upstairs in the building she passed, a raised voice commanded somebody about not shooting until they saw the whites of their eyes. She chuckled. A tenant enjoying an old movie.

More raised voices caught her attention, and she slowed. Unlike the ones from the apartment above, these were very real.

And coming from the alley to her right.

A sense of déjà vu invaded as she craned her neck to peek around yet another corner. But unlike her weak explanation of earlier, she truly was concerned someone needed help.

Although, if that were the case, she didn't know what she could do except run in the opposite direction.

No, honestly, she simply needed to know what was going on.

Three people faced off in a circle at about the midpoint of the narrow passageway.

Dave and Dewey, their friends from dinner.

And the purser, Neil Williams.

And neither of them appeared happy.

Dave's hands clenched into fists at his side as he leaned into Neil's face. Dewey stood to one side, tying her fingers into knots. And Neil, his head cocked at a jaunty angle, assumed a pose of nonchalance: one foot in front of the other, arms folded across his chest, his chin jutted out.

Dewey touched her husband's arm. "Dave, please. Let's just leave."

Dave shook off her hand. "Not until he pays us back."

Neil raised his hands to shoulder height. "Not going to happen, man. I lost as much as you did."

Dave poked the purser in the chest with a forefinger. "I don't believe you. Your type never loses. It's always us little people who pay the price. Your kind walks away with our future."

"Greed is what killed you, man."

"No. We listened to you. We believed you."

"Not me, man. The trends. And you could afford to take this trip, so you're not as broke as you let on."

Dewey gripped Dave's hand, still clenched. "Only because we paid for the trip before we invested with you."

"Water under the bridge, lady. If I had all the money, why would I be working on this ship?"

Dave stepped closer. "What better place to find a whole new pond of victims to steal from than a cruise? Captive audience and all that."

Neil shook his head. "Not true, man."

"If you don't give us our money, I'll go to the captain and tell him just what you're really like."

Neil planted his hands against Dave's chest and shoved him backwards a couple of steps. "Don't even think about it. I'll sue you for slander."

Dave laughed. "What do I care? I got nothing for you to take. They'll drop you off in the next port. See how far you get trying to rob these Alaskan bush men. You'll end up wolf bait."

"Don't threaten me, or I'll—"

"You'll what? Go to the cops and tell them you stole my retirement fund and I want it back? Who do you think they'll side with?"

Carly stepped back. So that was the story behind Dave and Dewey's financial problems. A crooked investment advisor.

No wonder there was no love lost between the couple and the purser.

So had Dave and Dewey chosen this cruise because they knew Neil would be here? If so, did they think he'd cave in and write them a check? Or have the cash on board to simply hand over to them?

Or did Neil request this assignment so he could rub their noses in their downfall?

Whichever way it happened, one thing was certain.

There would be no happy ending.

$ $ $

Mike studied the crowd behind him. Where was she? How could a person get lost going to the bathroom? And if she wasn't lost, what was she doing?

He moved forward another space as the line of people stepped through the ticket process into the former sawmill now converted into a mini amusement park of sorts. He had the tickets. If she didn't soon show up, he'd have to step aside and let others go ahead. Which wouldn't make her very happy.

So where was she?

Her familiar red hat bobbed and wove through the sea of people, heading in his direction. He exhaled. Finally.

When she neared, he held out his hands in question. "Where have you been? I was getting worried."

"Sorry. I got lost. And then I—"

"You stumbled into another conundrum, didn't you?"

"Well, not quite, but—"

"I hate it when you end a sentence in 'but'. It means 'yes but I don't want to admit it'."

"Okay. Fine. Yes, but I don't want to admit it." She peered past him. "Do you still need to go to the restroom?"

"Yes, but I'll wait until we get inside."

"Go now."

He shook his head. "No way. We're sticking together. I was dumb to let you go off on your own."

Her brow turned down. "You make me sound like a child."

"Not quite."

She relaxed her shoulders. "That's better."

"A child I could discipline. Send to their room. Know that eventually they'd grow up."

The ticket taker tapped Mike's shoulder. "Next, please. You're holding up the line."

She shoved him toward the entrance. "Yes, Mike. You're holding up the line." She smiled up at the man behind them. "He's always like this."

Mike gritted his teeth and handed over their tickets. A quick ink stamp on the back of their hands, and they were inside.

At least now she was kind of trapped. A ten-foot high fence all around. Their seats waiting. A show to watch.

He pointed to the small set of covered bleachers. "Find us a seat while I go to the bathroom. And don't get into any trouble while I'm gone."

She smiled at him then planted a kiss on his mouth. She tasted of toothpaste and cherry lip gloss, a nice combination he enjoyed sampling as often as possible. Then she stepped away. "Oh, Mike. What kind of trouble can I get into?"

He closed his eyes and counted to five.

That was a question he didn't really want her to answer.

Chapter 8

When Carly rode the elevator down to the meeting room for the third installment of Miss Dawson's talk, this one on investigative techniques, she did so with a rock in the pit of her stomach the size of Mount Saint Helen's.

After the snubbing earlier this morning, she wasn't certain what kind of a reception to expect.

Perhaps she'd find the author convinced all the other attendees to ignore her as well.

Maybe the romance maven arranged to move the meeting to another location, and she'd arrive to find geriatric yoga or a step aerobics class in full swing.

Instead, a roomful of folks sat in clusters and knots, chatting away like they were lifelong bosom buddies—which in some cases, they were.

She sighed and selected a chair near the back of the room, hesitant to shuffle to a middle seat in a row for fear of disrupting a discussion. Even though she'd love to be part of even a single conversation with somebody who wasn't belittling or deriding her.

Authors. Fans. A strange bunch, to be sure.

She tucked her feet on the crossbar of the seat in front of her and slid down onto her tailbone. Of course, she was one of those crazy fans.

Just not of this particular author.

Maybe she'd change her opinion after this talk.

In the front row, in his usual chair which seemed to have his name engraved in invisible ink on it somewhere, perched Teddy Bear. Ah-hum—Edward. He pushed his glasses up the bridge of his nose with a forefinger, then glanced to his left and then his right as though checking that everybody else was as ready as he for the event to begin.

He tossed a single nod to Monica, who sat poised in her appointed chair at the beginning of the row to his right, and she stood and approached the lectern.

After shuffling her notes—surely she wasn't going to read from them? That would be a disappointment. Then again, so had the guest speaker been. Maybe Ms. M. would be an improvement—Monica cleared her throat and tapped the mic. "Can you hear me?"

Carly closed her eyes then rolled them. The sign of an amateur speaker, to be certain. If they couldn't hear, she wouldn't get an answer, and then what? Raise her voice? Shout at them? And tapping the mic? Seriously.

Monica's face brightened half a degree with the broad smile that showed off high cheekbones and white teeth. "Good. Then let's get started. Thank you for attending. Miss Dawson will come shortly and give us her presentation about real-life investigation techniques."

Another eye roll. If what she witnessed in the changing room this morning was any indication of how to ask questions, Miss Dawson's grade would be Z minus.

"But first, let's conduct some club business."

Monica rattled off comparison numbers for the past few years of membership stats, bank account balances, and conference attendance, which Carly, for the most part, blotted out immediately.

Except the part about conferences. Who knew that three hundred people would gather in a wildly extravagant location like Florida to attend a fan club convention for Barbara Ann Dawson? And based on the next bit of information—the registration cost for next year's gathering—maybe that was something Carly should look into. Seemed holding conferences might be a way to make money.

She stifled a giggle. She could see it now—the Carly Turnquist Trouble-Mongers Conference. In Hawaii. A week of learning how to get into and out of trouble with the law, the mob, the justice system, crooks in general, and your neighbors.

She could truly teach that one.

In fact, a week might not be enough.

According to Mike, she was a trouble magnet. Maybe that would be catchier name: Trouble Magnet Conference. And it seemed she kept coming up with new ways to get involved. Like last fall, with the eclipse. A simple favor of babysitting for her son, and next thing she knew, a body, a kidnapping, and a drunk driving charge against Mike.

Yikes. Maybe he was right.

"And now, ladies and gentlemen, our guest speaker, Miss Barbara Ann Dawson."

Accompanied by varying degrees of enthusiasm—Teddy and Monica with wild abandon, most attendees with polite applause, and Carly doing the one-handed clap on her thigh—the author entered from a side door, bowed to the group, set her notes on the lectern, and surveyed her adoring fans.

And Carly.

Suddenly feeling exposed in the rear of the room, Carly slid down an extra inch, hoping to avoid the woman's eagle eye.

But no such luck.

The author's gaze froze on her like a wet tongue on an aluminum flagpole on a cold winter's day.

Carly held her breath. If she ducked down any more, she'd be on the floor. She leaned over and pretended she needed to retie a shoelace.

Except she was wearing slip-ons.

Luckily nobody else sat near enough to notice.

Once the author began speaking, and hoping it was safe to rejoin the group, Carly straightened then relaxed into her seat again.

Seemed the woman had the attention span of a peanut and had moved on to her favorite topic: herself.

For the next hour, Miss Dawson regaled them with examples from her books about how she gathered the material necessary to ensure a sense of realism in her stories. Tales of sitting in on police interrogations of suspects—unlikely. Of late night surveillance operations with private detectives—for that one, Carly snorted and had to cover the sound with a cough when the folks sitting in the row ahead of her turned around and stared.

Then the one she really wanted to hear about. The tale of the terrified housemaid. Almost word for word, the author recounted the bizarre series of questions and answers Carly overheard earlier. Except the setting wasn't aboard a cruise. It took place in Colombia. And the frightened miss worked for a local drug lord. And yes, apparently she had fallen victim to the amorous attentions of not just the big man himself, but every male over the age of ten in the city.

Ludicrous.

Outrageous.

But fodder for the type of books she wrote, apparently.

And for the type of books these people read, evidently.

In particular, Monica and Teddy scribbled copious notes. For their own works, perhaps? Or to communicate to those poor unfortunates who failed to attend?

Carly covered her mouth several times to stifle her yawns—no point in adding fuel to the fire of the author's dislike for her—and nodded off once, starting awake when the group applauded again to end the talk.

This time, Carly joined in wholeheartedly.

She checked her watch. Just enough time to get to the Faberge Egg talk.

Maybe something more interesting would hatch there.

$ $ $

After about ten minutes in the crowded display room, Carly felt like she was at a fireworks display. The *ooh*'s and *aah*'s of the folks crammed into the glass-cabinet-surrounded space breathed hot air combined with various smells of lunch, including one particularly obnoxious over-consumer of garlic in the far corner.

She shuffled sideways to get a better view of the Tenth Anniversary Egg, a delightful concoction of sky blue enameling flocked with spun gold and identical seed pearls, highlighted with the one and the zero in solid gold nestled on a velvet cushion inside the shell.

A husky-sized man, sweat staining the armpits of his dark shirt, bumped her off balance, and she grabbed at the table bearing the priceless artifact.

Kalim, the Faberge custodian, grabbed at the egg, which slid precariously toward the surface's edge. He missed and it slipped over the edge like a snowball racing downhill, gaining momentum as it went.

Several people gasped while Carly went to the floor in a heap, landing on her backside.

The Anniversary Egg landed neatly—and without harm—into her lap.

She beamed up at the circle of alarmed faces staring down at her. "Just goes to show a little padding comes in handy once in a while."

$ $ $

"I saw that." Mike pushed Carly's chair toward the table in the presentation room a few minutes later. "When are you going to learn?"

"Saw what?" She turned in her chair as he sat beside her. "I didn't do anything."

"You winced as you sat. Human padding isn't like a whoopee cushion, you know. It has feelings."

"I know that. And it wasn't my backside. It was my back." She shrugged and turned to face the front of the now-packed room. "These are good seats."

He clapped a hand to the side of his neck. "Ooh, whiplash at that change of subject."

She smiled. Which was a good sign. He hoped. Then again, sometimes she did that when she was up to something. "Well, they are. I'm trying to adopt an attitude of gratitude."

He groaned. "You are up to something. I just know it."

"Not at all." She leaned close and extracted their camera from his shirt pocket. "Hopefully you got some good shots of those eggs. I think they're beautiful, and you never know, I might want one someday. So I'll need pictures to show you which is my favorite."

He pulled the camera from her grip. "And what happened to being grateful? At the prices they're asking—which, by the way, could buy two new cars—I'd think you'd be happy to receive even the cheapest one."

She chuckled. "Seriously, if I had something like that, I wouldn't know where to put it. And I'd be scared silly to leave my house. Ever. Again."

"I agree. Imagine our insurance rates."

She touched a forefinger to her chin. "Unless I could find some way to write it off as a business expense."

Mike's brow raised. "Could you do that?"

She mock-punched his arm. "Not legally."

Kalim crossed the room from where he'd been chatting up a couple of wealthy Texans—at least, they looked like they were from the Lone Star State to Mike, cowboy hat and boots, lots of silver jangles and turquoise jewelry—and cleared his throat to get the room's attention. "Thank you, ladies and gentlemen, for following me from the display room to hear the presentation. I will give you some history about the eggs, how Faberge became involved, talk about counterfeit eggs, and bring you up to date on what's happening today, both with Faberge and with the eggs."

Mike settled in to listen. Sure, he'd love to be able to gift Carly with an egg, but really, they'd probably both enjoy a new vehicle or another cruise much more. He glanced at his wife. She nodded at what Kalim was saying, the laugh wrinkles around her eyes and the worry creases on her forehead relaxed. For the first time in a long while, he had some hope this vacation would be different. She already had her moments of excitement at the Space Needle, and really, the people on the ship were so nice, there was no reason to think. . .

She gripped his arm. Hard. "Did you hear that?"

He blinked. "No. What?"

She stared at him. "Where were you?"

"Thinking about you."

She narrowed her eyes. "Sure."

"Really, I was." He quirked his chin toward the speaker. "What did he say?"

"Just that there's a mystery surrounding the location of several of the eggs. Stolen during the Russian Revolution, when the Czar and his family were dethroned." Her eyes watered. "Which is so sad. I mean, if they didn't want them to be king or whatever any more, couldn't they have just told them?"

Oh, how he loved his wife's tender side. "You know how difficult it is to oust an elected official in our country. Imagine if that person were the supreme dictator of the country. Kind of like in Cuba. They might say they have democratic elections, but it's hard to believe a country would keep voting for the same kind of tyrannical leadership, years and years in a row."

She sighed. "I guess. And I suppose the Czar had a vested interest in staying in power. That's where his support came from."

"Right. Seems the monarchy in England made a wise choice. Have less input into government, but keep the figurehead. That way the people support them because they love them, not because they're afraid of them."

She nodded. "Oh, just listen. He's talking about private collectors who buy up stolen artifacts. Maybe that's where the missing eggs are."

Kalim continued on about the atrocity of purchasing great works of art on the black market, how these privates—as he called them—couldn't even safely display their stolen treasures, so they often kept them in secret vaults or locked rooms where nobody could enjoy them. "The Faberge Company, together with INTERPOL and national security agencies, works diligently to return these stolen artifacts to their rightful place. Just recently, an original of Rembrandt's *Madonna* was stolen and is still on the missing list. The *Mona Lisa*, by Da Vinci, has been stolen and returned several times, although its theft was not always made known publicly."

Carly raised a hand.

Kalim nodded toward her. "Yes?"

"Why not?"

"They didn't want to start a bidding war amongst potential black market buyers. When it's know that a masterpiece is available—even illegally—the worms come out of the wood."

She waggled her hand again.

Kalim sighed. "Yes?"

"Does the fact the painting is stolen increase its value to potential buyers? I'd think since they knew it couldn't be put on display or donate it for the tax write-off, folks would be less inclined to pay that huge price tag."

"That is a good question. Since these are all one-of-a-kind, whether a painting or a Faberge egg, the value to the collector is in owning something that nobody else has. While some try to justify their actions by claiming they are actually preserving the piece for future generations by keeping it in a safe place, in a good environment, that is nonsense. There is an international organization that monitors museums, and if a piece is not kept in a secure and environmentally-controlled atmosphere, they can step in and either offer a grant, a loan, or an alternate location to preserve the piece."

He then went on to explain how many Egyptian artifacts were looted from the pyramids under the pretense of preservation, working himself up to the proclamation that these pieces should be returned to their rightful owners.

Mike sighed when Carly raised her hand again. "I've seen lots of those mummies and stuff in museums in the US. How come nobody wants them back? It's not like they're hidden away. And, in fact, most of them don't look like anything valuable or culturally important."

"Are your parents still living?"

Her brow drew down. "No."

"So if their coffins turned up in a museum in Cairo and were put on display for folks to ogle, would you feel the same way?"

"Well, but that's different."

"Not really. Urns of ashes and mummies are somebody's family."

"From thousands of years ago."

Kalim smiled and jerked his gaze back to the rest of the audience. "Are there any other questions? If you're wondering about pricing, please wait until after the talk and I will make an appointment to discuss the item you're interested in."

The Big Texan raised a hand. "It seems as though the eggs on the ship are well-protected. Why is that?"

Kalim's shoulders relaxed. "Yes, it is true that we have a state-of-the-art security system. Newly installed, by the way. A first for this cruise line, in fact."

Tex's hand went up again. "Have you had attempts to steal them?"

Kalim's eyes widened, the whites contrasting starkly with his olive skin. "I didn't say that. The cruise line simply wants to ensure the safety of the eggs."

The Texan persisted. "So you haven't had any threats or attempts?"

Kalim's jaw muscles tightened. "I didn't say that either." He scanned the crowd. "Any other questions before we dismiss?"

When Carly's hand twitched, Mike grasped it in his own, stood, and offered his arm to her. "He obviously doesn't want to talk about why they increased security, so please don't put him on the spot. And we aren't making an appointment because we aren't seriously interested. I don't want to waste his time—or ours. I've had fun, but surely it's time to move on to something more interesting. Like dinner."

She resisted a moment then perked up at the mention of food, even though he knew her well enough. She was dying to pester the poor man with more questions. Argue her point of view about the museum pieces. If she even had a point of view. "Sounds good. Tonight is a casual night. Buffet or restaurant?"

"Restaurant. I like being treated like I could afford this meal if I was dining ashore."

Plus, the fact that they would sit at a table and she couldn't wander off to eavesdrop on conversations meant they could likely get through another evening without her looking for—or conjuring up—a mystery.

At least, he could hope.

Chapter 9

Carly surveyed the gathering scattered around The Captain's Table. "I guess since it's not a Gala Night, people are choosing to dine more casually."

"Or else they're going to eat later."

"Maybe." She sipped her iced tea and considered her menu. So nice to eat out somewhere classy without looking at prices. Not that there were any on the single sheet card before her. Not nearly as fancy as the Gala Night menu, tonight there were but two of each course to choose from. "I think I'd like the shrimp cocktail, the carrot bisque, the pork tenderloin again, and I'll skip dessert."

Mike glanced up at her over his own card. "Sounds good, except I'll have the escargots first and Baked Alaska for dessert. You can have a taste."

She patted her tummy. "Okay. I promised myself I'd save dessert for special nights. Although baked ice cream does sound good. Maybe I could have that tonight, and skip dessert the next Gala Night?"

"Why? You can taste mine. And still enjoy your own sweet on Friday."

She patted his hand. "You're always so logical. Good thinking."

They gave their orders to Emehlia, their server again, and settled in to wait. Carly scanned the other diners. Miss Dawson and her entourage of Teddy Bear and Monica entered and were seated at a table near the windows overlooking the stern of the ship. Three tables to her left, Bill and Belle sat, Belle's shoulders stiff and her hands clasped in her lap. They weren't speaking. When Carly waggled her fingers in his direction, Bill responded with a wan smile.

Oh, oh. Something wasn't right.

Carly shifted her chair a few inches to the right so she could keep them in her circle of vision.

Mike frowned at her. "What are you doing?"

She tossed him a flirty smile. At least, she hoped he thought she was being coy with him. "Just wanted to get closer to you."

He followed her line of vision then rolled his eyes. "Oh, no. Can't you let it rest for one meal?"

"Let what rest?"

"The snooping gene."

"I'm not snooping."

Their server appeared with their appetizers, which halted their conversation.

Or fight, depending on who was asked.

Conversation to Carly.

Discussion to others.

Fight to Mike.

Really, he was so sensitive.

She dipped a jumbo shrimp into the cocktail sauce and bit off a huge chunk. "Ohh, that is so good. I'd like to get the recipe for their sauce. I'm sure that's what makes it so delicious."

Mike addressed his escargot with diligence. "That, plus the fact it was probably caught fresh yesterday."

"Makes a difference, I'm sure. But it sure tastes better even than the fresh-caught shrimp we get at home."

"Maybe it's the Pacific versus the Atlantic. Water temperature. Way it's processed." He popped a morsel into his mouth, closed his eyes, and chewed. "Mmm-mmm. Garlic and butter."

She wrinkled her nose. "I don't know how you can eat those. No matter how much seasoning you put on them, they still taste like dirt-flavored inner tube."

He chuckled. "You've eaten everything." Another snail into his mouth. "You have no appreciation for fine food."

"I'll stick with my shrimp."

Movement at Bill and Belle's table caught her attention, and she glanced up as Mike dug another gastropod from its shell and forked it into his mouth, closing his eyes once again to savor the taste.

Neil Williams, the purser, hovered near their table. When he met Belle's gaze, he gave her a curt nod and waggled a slip of paper he concealed in his hand. Emehlia, their server also, neared the table, and Neil extracted the pitcher of iced tea from her hand. The young woman frowned when he spoke to her then turned on her heel and strode away.

Apparently the purser claimed rank.

Although, it was strange he was even here, in the restaurant, let alone offering to serve a table. As Carly understood it, his role on the ship was in the area of finances and administration, serving as a liaison between crew and passengers.

Unless he had something important to communicate, he wouldn't normally have any reason to be in The Captain's Table.

Carly kept her eyes on him as he bent over the table and topped up Bill's glass while dropping his note-holding hand beneath the surface of the table. Belle's hand groped around the edge of the cloth, finally grasping the note which she held in her lap, unfolded, and read.

Even from this distance, Carly saw her new friend's cheeks pale.

Could it be bad news from home?

Or simply bad news?

Carly held up her near-empty glass as Neil turned from the table, but he averted his gaze and headed for the door, plunking the pitcher on the hostess lectern before shouldering his way through the potential diners gathered in the entryway.

Strange. If he was here to serve, why did he ignore other diners who raised their glass for a refill?

And if he wasn't here to wait on tables, why was he here?

Other than to pass Belle the note, Carly saw no good explanation for his furtive actions.

And where no reason existed, a mystery did.

No matter what Mike might say about the situation, she would get to the bottom of this.

$ $ $

Back in their stateroom after dinner, Mike sighed as he hung up his nicer pants, shirt, and sports coat. "That was such a good meal."

Carly sat at the desk and looked over the next day's itinerary. "And Sam and Shandra did such a nice job with the towel whale."

He headed for the bathroom. "I'm going to take a shower before bed. Want to join me?"

Ignoring his waggling eyebrows, she shook her head. "I think I'll look at our schedule for tomorrow."

"Hot water might do your aching muscles and tender tush some good."

"Later." She buried her nose in the brochure. "Busy right now."

"Your loss."

He pulled the door closed behind him, and in seconds the water turned on and he started singing.

She gathered her room key and slipped into her windbreaker before heading for the door. Knowing Mike, he'd be in there for at least twenty minutes. Long enough for her to stroll up on deck and see who was there.

Well, actually, see if Belle was there.

When Carly and Mike left the restaurant, she overheard her friend telling her partner she wanted to get her mile in after such a delicious meal. They were still dining when she and Mike left, so hopefully, with any luck. . .

Luck, it appeared, was with her. As she climbed the steps to the Promenade deck, Belle strode past, her head bent into the wind. Carly slowed and stepped quietly onto the deck. A door to a third-deck passageway opened, and the purser stepped out.

Belle froze as he neared, and Carly ducked behind a pillar to remain out of sight. But still within earshot.

Belle shook her head. "Why won't you leave us alone?"

"Because you have something I want."

"No more."

Neil took a step closer. "I'll say when I've had enough."

Belle planted her palms on his chest as though trying to put space between them. "Please, you'll ruin my relationship with Bill. If that happens, there will be no more."

The purser chuckled and loomed over his victim.

At least, that's how it looked to Carly.

What were they talking about? More what? Money? Stock tips? Carly grimaced. Surely nothing physical. That was too disgusting.

Belle's voice cracked, almost carried off by a gust of wind. "I'll go to the captain and tell him what you're doing."

He gripped Belle's arms and held her in place. "I've worked long and hard to get where I am. If you ruin that for me, you'll regret it."

"Why can't you leave me alone?"

"Like I said, you have what I want."

"You're a beast."

He released her. "I remember when you used that word with much affection."

Belle's brow wrinkled. "That's changed. I'm not the person I was then. I don't want anything more to do with you."

He shoved his hands into his pants pockets and assumed an air of nonchalance. At least, that's the look he was trying to accomplish, from where Carly stood. But his stiff shoulders and clenched jaw muscles belied his subterfuge. "Well, I'm not done with you. Yet. Maybe soon. Maybe somebody will do us both a favor and put me out of my misery."

Belle snorted. "Misery? You? You enjoy putting me through this torture."

"Maybe not as much as you think. For now, it's a necessity. At some point, when I don't need you—or your money—I'll set you free as the proverbial bird."

"Why are you doing this?"

Carly stifled a snort of her own. Obviously, for the money, as he said. But what could the purser have that was worth paying for? Had they had an affair? Had to be since she met Bill, because if before, that wasn't a secret worth paying for. Had they done something illegal? Immoral? That she didn't want Bill—or her society friends to know about? Possible. But stuff like that was common news anymore.

Neil moved a few feet away and stood at the railing, one hand resting on the metal barrier. "It's nothing personal, *ma bella.*"

"Well, it's very personal with me. I had to lie to Bill tonight."

"Not the first one you've told, is it? Seems like your entire life is a lie."

"I should have told you to go to hell when you first approached me for money."

He laughed then leaned against the railing. "Yes, before it became more important to keep your little secret." He glared at her. "And don't think about siccing your boyfriend on me. I have pictures."

Belle staggered back a couple of steps. "What?"

He shrugged. "You heard me."

"You said you destroyed those. I believed you."

He spread his hands in front of him. "I don't always tell the truth though, so I?"

Belle crossed the deck and gripped his arms. "Well, tell me now. Did you? Or didn't you?"

He laughed. A cruel, nasty sound void of joy or compassion. In fact, the tone mimicked a demented serial killer in a true crime show Carly recently saw on television. A man who murdered more than a dozen people for the sheer delight of seeing the life-light leave their eyes. "That's for me to know and you to find out." He pushed her away. "Now, get out of my sight. Your weakness and begging sickens me. I don't know what I ever thought I saw in you."

"But I did that terrible thing for you. Because you said you loved me."

He snickered. Seemed nothing the poor woman said to him made a peck of difference.

Probably related to my first husband. He was the same way.

"Your choice."

Belle grasped his jacket in both hands. "Not my choice. You pressured me. And as a result, I've never had my own children. You stole that from me."

She released her grip and planted both palms on his chest, then pushed. "I wish you'd fall overboard and drown. Be out of my life, once and for all."

As though watching a scene in slow motion, Neil staggered backwards two steps, mouth open wide, eyebrows raised almost to his hairline, arms flailing at his side. The anchor footing for a column caught his heel, and he tilted precariously toward the handrail.

Carly froze in place, unable to move or even to call for help. Belle remained where she was, like a statue, arms still extended, a curious look of calm on her face.

Did she really mean what she said? That she wished he'd go overboard?

Carly glanced at the furious wake left by the fast pace set by the ship for night sailing. White water churned, spreading out in waves beyond the railing and vanished in the black of the night.

Surely, if somebody did go into the water, there could be no hope of recovery. By the time the alarm sounded, the ship slowed and turned around, either the cold, the shock, or the water itself would have claimed its victim. Swallowed down into the depths.

She shivered. What a horrible way to die.

One more step, and Neil rested against the railing, bending backwards with the momentum and the rolling of the ship at just the right moment. Then his right hand gripped the metal and he caught himself, straightening with both hands on the barrier behind him.

He breathed heavily a couple of times before pointing at Belle. "You're going to pay for that."

"No, I'm not. I've already paid for what I did—and what we did—with my life. I am not giving you anything else. Starting right now."

His mouth lifted in a sneer. "You're brave now. Let's see what you say when I tell Bill the truth."

She lifted her chin. A sign of defiance.

Here comes the punch line. Watch out, Neil. You might fall over in surprise.

"Bill already knows."

"You're lying."

"I told him about it over dinner. I think *you're* the one who better watch out. He wasn't happy to hear how you treated me then. Or since."

"I don't believe you."

She shrugged. "Then take your chances. Only I'll warn you now. Bill has a mean right hook. I suggest you not meet him out here." She quirked her head toward the ocean. "He'd probably just pick you up and toss you over. And *not* call for help."

Neil leaned toward her again. "You know, one of these days one of us will be dead and gone, and it will be too late for us to be friends."

She snorted. "I see now that we never were friends. I thought we were, but apparently you have a different definition."

He chuckled. "Live and learn."

She shook her head. "I wish you'd just curl up and die."

He stared at her a long moment before he tugged at the lapels of his jacket then stalked toward the same passageway he recently came out of, slung open the door, and disappeared from sight.

Belle slumped against the wall and took several deep breaths, her hands on her knees. Then she turned in the opposite direction and returned the way she'd come just minutes before.

Carly shrank back into the shadows, her heart—and mind—racing with this new information.

Whether Neil Williams knew it or not, he evaded death by a hair's width.

And he might need to be just as lucky again.

Because knowing what she knew now, she just joined the ever-growing group who wouldn't call for help if he went overboard.

Chapter 10

The next morning—Wednesday, day four of the cruise—and Carly headed for the next digital workshop, this one about archiving digital files. Not exactly a hot topic for her, since she preferred paper files, but maybe it would be the next new thing. According to the day's brochure, there was even going to be a short discussion on something called The Cloud.

Whatever that was. Or would be, someday.

She traveled in the elevator up to the Exploration Deck where the Explorer's Lounge resided without talking to anybody. Funny how once the car doors closed, so did people's mouths. Which was all right with her. She needed time to think. Mostly about the scene she witnessed—okay, spied on, according to Mike—the previous evening. Sounded like Belle had a real hatred on for Neil Williams. Which made her mind leap in all directions—the only kind of exercise she considered worthwhile—about the meaning behind her new friend's words.

And then that vicious push.

Neil stumbling and almost going overboard.

But worst of all—the smirk on Belle's face.

Cold.

Even the memory was enough to make her shiver, despite the fact she was indoors and well-dressed. She wrapped her arms around herself as she turned left out of the elevator and left again then straight into the back row of the room which was now filled with tables and chairs set up classroom style.

She selected the last chair furthest from the door and closest to the windows overlooking the starboard ocean view. At least if the class was boring, she could check out the scenery.

After settling in, she surveyed the rest of the class. Nobody she knew. Double win for her. But then defeat snatched victory from her grasp. The door opened again and Belle stepped in. By now, the only empty chair was beside Carly. As much as she wanted not to talk to anybody, if she had to, Belle was the one she'd choose.

She tossed the woman a smile and patted the chair. Belle surveyed the room then turned back to Carly, her shoulders slumped. Resignation? Disappointment?

Carly did an internal shrug. As Mike would say, *whatever.*

Belle perched on the corner of her chair furthest from Carly, facing the front of the class, her purse clutched in white-knuckled hands. Strange. Carly wouldn't have pictured the woman as being interested in anything digital, unless it was a bathroom scale or a thermometer, perhaps.

A pert blonde standing at the front of the room chatting with a male attendee stepped over to the lectern and smiled at the class. "Thanks for coming today. I know you could have been doing something else, but you chose to be here. Let's get started."

The young woman, who introduced herself as Ivy, launched into an impressive CV about her education, training, and experience that included employment with several Fortune 500 companies. Apparently she wasn't quite as young as Carly first estimated, since she had more than twenty-five years combined years—if what she said was true. Carly was well aware some folks made themselves sound more than they were by pumping up their resumé.

But really, an instructor on a cruise ship? Why would she bother? And who would check her out anyway?

Ivy continued. "Archiving digital files is a lot like archiving your paper files."

Carly settled in. That made the whole thing sound easier. Not so foreign.

The instructor smiled. "You just don't need to lug boxes around, or build a storage shed. Or hire out space in a warehouse."

This was sounding better by the minute.

Particularly the part about hiring out space.

And, eventually, a document shredding company for the boxes of old files.

"Everything is stored on a server. Most likely, the one that currently provides either your email service or your website provider."

Hold your horses! Website?

Ivy held up a hand. "And I see it in your eyes. You don't have a website. Well, perhaps by the end of the cruise I'll be able to convince you—and your business— why you might need one. But for now, let's focus on how to store documents and files digitally, and we can discuss the where later."

Carly leaned toward Belle. "Do you have a website?"

Belle looked her up and down a couple of times, her nose wrinkled as though Carly had something disgusting stuck to her shoe, before she gave a quick shake of her head.

No words.

Just the look. The semi-sneer. And the shake.

Carly thought they got along better than that. Then again, the woman did have some problems on her mind. Major ones, judging by what she heard the previous evening.

Maybe she'd try to lighten the mood. A little self-deprecating accounting humor, perhaps. She tossed Belle a smile. "Did you hear that old accountants never die?"

Belle stared at her as though she had three heads.

This was going to be tougher than she thought.

"You know, the old fill-in-the-blank occupation line jokes?"

Carly glanced to the front of the room. Ivy was still explaining to a couple of old geezers why having digital documents was easier, better, and safer than paper. Right. Until your computer crashes. Or your internet goes down. After all, what's easier? Carrying a file folder or a forty-pound desktop to a meeting?

She turned her attention back to Belle. Still no response. "Sure, you know, they just lose their balance." When her acquaintance didn't crack a smile, she pressed in. "You know. Accountants balance financial records. Lose their balance. Get it?"

Still nothing.

Feeling out of her depth, she laid a hand on Belle's arm. "Can I help in some way?"

This pulled the woman out of her coma. Or wherever she was. "Help? For what?"

Carly shrugged. Best not to let on she overheard the spat last night. "Whatever has you down in the dumps. You were friendly and chatty at dinner the other night. Now you're treating me like I have bad breath." She clamped a hand over her mouth. "Oh, no. Did I have too much garlic at breakfast?"

Belle faced forward again. "I don't want to miss this part."

Way to change the subject. Carly occasionally employed that little tactic herself. Which is why she would not be diverted from her focus: get Belle to spill the beans. "It's in the handout. Bottom of page two." She jabbed a finger on the paragraph. "Right there."

"Later. We'll talk later."

Ooh, exactly what she wanted to hear. "When?"

"I'll call you."

Ooh, not what she wanted to hear. "When?"

"Later. Now please be quiet."

Ivy called from the front of the class. "You, in the back, is there something you needed to ask?"

Carly met the instructor's gaze. Oh, she was talking to *her*. Several heads swiveled to get a good look at the troublemaker. Great. Now she'd be on *two* naughty lists. Miss Dawson's and Ivy's.

She smiled. "No, thank you. I was just showing this lady where we were in the handout."

For an introvert who didn't like the limelight, she sure managed to end up center stage often enough. Maybe Mike was right.

She *was* a full-time job.

$ $ $

Somehow she managed to make it through the rest of the workshop without once drawing the instructor's attention—or a response from Belle, either.

She waited while the room cleared out before exiting. Belle stood in front of the bank of elevators, but when the woman saw her, she wheeled about and headed down a passageway.

Carly did another internal shrug. Belle's loss.

She pulled out the daily itinerary to see what was next. She had a couple of hours before Miss Dawson's next lecture. Maybe she'd take a jaunt over to see what the purser had to say for himself before joining Mike at the Lanai Buffet.

Up the stairs to the fifth deck—wouldn't Mike be proud she skipped the elevator?—then she headed for Guest Services, hoping to find him in his office.

Which he was.

Although he wasn't nearly as happy to see her as she was to catch him there.

Particularly when she started asking questions.

She started by introducing herself, her occupation, and explaining her interest in onboard security. "So, you see, I've read about these cameras that are motion detectors and can alert the crew if somebody falls overboard."

He nodded and stood. "Let's get out of this stuffy office. I need a break anyway."

She hadn't thought his space was particularly stuffy, but she was open to just about anything. "Sure."

She followed him to the common area near the stairs where tables and chairs were arranged in cozy but private groups. He indicated a table and chairs in an open area. "Let's sit."

They did.

"Why did you want to know? Not planning to throw anybody over the side, are you?"

No, but his smarmy attitude just moved him a couple of notches closer to the top of her list. Just the fact Belle didn't like him was enough for her to even have him on a list. "Nothing like that. Just wondering. As I said, I read an article."

"They're still in the development stage. Actually, not even that far. We realize the need, but so far camera specs and hard drive requirements limit the actual functionality of a system that complex and prohibits us from installing a prototype."

Sounded like the company line to her. "So what kind of security do you have on the ship?"

"Fully trained staff. Honest crew who promptly report problems. Emergency drills like the one you experienced your first day on board. Ongoing fire and evacuation training for staff and crew."

A vein bulged at his left temple. He didn't like these questions.

Well, she didn't really like his answers. She could have read this in the in-stateroom guest binder. Which she had. She wanted something new. Something juicier.

She leaned closer. "What's the worst crime that's ever happened on this ship?"

He blinked at her a couple of times. "This ship?"

"Yes." She peered around. "The worst?"

A tiny smile tickled his mouth. "There was that time—" He straightened. "No, you're not interested in that."

"I am. Really."

Would it be murder? Assault? Theft? Impersonation of a crew member? Stowaways? Attempted hijacking? What?

"Well, there was that time when the chef overcooked the prime rib. Burned it to a crisp."

Carly straightened. He'd played her at her own game.

And well he knew it.

She smiled and nodded. "Good one. But seriously, when was the last man overboard alert?"

He stood. "I'm sorry, but I really must get back to work."

She stepped in front of him. "What should somebody do if they think a crime is about to be committed?"

"Such as hiding a pesky passenger in the cargo hold?"

She blinked up at him. "Surely there's no expectation that my asking a few questions will cause a problem?"

"Only in my workload. Excuse me."

"How about blackmail? Is that serious enough for Security to get involved?"

He froze in his tracks then turned slowly on one white soft-soled shoe until he faced her. "That is a serious allegation."

"Not one I'd make frivolously, I assure you."

"And are you lodging that particular complaint?"

"No. Just asking on behalf of—of an anonymous person. Who shall remain nameless. Just an example, really. I could change it to murder, if you like."

"Well, now, murder is much more serious, as I'm sure you can appreciate. Messier, what with a body to deal with. Weapon. Motive. All that."

"Unless the body and weapon go overboard."

"Ah, I see. Back to the overboard thing again."

She spread her hands wide. "It's a great big ocean. Just using it as an example of an easy way to dispose of a body. And evidence."

Neil stepped closer, hands clasped in front of him. "You have a vicious *little* mind."

His overt emphasis on the second adjective wasn't lost on her.

When he took another step, invading her personal space with his frame, she stood her ground. "Mr. Williams, you have just proven my theory. Thank you."

His brow pulled down. "What theory?"

"That you can't judge a person by the color of their shoes."

"Huh?"

"As an officer, you wear white shoes. Sets you apart from the rest of the crew and the staff. Sort of like stripes. But it appears that not all officers are gentlemen."

He sniffed. "And not all women are ladies, I assure you."

Enough bantering. She would have the final word.

"Well, you have been busy. That you would deign to believe you know all women."

She turned and headed for the stairs. As she passed the large steam-punk-style clock that filled the stairwell between the deck below and this, she caught his reflection in a mirrored panel.

Good.

He looked worried.

Chapter 11

After lunch, Carly headed to Deck Four and the Explorer's Lounge to take in Miss Dawson's talk about "Red Herrings, Suspects, and Motives" while Mike went up on the forward deck to do some whale watching. He was determined to see something more than a water spout in the distance—if it meant camping out in the wind and cold.

Carly stepped out of the elevator with two or three other women she recognized from previous lectures, lagging behind to let them go in the room first. Nothing worse than choosing a seat where she hoped to sit alone only to be surrounded by a bunch of latecomers who wanted to gush on and on about the author, or chat about an inside story of their little group.

No, siree. She'd wait and slip into the back row at the last minute before the doors shut.

Because one thing she'd learned about these talks—nobody wanted to sit in the back.

She lingered in the hallway—called a passageway on a ship—near a darkened alcove, wishing she'd thought to get a coffee. Her lunch of salad and salmon was making her sleepy. She peered around the corner. Wasn't there a name brand barista around here somewhere? She could swear she vaguely remembered it from one of her strolls.

Hushed voices greeted her and she paused. When people talked that low, they generally didn't want to be overheard. The right thing to do would be to backtrack and step out of earshot.

Not that she was famous for always doing the right thing.

And seriously, when she signed up for a cruise with over two thousand of her closest friends, she expected privacy in her own stateroom, but was under no delusions of being alone anywhere else.

Except a bathroom stall in the common areas, of course.

Which this wasn't.

She peeked around the wall again.

Two people. A man and a woman.

The man, slender. Dressed in white. Crew? Or staff?

She checked the shoes. White. Officer.

Dark hair. Casual stance.

Purser Williams, no doubt.

And the woman?

Williams partially blocked her view, so she sidled into the hall—passageway—a few inches. Big hair. Patent leather boots.

Miss Dawson, no doubt.

A suspicion confirmed an instant later when the woman raised her voice. "This isn't the end of it. Do you understand?"

The purser's low chuckle was clear enough, but his response wasn't. Miss Dawson pushed him to one side and stepped out of the alcove, heading directly for her. Their eyes met across the room. Miss Dawson glanced back at Williams, who ducked his head, shoved his hands in his pockets, and walked in the opposite direction. The author's cheeks colored as she brushed past Carly in a wave of hairspray, sickly cologne, and yards of a filmy taffeta jacket.

Carly stared after her. Funny, their reaction. Like they were embarrassed.

Or guilty.

What were they up to?

And how did Williams manage to upset so many women? Not that he was likely to win Mr. Congeniality anytime soon. He ticked her off, too, with his smarmy attitude and self-assuredness that topped most Hollywood stars and all politicians. Really, nobody could be that confident about themselves, could they?

He did put on a good act. Except the couple of times she called his bluff and noted a momentary drop in his façade.

Carly followed the author into the room and selected a seat in—yes!—the last row as Miss Dawson headed for the front and the lectern. She settled in while the author made a great show of finding her reading glasses and tamping her notes into perfect place before scanning the room. A smile lit her otherwise dour expression—until her gaze landed on Carly.

Barbara Ann's eyes narrowed and her upturned lips upended themselves into a frown. She held that position for what felt like forever—but was likely just a few seconds—before moving on to the next person as though Carly didn't exist.

Which, at that moment, is exactly how she felt.

But not for long. The next time the author scanned the room and her eyes lit on Carly, her expression didn't waver for even an instant. The great woman had regained control of herself, it seemed.

Because now she was in control. She commanded the microphone, stood at the front of her adoring fans, and expounded on the importance of planting suspects with good motives and misleading clues with a reason to be where they were in order to keep readers turning the pages.

At the end, she opened the floor for questions.

Carly raised a hand. Surely the author wouldn't—couldn't—ignore her now.

But apparently she could. When Carly's arm grew tired of its vertical position, she braced it against her other hand and her head. But still no acknowledgment. After a minute or two of nodding to other attendees and taking their questions, the room fell silent.

Carly cleared her throat and stood. "I guess you couldn't see me way back here." She glanced around at the faces now turned toward her. "That'll teach me to sit closer to the front."

She chuckled at her own humor, although apparently nobody else found it particularly funny. What? Had she missed a memo or something? *Nobody talks to or even pretends to notice the pesky accountant.*

She persisted. "I was wondering why some authors think it's okay to hide things from readers? Like when they see something in a picture, say it's important, but don't tell the reader what they saw? I hate when that happens. It feels like they're cheating. Like they don't want us to figure out whodunit."

Miss Dawson smiled, but only half her mouth turned up. The other half somehow managed to turn down. "It's a matter of style. I've used that technique myself. What does everybody else think?"

Well, it seemed everybody else couldn't help but jump all over themselves in an attempt to assure Miss Dawson that she was absolutely correct that it was sometimes permissible to hold back information from readers.

Carly tried again. "Despite the fact you've used that particular *easy* way out, do you think it's fair to readers? I mean, up to this point, the reader knew everything the character knew. And suddenly, when it's really critical, information is withheld."

The author stared at her as though wishing a hole would open in the floor and swallow her. When it didn't, she turned again to the audience. "Well, thank you for your questions. I hope you will attend the lecture tomorrow which begs the question about whether you prefer a standalone or a series. See you then."

Carly sat. Talk about rude. Belittling her first question, then ignoring the second. It was like she didn't want to answer, or she didn't know the answer. Why? If she didn't want to give away some trade secret, like a magician's guild or something, simply say so.

But if she didn't know the answer, that was an entirely new kettle of wax. Or ball of twine. Or whatever the saying was. Though what wax or twine had to do with not answering a question, she wasn't certain.

One thing she did know: Barbara Ann Dawson and the purser were up to something.

And she was just the person to find out what.

$ $ $

Exhausted from the mental gymnastics required to attend a simple lecture, Carly headed for the stateroom for a nap. Mike was either still on deck looking for whales, or he was in the afternoon matinee of *Shark Tale*. Either way, he wouldn't be back until almost time to dock in Sitka.

Which was fine with her.

She would enjoy a nap, maybe read some—not a Barbara Ann Dawson, to be sure—shower, then change for their time ashore. Not to mention time to ponder, without interruption, the events of the day—and last evening—and try to fit them into a picture of what was going on.

Because although she felt like a goldfish looking into the bowl from the outside, she knew one thing for certain: everybody she'd met so far was trying to hide something.

And she was just the one to figure out what.

At the last turn before their room, Sam their steward stepped out of a room with an armful of towels and linens. He smiled. "Good afternoon, Madam. How are you today?"

"Doing fine, Sam. And you?"

He ducked his head. "Very well. Always busy, as you can see."

"Yes. Seems so. Thank you for taking such good care of our stateroom. You're in there, what? Three times a day?"

"At least. To make the bed in the morning. To tidy the bathroom and empty the trash in the afternoon, and of course, to do the towel animal and leave chocolate and the itinerary for you in the evening."

"You do a great job. It seems like we never see you. You always come when we're out. It's like magic."

He smiled and bowed again. "Thank you. Is great compliment." He glanced up and down the hallway and took another step closer. "I tell you this in confidence."

Her heart pounded. What would he divulge?

"Please to use the safe in the closet of your stateroom for valuables. You have jewelry?"

"No, nothing besides what I always wear. Why do you ask?"

"Passport? Special documents?"

"Yes, we brought our passports. What is going on?"

"Please to not tell anybody else."

"I will tell my husband, of course."

"Yes, of course. But nobody else. Promise?"

This was serious if he was intent on extracting her word before she even knew what it was. "Promise."

"Several passengers say they missing valuables."

"What kind of valuables?"

"Jewelry. Gold lighter. Cuff link. Money."

"From their staterooms?"

He nodded. "Make us stewards look bad. We have master key, so of course must be one of us. That is what officers think. They watch us all the time."

"I can see how that might look bad for you. Is it only on this deck?"

He shook his head. "No. Also on Promenade Deck and up on Lanai Deck where apartments are. They more rich so they have more taken. But since is on every hotel floor, room stewards being watched."

"But you aren't the only crew who go into staterooms, are you?"

"No. Security has key. In case somebody fall or missing. Like the woman from the evacuation drill on Sunday."

"Yes, I remember seeing men in suits go into her room. Was she all right?"

He shrugged. "She lazy. No think rules apply to her. They threaten to put her off at next port, but she one of their stars." His mouth turned down. "I think it not first time she did that."

"She likely gets away with it so she keeps doing what she likes."

"So promise you put valuables in safe? And you not tell anybody. Except Mr. Mike."

"Promise." Carly crossed her heart with her forefinger. "Thanks for the warning."

"Not supposed to tell anybody, but am telling special people. Like you and Mr. Mike."

Carly proceeded to her stateroom, Sam's words warming her heart. Maybe she should sic him on Miss Dawson. And Teddy Bear. And Athena. And Neil Williams. And now Belle.

Goodness. Did she have *Typhoid Mary* emblazoned across her back?

Seemed she'd alienated half the people on the ship.

Well, not half. Only five.

But five more than disliked her when she boarded.

Must be a new record. Even for her.

.

Chapter 12

Carly sipped her second—and final—cup of hot chocolate as the ship nosed into the berth in the small fishing village of Sitka. Although it was much bigger than she expected. She envisioned huts, drying racks, and perhaps rowing to the community pier. Bear Cove was a small town, four hundred souls at the height of lobster season, and Sitka looked much larger.

Then again, perhaps the dozens of jewelry and souvenir stores lining the main street created—or at least contributed—to that effect. Flashy neon lighting, signs proclaiming LOWEST PRICES, SALE, or EVERYTHING HALF OFF detracted from the towering pines hugging the edge of town, or the picturesque seagulls decorating the tops of the wooden piers, or the bald eagles riding the air currents.

Now *that* was the Alaska she expected.

Mike nudged her foot beneath the table. "Are you ready to go ashore?"

She set her cup down. "I am. Figured we could walk around a bit and build up an appetite."

He grinned. "Or buy a few trinkets."

She shook her head vigorously. "Not me. I do want to get my free things, though." She dug through the shoulder sack she intended to collect her stuff in. "I have coupons for charms, coins, and something that changes color in response to heat."

He chuckled. "That would be me. I sunburn easily."

She swatted at his hand. "Seriously. This is a trip of a lifetime, Mike, and I want to remember it."

"I think you will, whether you have a charm from this town or not. It's probably made in China, anyway."

"Maybe so. But it's the principle of the matter."

"No, it's your principle. Collect everything free." He rolled his eyes. "For that, we'll stand in line in crowded stores that are trying to sell you something you don't need and likely can't afford."

"But it's the adventure of seeing how low they'll go before we walk out the store."

He sighed. "Maybe I'll let you build up your appetite your way, while I build mine elsewhere."

"Oh, you can't do that. Some of these require both of us to be present."

"Sounds sexist. Like a woman can't make her own decisions?"

"I think it's so they can work on you and guilt you into buying me a lovely gift."

He shook his head again. "I'm not taking any plastic with me. Just enough cash for dinner. And I suggest you do the same."

She stuck out her bottom lip like a defiant child. "I might want to get a few souvenirs for the grands. And maybe something for Doc." She glanced out the window where a large marmalade cat stalked a gull. "A collar, maybe, with *Alaska* on it."

"Right. Like he'll keep it on for more than ten seconds. He never does."

"He'll be so happy to see us he won't care."

"More likely he'll be so glad to be home from Denise's and the kids he'll collapse from sheer exhaustion."

"Anyway."

Mike stood and offered his hand. "Time to go. Leave the plastic in the safe."

"Shhh, keep your voice down." She stood and grasped his arm.

"That's supposed to be a secret."

"I was just saying. . . ."

"I know. But—" She made a zipping gesture across her mouth. "Loose lips sink ships, and all that."

They headed back to their stateroom for a quick freshen-up before going ashore. While Mike was in the bathroom, she stored his credit card in the safe but tucked her own into a back pocket of her jeans. No point in taking a chance of being unprepared, she always said.

Well, not always. Most of the time she jumped in with both feet before looking to see how deep the hole was. At least, that's what her son Tom said. With a glint of mischief in his eyes and a smile on his face, of course.

She turned her attention back to the day's itinerary. Maybe there was a coupon for a nice restaurant. After all, everything in town had to be flown in or brought by boat. No telling how expensive food might be. And there were few things more embarrassing than not having enough to pay for the meal—after they ate it.

Oh, here was one. For a place that looked nice, at least according to the picture. *The Bait and Tackle*, a seafood restaurant that also served moose, caribou, and bear. She wrinkled her nose at this last one. Didn't sound too appetizing.

Maybe she'd stick with the seafood.

And the ad came complete with a "buy one, get one free" coupon.

Sweet!

By the time Mike emerged, she had her game plan in place, having marked off the four stops she wanted to make before dinner. When he protested, she explained her reasoning. "Everybody else will rush to the restaurants first and then get to their shopping after. My plan is to hit the shops first, then eat when the place is less crowded."

He smiled. "There are over two thousand people on board, most of whom will be going stir-crazy now and so they'll go ashore. Not to mention whatever percentage of the crew and staff who have the evening off. The place is going to be crowded. For hours. And hours. If we don't head to the restaurant first, we might not get to eat."

She considered his words. Which would she rather miss—eating or shopping? "We can always eat later onboard. And the food here is great. And we get seafood at almost every meal."

"Fine. We can eat here first then go shopping."

"But—"

"Gotcha." He looped his arm around her waist. "Come on. Let's go ashore and see where the longest lines are, then go somewhere else."

That sounded like the best plan. A self-proclaimed introvert, she didn't really like crowds.

They rode the elevator to the first deck then walked forward, following the lines of folks ahead of them, stepping over bulkhead barriers, through narrow doorways, up three steps, then onto the ramp that would take them to *terra firma*.

As before, however, dry land didn't feel so steady for the first few minutes, the natural effect of the ship's rolling motions having affected her inner ear in only four days. But the more they walked and the more fresh air she breathed—and the less she focused on the sights and sounds of the town—the less the rocking seemed. By the time they reached their first destination—a tanzanite jewelry store promising them a free tanzanite bracelet—the better she felt.

She pulled him inside the store. "Come on. Two minutes and we're out of here."

He pasted on a smile and accepted the coupon she handed over. "One for Denise, one for Sarah, I presume?"

"Right. Exactly."

But three minutes later, she was still standing behind a woman who was almost as wide as she was tall, including the added height of a crazy-cloth turban-like hat that must have come straight from the '60's. Or a thrift store.

And ten minutes later, they'd moved all of about two feet forward.

This would never do.

She turned to Mike. "You stay here, while I suss out other opportunities."

"Like what?"

"Another clerk who is faster at their job."

She left the line before he had a chance to complain and headed for the rear of the store where a thin young man in a suit surveyed the crowd. Probably counting the dollars coming in. Well, not from this landlubber.

She paused in front of him. "Excuse me."

His gaze never left the crowd behind her. Maybe he was store security.

"Can you help me?"

"What's the problem?"

Still no eye contact. Now that was just plain rude.

"I want to get my free bracelet. And so does my husband."

"And so do half the people in the store."

"Right. But I'm not going to buy anything. I just want my gift."

His eyes finally rested on her. And a most disapproving look it was.

Maybe she was better off when he didn't make eye contact.

She sighed and shifted her weight to the other foot. "I don't want to waste your time. If I promise to walk right out and leave the real buyers more room, and if I wave the bracelet around and say what a bargain I got in here, will you just get me my gifts? I'm hungry, and tired, and when I get both hungry and tired, well, you won't want to be anywhere near me." She waggled her fingers at Mike, still standing patiently in line. "My husband will tell you."

The young man's gaze followed hers to where Mike stood. To his credit, her husband lifted one shoulder in a half-shrug, a look of resignation pinching his eyes.

"Fine." The clerk whirled around and turned back, two small plastic bags in hand. "Off with you. Thanks for coming in."

She snatched her goodies, quirked her head toward the door, and headed toward the door while she tore one bag open. Holding her treasure aloft, she called back to Mike. "You should see the bargain I just got. Isn't it lovely?" She dangled the bracelet toward a middle-aged woman peering into a display case. "Talk with that nice young man back there. He'll get you one just like it."

The woman nudged her shopping companion, another woman about the same age, and both hustled to the rear of the store.

Carly laughed as Mike caught up with her and they took a sharp left outside the store, heading for the next stop.

Mike laid his arm across her shoulders. "I don't know how you do it. I probably don't want to know, do I?"

"Give them what they want. It's a win-win for everybody." She glanced back. "I sure hope those two women buy something fabulously expensive." She pointed. "Looks, there's the next place. Something that changes color in the heat. Although this seems a strange place to sell that kind of stuff."

"How so?"

"Well, I wouldn't think of Alaska and heat, would you?"

"Not necessarily, but they do get summer here. Maybe it's short, and not too hot, but it's still summer. Not to mention that pretty much all the tourists are from somewhere else that probably gets a longer summer."

"True. Still, free is free, isn't it?"

"Depends on how much the free stuff costs."

She sighed. Sometimes Mike could be so practical he was practically boring.

After all, how much could free stuff cost?

$ $ $

An hour, three stops, and a sack of treasures later, and Mike and Carly arrived at the *Bait and Tackle*. And a lineup. When he checked with the hostess, however, he was informed most of the people ahead of them were a single large party, and their wait should only be about ten minutes. Despite the ache in his lower back, he agreed this was likely the shortest line in town.

For sure it was the shortest he'd stood in all day.

The hostess was wrong.

They waited seven minutes.

Inside the quaint Old English-style pub/restaurant, the cute teenager with green hair led them to a table in the corner. "Will this do, sir?"

He nodded. "Nicely, thank you."

She set menus on the table. "Your server, Paul, will be right over."

Mike pulled out Carly's chair and helped her sit before taking his own place. No way would he be outdone by the waiters at the Gala Night dinners. This was a special time for them, and he'd do whatever he could to enhance that experience for Carly. Even his objections to the shopping thing were half-hearted. He had nothing special planned for this time. He'd go along and do whatever she wanted.

But he'd never let her know that, of course.

Carly in control could quickly become Carly out of control.

Dinner passed uneventfully, for a change. She concentrated on their conversation instead of trying to eavesdrop on those around them. And not once did she point out another customer or relate a story of something she'd seen—or accidentally overheard—on the ship.

Maybe he overreacted sometimes to her snooping. Blew it all out of proportion. Exaggerated.

Perhaps in some ways they were more alike than he wanted to admit.

Still, it was nice to eat at least one meal without interruption.

As he sipped his coffee and contemplated whether to finish the last two bites of mocha cheesecake, Carly stiffened, her eyes fixed on something behind him. He swiveled in his seat.

Now what?

A parade of folks trooped through the restaurant, following their hostess like the children in the Pied Piper story.

A parade of strangers—almost.

Dave and Dewey, and Bill and Belle followed in the wake of three women he didn't recognize.

He tapped Carly's arm. "Who are they?"

"Nobody."

"Nobody? So why are your hackles up?"

She turned to face him. "No reason."

"Don't give me that. I know four of them. Who are the rest?"

"Just the other three people in addition to our new friends who have the most reason to hate the purser, Neil Williams."

"Why do they hate him?"

She waved off his question. "Various reasons."

He rolled his eyes. He'd spoken—or thought—too soon. No way would he get off this easy. "Don't tell me you're getting involved in another mystery."

She shook her head. "It's no mystery *why* they hate him. The real mystery is why they're all together. I didn't even know they knew each other." She leaned toward him. "It's like a remake of that great movie, *Murder on the Orient Express.*"

"Except we're on a ship. In Alaska."

"Not that part. The part about all the killers knowing each other."

"All the killers?" He glanced back at the party being seated at a large table in the rear of the restaurant. "Who did they kill?"

She smiled at him.

"Nobody. Yet."

$ $ $

Her tummy full and eyes heavy, Carly slipped her key into the stateroom lock, flipped on a light, and entered, wondering what neat towel animal Sam or Shandra left for them tonight.

And looking forward to a piece of bedtime chocolate.

Instead, the next day's itinerary lay on the floor, crumpled into a ball.

And scrawled on the mirror over the desk, in some kind of black ink, a message: STOP POKING YOUR NOSE INTO OTHER PEOPLE'S BUSINESS!!!!

The multiple exclamation points illustrated the writer's agitation, it seemed.

She glanced around.

No towel animal or chocolate, either.

Mike stood close, his arms around her waist. "What's wrong?"

She pointed, first to the wad of paper, and then to the mirror. "Not the top-notch service we're used to. Do you think we made Sam angry? You did mention putting the credit card in the safe quite loudly in the restaurant."

He nuzzled her neck. "I don't think that's the cause of this." He released her and stepped to the phone on the bedside table. "Let's call him."

He did, explained the situation, and within a few minutes, a light knock sounded. When Mike opened the door, both Sam and Shandra stood there, the younger steward wringing his hands into knots.

Sam stepped forward and ducked his head. "Apologies." He looked at the detritus, and his eyes widened when he spotted the message. He hurried forward, pulling a white cloth from a pocket. He scrubbed at the words, which disappeared beneath his ministrations. "Dry erase marker."

Carly exhaled. At least their intruder didn't expect them to either finish the cruise with no mirror or be forced to look at those awful words for the next three days.

Sam returned to the open doorway. "I was employed at other end of the passageway, and Shandra prepared your room for the evening." He stepped aside and lowered his voice, speaking to his junior steward. "Tell them."

Shandra shuffled toward them. "I make up your room. Make towel monkey. Leave two pieces of milk chocolate. Empty trash. Set out itinerary as usual."

Mike nodded. "And then what happened?"

His shoulders slumped. "I think I forget to lock door. But I remember when in trash room, so I hurry back. But door is locked, so I think I am being foolish."

Carly stepped around Mike. "Did you look in?"

"No. Sorry." He shuffled back into place just behind Sam. "I sorry Mr. Sam."

Sam cast a stern look on his junior. "Not me who needs apology. But you shame us both. Search for towels and chocolate. Now."

Shandra nodded briskly and wheeled out of sight. Sam tossed a smile after the agitated youth. "He will remember this. Not happen again. He need this job."

Mike dug into his wallet and pulled out a couple of bills. "Thank you for looking into this so quickly. And so late at night. Sorry to disturb you."

Sam shook his head and stretched out his hand to block Mike's offer. "We cannot take money when it is our fault. His fault is mine, too. Reflect poorly on me that I distracted with other work and not check up on him. Won't happen again."

Carly gestured to the chair at the desk. "Can you sit a minute until he comes back?"

But the steward stepped back and folded his hands in front of him. "Not permitted. I will wait here." He indicated their stateroom with his hand. "Please. I will knock when he returns."

Mike ran his fingers through his hair. "That will be fine. Thank you."

Carly perched on the edge of the bed. "Why would somebody do this?"

"If Shandra is to be believed." He sat beside her and pulled her close. "Maybe the boy isn't telling the truth?"

"He doesn't seem the type to be well-versed in subterfuge. So if he's lying, that means he did this damage. And why would he do that? He needs the job. Did he think we wouldn't report it to Sam? Or somebody at Guest Services?"

Mike released her and flopped back onto the bed, hands clasped behind his head. "True. And he did look pretty upset."

"As was Sam. I think they have a deeper sense of shame than we Americans do anymore. I mean, singers can wear their underwear on the outside of their clothes and think nothing of it. Yet this little incident reflects poorly on the entire cruise line and the country of Indonesia. At least, according to Sam."

At the second light tap on the door of the night, Mike crossed the small room and admitted both stewards, Sam first, with Shandra close behind, his arms filled with rumpled towels.

Carly stood beside Mike. "You found them?"

Shandra indicated two googly eyes clumped together in one facecloth. "This was his face. I know, because we only give these to special passengers."

Carly smiled. "Really?"

"Yes. These are large size with eyelash. Special. For you and one other couple on this deck." He held up two empty chocolate wrappers. Milk chocolate. Carly's favorite. "And these were in hamper also."

Sam nudged the young man out the door. "Very sorry this happen. Double chocolate for rest of cruise." He handed Mike four squares of milk chocolate, which Carly grabbed. "Good night."

Mike nodded. "Make it two dark and two milk chocolate each night, and you've got a deal."

Sam bowed and backed away, nattering at Shandra in their mother tongue. Mike closed the door and leaned against it, quiet.

Too quiet.

Oh, oh. This won't be good.

He exhaled loudly and walked toward her. "Carly. . . "

She held up one hand. "I know what you're going to say."

"No, you don't."

"Yes, I do. You're going to say I need to stop asking questions. Stop listening in on other people's conversations. Stop walking in at awkward times. Stop looking for mysteries where there isn't one."

"You've been doing all that?" He rolled his eyes. "I declare, I can't let you out of my sight for two minutes."

"It's not like it's my fault. It just—"

"I know. It just happens." He smiled. "That's not what I was going to say. In this case, somebody is worried. Very worried. To leave a message like that indicates you're getting close to the truth. Whatever that is. This was deliberate. Most of your bumbling around into other people's lives isn't. So what I was going—"

"Bumbling? What do you mean? I am a highly trained professional—"

"Bumbler." He stretched out his hands in front of him. "And I was going to say: give me some chocolate."

"Not on your life."

Her words sobered her—but just for a moment.

Mike pressed her down onto the bed as she clutched the chocolate in her hands.

No way was he winning this time.

Leeann Betts – Silent Partner

Chapter 13

After a good night's sleep and a hearty breakfast—really, there was no other kind on this ship—Carly and Mike headed for an on-ship excursion included in their gift cruise. A couple's massage. And although Mike wrinkled his nose when the coupons appeared at the slot outside their door that morning, accusing her of arranging this—which she vehemently denied—he admitted some curiosity about the entire thing.

He nodded when they passed another couple coming in the opposite direction. "Any idea what to expect?"

She shook her head. "None at all."

"So why do you think it's called a couple's massage?" His eyebrows waggled like drunken caterpillars. "Are you going to rub my feet while I rub your back?" He pondered that a moment. "Sounds interesting. But we could have done that in our room."

She mock-punched his arm. "No, silly. Somebody else gives the massage. We just lie there in our all-together, hold hands, and enjoy it."

His brow raised. "In our all-together?"

"Yes. And if you're nervous, I'll hold your hand."

"Do you mean—"

She lowered her voice as they threaded their way through the exclusive shopping area, now heavily populated with folks looking for onboard deals. Of which there were plenty. "Our birthday suit. You know."

He shook his head and jutted out his chin. "I didn't come all the way to Alaska to get naked in front of strangers."

She chuckled. "Did you see the look on that woman's face when she heard you?"

His cheeks colored. "She heard me?"

Carly nodded. "In fact, she's ogling you now." To prove her point, she paused, forcing him to stop since they were holding hands. "See."

Sure enough, a woman older than them by several years—judging by the wrinkles, penciled-in eyebrows, and white hair—touched a forefinger lightly to her cheek and smiled coyly at him.

He wheeled around and practically dragged Carly the remaining distance to the spa. "Getting naked with two strangers sounds good about now."

She giggled as they checked in at the reception desk where a young man with spiked purple hair and several piercings—not all of them in his ears—checked their names off a list. He looked them up and down—sizing them up for something, perhaps? Carly squirmed at the thought—then looked back to the list. "You are signed up for the couples massage, correct?"

Carly smiled. Might as well make the best of this. "Ye-e-s-s."

"Would you like to upgrade to the intimate couples massage? For just ninety-nine dollars, each, you can be completely *au naturel.*"

Mike squinted at him. "So for the couples massage, we'll keep our clothes on?"

"Well, not *all* your clothes, of course. But you will be modestly clothed during the entire procedure, yes. But if you want the intimate—"

Mike interrupted. "No, we don't want the intimate. We want just the plain, old, couples thingy. Because we're just a plain, old couple." He grinned down at Carly. "Right?"

She nodded. "Right."

Jon, as identified by his name tag, led the way. "This is your dressing room." He eyed Mike up and down again. "Or would you prefer separate dressing rooms?"

Mike chuckled. "We're not that plain and old."

"Very well." Jon opened the door and gestured to the hooks, hangers, and bath robes. "Change into these robes and go out that door. Your masseuses will be on the other side."

Carly closed the door and latched it, then slipped out of her shoes and pants. "I'm keeping my undies on."

"Me, too."

She hung up her blouse. "All my underwear."

He shrugged. "Suit yourself." He looked at his feet. "What about socks?"

"They have these little booties here."

"Right."

She glanced at the door leading to the massage room. "I just have a horrible feeling that when we walk through that door, we'll step onto a live audience stage. In our underwear. With people laughing at us."

He hugged her close. "Don't worry. At least we'll have robes on."

For some reason, the added layer didn't increase her comfort with the situation.

What was she getting them into?

But when they opened the door and peered into the room, two cushioned massage tables surrounded by several cabinets and push carts of supplies greeted them.

As did a male and a female masseuse.

Maybe this wouldn't be as bad as she thought.

Using the small step stool, she clambered up onto the table, sitting upright. A woman of Chinese descent bowed before her. "Please untie the belt of your robe and lay on your stomach."

She glanced over at Mike, who lay down already, eyes closed, as though ready for a nap. His male masseuse slipped her husband's robe down around his waist, then applied oil and began working on his back.

Mike groaned. "Oh, that feels good." He opened one eye and grinned at her. "Told you this was a good idea."

Carly undid the belt and lay as instructed. Maybe if she kept her eyes on Mike, this wouldn't be as embarrassing as she imagined. Her breath caught in her throat when the young woman released the catch on her bra, however, although the warmed oil did feel good. But she gasped at the woman's first touch, a combination of knuckle and palm in the muscles just below her shoulder blade.

The masseuse eased off a mite. "First massage?"

"Uh-huh."

"Thought so. You're very tense." She shifted so Carly could see Mike better. "If you like, you can hold hands."

"I'd like that." She grasped for Mike's hand which dangled over the edge but couldn't quite reach it. "Mike. Wake up."

He opened his eye again. "Huh?"

"Hold hands with me."

He laced his fingers through hers then closed his eyes and was soon snoring. Again.

She sighed. Maybe if she pretended she was comforting him. . .

She closed her eyes. Maybe she could fall asleep, too.

No such luck, as their two attendants began chattering about their schedules, their own aches and pains, their families back home. Mesmerized by the voices, Carly drifted off into a light snooze until a familiar name caught her attention.

Miss Dawson.

Feigning sleep, she stayed still but turned up her hearing.

The female masseuse, working on a spot in Carly's lower back, continued. "She is so demanding. Never happy, no matter how much time I take with her."

"I've heard the purser say some unkind things about her in here, too."

"Oh, such as?"

Yes, what?

"Like she shouldn't be teaching things she doesn't know anything about."

"Ooh, does he mean she doesn't know about writing? I hear she's written lots of books."

"I guess that's what he means. She's doing that whole lecture series on the cruise."

"Maybe he means about writing mysteries. I heard from somebody else she doesn't do those very well."

"I think that's what he means. And he said if she didn't 'fess up about who the real expert is, he'd out her."

A gasp. "You mean he'd kill her?"

A chuckle. "Not off her. Out her. Tell the truth about her ineptitude."

"Well, Miss Dawson said that Neil Williams isn't a nice man. Something about taking his bad boy persona too far."

The male masseuse chuckled again. "Some women like bad boys."

"I think in this case, it was something worse than that. She said he hurt a lot of people, and somebody should teach him a lesson. Put them out of their misery. That's how she put it."

"I heard they once dated."

"She's like years older than him."

"Only three or four, I understand."

"Is he like one of those playboys, do you think?"

"You mean a gigolo?"

"Yeah. Like that." Another hard jab at Carly's back, like a period at the end of the woman's sentence. "I hear some women like that kind of bad boy."

"Dunno. But from what Mr. Williams said, he doesn't like her anymore. Said she did him wrong, and she deserves what she got. Something like that."

"Ooh, sounds like a regular soap opera. And imagine them being on the same cruise together. Did that happen a long time ago?"

"Years and years, according to him. When he was young, and she was young and foolish. Whatever that means. Could be three years. Could be ten for all I know."

"I heard a couple of my ladies talking the other day about money missing from their cabin. Do you think that burglar is at it again?"

"Thought they caught that guy?"

Really, there could be more than one thief? Yikes.

"Nah, that was the fellow who was stealing food. A stowaway on the South Pacific leg of the tour. This is something different. The stewards have all been questioned, and Security is looking into the rest of the crew and staff now. Especially if they have a lot of debt."

"Like they owe a lot of money?"

"Yeah, apparently that's a reason why people steal in situations like this. Or if they have a gambling problem."

"I always wondered why they bottled us up on these ships with no internet, no phone, but lots of slot machines and gaming tables. Seems like they cater to that kind of person."

Carly's masseuse switched to a gentle patting motion up and down her spine. "Another way to make money, I guess." She patted her shoulder. "Wake up, madam. All done."

Carly waited a couple of heartbeats before opening her eyes slowly, raising her head, and peering around. "Oh, that was lovely."

Yes, indeed it was. She learned a lot during this time. Mostly about Miss Dawson and the purser, of course, but also about herself.

She had a knot at the base of her neck the size of a golf ball. When she got home to Bear Cove, she'd look into some chiropractic treatments.

$ $ $

When she suggested they do a little onboard shopping, Mike said nothing doing. He was going back to their stateroom to sleep off his massage. Carly kissed him and sent him on his way, glad he wasn't planning to hang around.

He hated shopping, which she well knew.

To provide a cover for her time, she ducked into the first shop and bought several bags of popcorn and chips, as well as two gourmet granola bars and a bottle of fragrant oil in case they decided to rub each other's feet some night.

Armed with her alibi, she headed for the elevator.

Her masseuse, her tongue loosened with an extra ten dollars, revealed to Carly when she went back on the pretense of asking a question, that the entertainers—apart from Miss Dawson—were housed in small cabins on Deck One, just aft of the main elevators, and that's where Carly headed now. The talk about Miss Dawson and the purser peaked her interest, and she hoped she might learn more by seeing where he lived while onboard. Plus, she had some questions she'd like to ask the lounge singer, Penny

Goodnight.

If nothing else, perhaps she could ask questions of their steward. She'd have to save questions about the romance novelist until later, as Miss Dawson's stateroom was on the same deck as her own. Perhaps Sam's chagrin would loosen his tongue later.

Down she rode, waiting patiently as folks got off on each floor, until she was left alone to descend the single floor below her own. When she stepped out, it took her a moment to get her bearings. No mahogany paneling on the walls. No brass handrails. No plush carpet here.

Instead, painted walls, wooden handrails, and indoor-outdoor carpet reminded her of a cheap hotel in a bad part of town. Apparently the cruise line was more about impressing the passengers than making the crew and staff accommodations extra-nice.

Down the drab passageway she trekked, feeling as though she stepped into an Oliver Twist-like world, where, in the next instant, either the miserly Mr. Bumble or the kindly Mr. Brownlow would stick their head through a doorway and ask if they could assist her.

Instead, a familiar face greeted her: Sam.

She smiled. "Hello, Sam. Fancy meeting you here."

He tossed a pillowcase filled with dirty laundry into the hallway. "Madam, did you get off on the wrong floor?"

"No. I was hoping to talk to Miss Goodnight. Is she in her room?"

He glanced down the hallway, his shoulders tense and eyes wide. "She is, but I think she doesn't want to be disturbed."

Carly breezed past. "Oh, I won't disturb her. I just wanted to tell her how much—"

Sam pushed past her and stood with his back to one of the cabin doors. "Passengers are not permitted in the crew section."

"Oh, Sam. But you know me. Surely it can't hurt."

He hesitated, just long enough for Carly to hear movement behind the door.

She smiled. "See, she's in there. Let me just tap."

She raised her hand to knock but froze when a man's voice came through the door. "I didn't mean nothing."

Penny answered. "You almost got caught. I told you to stay out of sight."

"Wanted some fresh air. Then I saw her."

"Look, I bailed you out once. You get caught again, you're on your own."

"You can't do that." His voice took on a distinct whine. "I'll tell them you helped me."

"Don't pull me down into the cesspool you live in. Do you hear me? I won't let you."

"You don't have a choice. You're in it with me now."

Sam gripped Carly by the forearm and pulled her away. "You must go now."

"But I just want—"

Penny Goodnight's door opened and she stepped out. "What's going on here?"

Carly wrestled herself free of Sam's grip. "Are you having a problem?"

Penny looked back into her cabin. "In here? No." She chuckled. "Just watching an old movie. Cops and robbers."

"Sounded like you were talking to someone."

"Me? No. Just a movie." She smiled at Sam. "Besides, I'm not allowed to have anybody in my cabin, am I, Sam the Man? Particularly not a man. Against the rules and all that."

Carly headed back to the elevator, her shopping bag banging against her leg in time with her steps. An interesting development, to say the least.

The woman said she didn't have a man in her room.

Carly never mentioned the gender of the person she heard.

As Alice in Wonderland would say, curiouser and curiouser.

Chapter 14

"Oh, this is going to be so exciting." Carly led the way down the ramp to shore. "I can't wait to see the glacier. And the bears. And—"

Mike slowed and laughed. "No guarantee you'll see any bears. But unless a heat wave hit, the glacier should still be there."

She tugged on his hand. "Come on. I want to get a good seat on the bus."

"We have a reserved seat. They can't leave without us."

"True, but it's important to sit where I can see everything. I don't want to miss a thing."

He relented and picked up speed to catch up with her. On the other side of a white fence-like barrier waited a line of buses, each identified with a sign as to its destination. Theirs was the third from the front, and Carly happily showed her ticket and plunked into the second seat behind the driver.

She'd have sat in the first row, but it was marked as reserved for handicapped passengers.

With camera in hand, she practically bounced in her seat. Mike sat and inclined his seat. In moments, his eyes were closed and he was snoring. Just like a bear she hoped to see soon.

The city of Juneau spread about on all sides of them, and although the cruise terminal wasn't the center of town, it sure felt like it. Large warehouses sprawled across acres of harbor-front property, small boats bobbed against the marinas like corks on the end of a fishing line. Forklifts and skid steers moved cargo into and out of the ships, while a large glass-walled structure that reminded her of a control tower at an airport overlooked the entire operation.

A small parade of passengers boarded and settled into their seats, and soon after, the driver—a corpulent man already sweating in the cool morning air—heaved himself into his seat and adjusted several knobs and switches before picking up the hand-held mic.

After a sharp whistle indicated he turned on the system, his voice—a combination between Georgia sweet tea-drawl tinged with smoker's cough—echoed through the bus. "Good mornin', ladies and gentlemen. Welcome to the cemetery tour." He paused while a murmur raised from those on board before continuing. "Just kiddin', folks. Settle down. Seriously, we're headin' for the glacier where I'll let you off for about ninety minutes. Then we'll head on back to the ship. You can do your shoppin' then. And don't worry, you'll have plenty of time, and I can guar-on-tee you they won't run out of stuff."

A chuckle rippled through the bus, and Mike opened one eye and mouthed his response. "Told you so."

Despite their conversations earlier about getting off the ship early and going shopping, that didn't happen. They were both so relaxed from their massage that they fell asleep right after lunch and didn't awaken until the final announcement for disembarking for tours.

At which point, Mike remembered he booked this excursion for them. Carly was willing to skip it, until he reminded her he also paid for it.

Carly's frugal nature—or cheapskate as some of her friends said—kicked in. No way would she miss something when money already changed hands.

The ride to the glacier was an uneventful twenty minutes. The lush green surroundings surprised Carly, who always envisioned Alaska as buried beneath at least ten feet of snow year-round. Tall lodgepole pines, stately and elegant although totally unsatisfactory as a Christmas tree or even a windbreak, towered over them. She craned her neck but wasn't able to see very many tops. And at ground level, thick underbrush cluttered the base of the trees, serving double duty by providing cover for small animals and holding in the moisture.

The driver kept up a running commentary about various landmarks and buildings they passed. "Over here on your right is the first fish processing factory in Alaska. Built in the early 1800's, it still operates today." A few minutes later, "And over here is a cluster of totem poles built hundreds of years ago by the local natives. Each one tells a story, and contrary to what we say, being on the bottom of the totem pole is a place of honor. That person, animal, or being actually holds up the rest."

Interesting concept, to be sure. Sometimes she felt that way. What with work, and family, and the town and its goings-on, and her most recent escapade in the Space Needle. Sometimes she wondered what she did with her time, but when put into context, no wonder the days and months slipped by so fast.

A turn off the highway and up a winding road, and Carly had the impression she headed into a secret world through which she might not return. The trees blotted out the sun now, and a light mist clung to the road ahead of them.

A final turn into a parking lot and the bus slowed.

The driver intruded into the rustling of passengers gathering their belongings for their trek onto the glacier and surrounding paths. "Okay, folks. Meet me back here at 3:00. Set your timers for ninety-three minutes. A five-minute delay will result in a thirty-minute walk back to town for you, so I suggest you plan to be on time."

Mike chuckled as he stood and offered a hand to Carly. "Do you want to split up, or go together?"

"Let's stick together this trip, okay?"

He led the way off the bus, assisting her down that last giant step. She clutched her camera with extra batteries close to her chest while zipping her jacket. Mike tugged his hat tighter on his head against the brisk wind, and

Carly was glad she thought to tuck her ear warmers into a pocket.

Suitably attired, they headed first for the glacier, bowing to Mike's suggestion that since that was the furthest trek, they could adjust the time remaining as needed to view the museum, gift shop, and maybe go down the path where bears reportedly lurked.

Down over a gravel bank, hopping across a shallow but very cold stream judging by even the tiny splash over the tops of her sneakers when she lost her balance for about a millisecond, and employing the log and several large rocks placed conveniently for tourists, they made their way across the beach. In about ten minutes, they stood looking across a pristine lake at a glacier that reminded her of melting ice cream oozing out of the container on a warm summer's day.

Across the water, several groups of hikers headed toward the glacier field. One of them—a woman taller than the rest—led the pack. Blond hair pulled into a ponytail, baseball cap, lithe limbs—Carly squinted in the afternoon sun. The figure looked familiar. Using her camera, she focused on the woman.

She was right.

Penny Goodnight.

Well, even in the bar the other night, the woman's fitness was obvious. Well-muscled arms and an overall air of good health exuded from the woman's pores. Even the obvious sadness behind her original song couldn't overshadow that.

Carly shifted her camera and took in the rest of the singer's attire. A sweater or jacket tied around her waist. Fanny pack with water bottle. Walking stick. Leggings that hugged her thighs and calves. Leg warmers bunched around her ankles, crowning the tops of her hiking boots. Head down, arms pumping, Penny Goodnight looked like she was leading an excursion to Mount Everest.

Carly scanned the parade of about ten hikers who followed in her wake, each attired in various degrees of hiking acumen, most likely best illustrated by their position in line. Two chubby women in the caboose position appeared to struggle already, their cheeks puffing in and out, faces red from the exertion. And all the while, Penny threaded her way along a path strewn with fallen trees and rocks.

Ahead, boulders as big as wheelbarrows peppered the field of snow like chocolate sprinkles on a sundae, and—Carly shook herself from her musings. She shouldn't be hungry, even though she ate only salad for lunch. No more thinking about food.

She turned back to point the singer and her hiking entourage out to Mike, but they'd gone down over a hillock and were out of view. Oh well, another time.

Mike peered through his own camera, zooming in on where the ice met the water. "Those rocks are actually boulders." He pointed. "See that boat out there?"

She nodded. A toy canoe paddled across the lake. "It's small, isn't it?"

"It has six people in it."

Not as small as it appeared from here. Large, in fact.

"And the rocks at the base of the glacier dwarf the canoe."

Funny how at this distance—over a mile—size could be distorted.

A deep roar like large planes passing rumbled over them like a tidal wave. Carly looked up, expecting to see several Air Force jets—or something big and fast enough to make a noise like that—but the sky was clear except for a few clouds in the distance.

When those around her gasped and pointed back at the glacier, she turned her attention just in time to see the canoe dancing atop a series of three-foot waves.

"Oh, Mike, are they in trouble?"

He shook his head, still focusing through this camera. "No. They were expecting it. A huge chunk of ice fell into the water. Got it on video."

Great. Well, she'd see that later. On to the next thing.

She turned and headed back the way they'd come. "Let's go see if we can find any bears."

But by the time they got back to the museum, she wavered. "I'm getting chilly. Maybe I'll tour the inside, and you look for bears." After all, if she had to watch the glacier calving tonight, she could watch wildlife on video too, right? "That okay with you?"

"Sure."

She planted a kiss on his cheek and he headed off on his next adventure. She smiled at his retreating back. Mike was so easy-going. Calm and stable. Even though sometimes he could be obstinate. Pig-headed even.

But she loved him anyway.

Inside the museum, she made a pit-stop at the restroom first then sauntered around the displays. Most talked about a glacier-producing factory comprised of the cold, the terrain, the heavy snowfall, short summers, and lack of rainfall in the area. Apparently glacier country was limited to the perfect climate conditions, and even places like Siberia had fewer ice fields than Alaska.

After about twenty minutes, though, she was mesmerized by talk of millions of years for even a small glacier to sprout, and she headed for the observation windows. Superimposed on the glass were images of the ice constructed from data collected over the past hundred years or so and extrapolated to interpret what the field would have looked like—she squinted to read the small print—yep, millions of years ago.

Apparently, if she was here then, she would be hundreds, maybe thousands, of feet under the ice. So she hadn't missed anything, really, had she? In fact, by coming now and not then, she could see more.

She looked past the interpretation illustrations out to the beach and lake below. Two people stood close to each other, one leaning over the other with a hand raised as though preparing to strike.

She gasped.

The woman closest to her turned. "Read an interesting fact, dear?"

"Uh, no. I just thought I recognized somebody out there."

The woman looked. "How could you possibly recognize them from this distance?"

Good question. The stance. His military-style haircut, shorter than the norm. The white shoes, visible even from this distance.

Carly glanced around. Over there. The long-range viewers. She dug into her pocket for a quarter as she neared the oversized brass binoculars before dropping her coin into the slot and peering through the viewfinder. Fuzzy nothingness morphed into a crystal-clear view of the mountain towering over the ice field.

She adjusted the knobs, turning first one way then the other, then shifted the viewing field. Oops. Down too much. Now all she saw was the crowd outside the museum on the paths. Up a little. A little more to the— she stepped back and checked her field of vision again—to the right.

There. Bill and Neil. Pushing and shoving. Bill raising his hand again and—

The field went black.

Oh, no. Another quarter. She dug into her pocket. Then her purse. Back pocket? Nothing. She straightened. A small child stared at her. Carly smiled. "Wouldn't happen to have a quarter, would you?"

An adult—the child's mother—stepped between them. "I'll thank you not to approach my child."

Carly gasped. "I didn't approach her. I was looking through these giant binoculars, and when I straightened, there she was."

The woman folded her arms over her chest and lowered her brow. "You spoke to her." She turned to the little girl, now sucking her thumb and clutching a blankie to her chest. "What did she say to you, Gertie?"

The thumb popped out with a sucking sound. "Money."

Now it was the woman's opportunity to gasp. "Money. You offered her money." She glanced around. "Where is Security?"

Panic rose in Carly's chest like a tidal wave. "No, I didn't offer her money. I asked if she had a quarter." She turned to the view out the window. "I recognized some people out there, and I put in a quarter, but it didn't last long enough and I didn't have another quarter and—"

The woman grabbed the child's hand. "I see. First you spy on people, then you try to steal from a child. Where is Security?"

Sensing now was a good time to beat a hasty retreat, Carly did just that, slipping past the irate woman and thumb-sucking child, past the cash register, and down the steps to the ground level. Once outside, she headed for the path where she last saw Mike.

Even a grizzly wouldn't be as angry as that woman.

About twenty feet down the path, she spied Mike heading toward her. Casting another glance over her shoulder—the woman stood framed in the doorway, scanning the crowd—Carly ducked her head and made a beeline for Mike, looping her arm through his and whirling him around where he stood.

"Mike, so how was the bear tour?"

He halted, forcing her to do the same. "Great." He held up his camera. "I got some great footage here of a mother bear and—"

"Show me."

The sooner she got down this path and out of that woman's sight, the better. Hopefully she didn't call in the cops and search the buses. This could well be the end of her cruise.

She slowed as they turned a corner and the crowd thinned out. "What time is it?"

"About ten minutes until we board. We should head back."

She paused and breathed deep of the pine-scented air. "Let's just enjoy the outdoors for a moment."

He peered at her. "Are you okay?"

"Sure, I am. Why?"

"You didn't fall and hit your head?"

"No."

"You just never liked walking in the woods much, especially at the pace you were setting." His brow lowered. "What's going on?"

"Show me where you saw the bear."

His face brightened. "Over there." He pointed past the railing and down a slight incline. "She was just wandering around, digging under the bushes. She had a cub with her, like she was showing it how to find food, and suddenly a smaller cub showed up. It was neat."

"Were you scared?"

"No. There were other people here, and I knew I could outrun at least one old geezer."

"Seriously. You could have been hurt."

"There was a forest ranger here. She said for us to keep our hands and clothes on this side of the fence, and we'd be okay. She said we were more likely to be hurt by a porcupine falling from a tree than to be attacked by a bear."

Carly rubbed the top of her head. "That would hurt, wouldn't it?"

He nodded. "We'd best head back. There's a shortcut through here, but you have to walk carefully. It's a bit of an uphill walk, but the forest ranger said it would cut at least five minutes off the return trip."

She wasn't sure she wanted to go wandering off in the Alaskan wilderness. "Is it a marked path?"

"Sure is. Follow me."

He gripped her hand and led the way along a concrete walkway that ended about ten feet in, turning into a gravel path. Around some tall trees, over a picturesque bridge and a burbling brook, then through a cleft cut into a boulder as big as a house.

A rattling noise caught her attention, and she held back. A flash of color—blue—and a shape at the periphery of her vision. Was somebody there? Who? Another tourist like themselves beating a hasty retreat back to the parking lot?

Or somebody paralleling them?

Stalking them?

She glanced around. This would be the perfect spot for an ambush. Loose rocks. Loose trees. If something fell on them, nobody would be the wiser.

A footfall on rock. A grunt.

She looked up. At the top of the boulder, a person—man? Woman? She couldn't tell because of the hoodie pulled tight around their face—wrestled with a rock the size of a Thanksgiving turkey. She stepped back, but the passageway left no room to maneuver.

A scream froze in her throat as the granite eased over the downhill edge, gathering momentum as it headed for her.

And as if that wasn't enough, the person—surely a man. A woman couldn't be that strong. Could they?—shoved another rock over with their foot.

The hood slipped back, revealing a familiar face as she found her voice. Dark eyes. And moustache.

"Mike! Watch out!"

The pick-pocket from the Space Needle.

Grinning down at her.

Dusting his hands off as though his job was complete.

She recalled his parting gesture while being hauled away by the cops in Seattle.

I'm going to find you.

$ $ $

Carly stepped down from the bus, grateful Mike was at the bottom of the steps. She clutched his hand as her knees continued shaking.

That was a close call back at the glacier. And just a few feet from safety, too.

Her scream brought several park rangers running from both directions, but by the time she regained her wits, the boy—man, really—was gone. And despite knowing for certain what she saw, they assured her rocks fell in that particular area on a regular basis.

Her pulse didn't return to almost-normal until they were pulling into the cruise line parking lot, some twenty minutes later. Mike kept peering at her, asking if she was all right—of course she wasn't—and was she sure what she saw—of course she was.

At least, she thought she was back to normal—until she stood. Then her knees wobbled like a newborn calf.

Guess she wasn't as back to her old self as she thought.

She allowed Mike to lead her straight back to the ship even while she lamented the loss of her trinkets, but he assured her he'd give her double time at their next port-of-call. While not exactly the same, it would have to do. Truth be told, she couldn't have walked more than the length of herself feeling as she did right now.

At the top of the ramp, a security officer checked names off a list, the way they ensured all passengers were aboard and accounted for before leaving port.

She smiled at the security officer as he ran a practiced finger down the paper, nodding when he found her name. "Have you ever left somebody behind?"

"No, Madam. We are very careful." Luis turned to Mike. "Name, sir?"

Mike obliged and the man, identified as Luis by his name badge, placed a small check mark in the line below Carly's. "Welcome aboard, sir. Enjoy your evening."

Carly checked behind her. Nobody there. Maybe she had a couple of minutes to ask a few questions. She leaned closer and lowered her voice. "If somebody died on the ship, whose jurisdiction would it be?"

Luis stared at her. "Jurisdiction, madam?"

"Yes. Say two people got into a fight, and one of them died, what would happen?"

Luis glanced at Mike then turned his attention back to her, his face as impassive as though carved from granite. "The captain's, madam. He would decide what to do."

"Would the local police be called in?"

"I suppose. If it happened in port." He shifted his weight. "Are you also a mystery writer?"

She jabbed a thumb into her chest. "Me? No." She chuckled. "I'm just—"

Mike grabbed her arm. "Nosy. That's what she is. Nosy." He lowered his voice and whispered in her ear. "Carly."

She wrested her arm from his grip. "One more question. Why did you ask if I'm a writer?"

"Miss Dawson asked similar questions. I thought maybe she gave you an assignment. To write a story about a murder on a ship."

"And what did you tell her?"

"The same thing I told you."

"If the murder happened at sea, what would happen?"

"Whatever the captain decided. He is the ultimate authority while we sail. If he thinks he needs the police, the FBI, or the local national law enforcement, he will contact them." Luis smiled at her, but the gesture didn't reach his eyes. "But you are very safe on this ship, madam. We have never had a murder before."

"Always a first time for everything." At his widened eyes and stiffened shoulders, she tossed him another smile. "Not that I think anything will happen. I'm sure you're correct. This is a very safe ship."

Mike pulled her down the passageway, his voice hissing in her ear. "Carly, what did you think you were doing? Do you want to be arrested for suspicious behavior?" He rolled his eyes. "I knew it. I said you couldn't stay out of trouble. Always looking for a mystery here. A mystery there." He groaned. "What will I do with you?"

She planted her heels in the thick carpet then stuck her fists into her hips. "First of all, I am not a child to be done anything with, Michael Turnquist." She swallowed hard. "And second, I was only asking the same questions that author was asking. You don't see her getting arrested."

He held her gaze a long moment then pulled her into his arms, pressing her against his chest. "Oh, Carly. It's just that after the incident today with the rocks falling and almost bonking us on the head, you asking questions like that worries me."

"Worries you?" She pulled away a few inches and looked up at him. "Why? Do you mean you're taking me seriously? For a change?"

He pulled her close again. "I always take you seriously. Serious as a heart attack."

Chapter 15

After a long nap and a good dinner, Carly felt like a new woman. And despite Mike's protests that she had enough mystery today to last a lifetime, she didn't want to miss the next writing presentation that asked the question, "Prefer a series or a stand-alone?" The ambiguous title opened itself to interpretation, including for her to figure out whether Miss Dawson's latest offering was part of a series or a single book, or perhaps the real dilemma was where the most money could be made. Or maybe the author was asking participants if they preferred reading a series or would like to pen the next Great American novel.

Whichever it turned out to be, she didn't want to absent herself on the off-chance she might learn more about the characters in Miss Dawson's own mystery, namely the author herself, Teddy, Monica, Neil, Bill and Belle, and Dave and Dewey. Oh, yes, and Penny Goodnight, too. At one time or another, they all had interactions with each other. And nobody, it seemed, like Neil Williams very much.

Mike acquiesced because there was a movie he really wanted to see— *The Incredibles*—although why a grown man was so interested in a cartoon about superheroes was beyond her. Still, it was his cruise as much as hers, so he had every right to spend it as he pleased. They agreed to meet in the auditorium later to listen in on the Ask the Captain hour, then converge on the piano bar later. Tonight was Neil Diamond tribute night, one of her favorite artists.

Plus, maybe she'd learn more about the ship and the crew from the head man himself.

Once again, Carly sat in the back row, this time on the opposite side of the room. Sure enough, when Miss Dawson entered, her gaze went to Carly's previous position, and finding it empty, a tiny smile tickled the author's mouth.

At least, that's how it looked from back in her darkened corner.

But when the woman scanned the rest of the room, beaming at her adoring fans, her eyes passed over Carly then returned, one eye drawn down into a hint of a frown.

Seriously, the woman should work harder to hide her dislike of readers. Or of this reader in particular.

Carly scrunched down into her seat a smidge more, resolute in her decision to keep a low profile. After the near miss at the rocks and the witch hunt at the museum, she couldn't afford to draw any additional attention today.

Or indeed, the rest of the cruise.

As usual, Miss Dawson's lecture meandered around and about the topic, mentioning her own books as often as possible, without ever coming out and answering her own question. She seemed to prefer writing a series, except when a publisher—who shall remain nameless, she intoned, tapping a forefinger alongside her nose as though discussing the world's worst-kept secret—wanted a single book to fill a publishing slot, in which case they *always* came to her because she could *always* write another book at the drop of a hat.

Carly sighed. That's probably why most of her books seemed to be the same characters under different names, in the same situations caused by their same poor choices. A particular favorite was the good girl choosing the bad boy being rescued by the good boy who sweeps her off her feet and shows her just how wrong she was about him. And the bad boy doesn't want to let her go, so he stalks her, or threatens her, or tries to kill her, or tries to kill the good boy.

Same story, different title and names.

As bored with the talk as she was with the author's books, Carly scanned the room. Two rows ahead of her, Neil Williams sat at one end, while Penny Goodnight occupied a chair at the end other. Occasionally one glanced sideways at the other, always looking away when spotted. The purser's normal casual stance was missing tonight, and instead he sat straight up, shoulders tense, back straight. And the singer cross and re-crossed her legs as if in pain. Too much hiking, perhaps? When she shifted in her seat, Carly caught a glimpse of a cluster of bruises on her forearm before the woman tugged her sleeve back into place.

As though somebody grabbed her roughly.

More than once.

When Miss Dawson wound her talk down, she invited her audience to share something they'd read recently. Or been writing.

Nobody raised their hand, so Carly jumped in. Or rather, stood in. "I've been thinking about a murder mystery. Aboard a cruise ship."

Miss Dawson's chuckle echoed hollowly. "How unique."

"Well, as you said in one of your lectures, there are no unique plots. Only unique storytellers."

The author's brow lowered. "True. I did say that." She beamed at the rest of the group. "Nice to see somebody has been listening."

"Oh, yes. I've been doing more than listening. I've been doing some research."

One brow raised. "Oh, really?" She smiled at Teddy and Monica sitting in the front row, hanging on her every word. As usual. "What kind of research?"

While not completely true, Carly decided to fire for effect. "Oh, following people. Listening around corners." She nodded. "And do you know what? Just like you said, Miss Dawson. People have secrets."

Teddy whirled in his seat, his face red. "You could get in trouble for doing that. Stalking, the law calls it."

Carly pulled her mouth down in a half-frown. "Really? I didn't know that." She waved off his words. "But I don't think my little investigation and research jaunts could be called that. All in fun, you know."

The author interrupted. "So what have you learned?"

"Nice people sometimes do bad things. Everybody makes poor choices, as you just said in your lecture. And even an innocuous comment can be turned into a threat."

"Such as?"

Carly shrugged. "I could kill you for that."

Monica gasped and her face paled.

Carly chuckled. "Oh, I don't mean I could kill Miss Dawson. That was just an example of how our words can be taken in a different light."

Monica giggled and fanned herself with a hand. "I knew that."

Carly gripped the back of the chair in front of her. "And I saw a real-life example of a scene in a book. *Murder on the Orient Express*. By Agatha Christie, you know."

"I know." Miss Dawson's eyes blazed. "Anybody else want to share?"

But Carly pressed on. "For those who aren't familiar with the plot, a bunch of people set out to kill a mutual enemy. Which they do. And the hero has to figure out who killed him and why. And, of course, nobody tells him the truth." She tilted her head to one side. "Don't you think it's strange that folks tend to lie to the cops right out of the gate? Wonder why?"

"Well, that's an interesting plot, although it seems a little overdone."

Carly tossed her most winning smile at the author. "Well, you have so much experience, Miss Dawson, I'm sure you'd know."

Her words hung on the air for what seemed an hour, but was likely only a few seconds before the author thanked the audience for coming.

Carly headed for the singer, blocking her way from leaving, and introduced herself. "I haven't had a chance to hear you sing yet. Maybe tonight?"

Penny shook her head. "Not my gig tonight. Paul Turner is on tonight." She sniffed and rolled her eyes. "Doing Neil Diamond, I hear. Well, good luck to him on that."

"Is he not very good?"

"Oh, he's good all right. But really. Who listens to Neil Diamond anymore but old ladies and teenagers. The kids think that old music is new stuff. Like they wrote it themselves."

Behind the singer, the purser stood to leave. Carly gestured to him. "Have you two met? Purser Williams, this is Penny Goodnight."

Williams paused and acknowledged the introduction. "We've met."

Carly waved off his words. "Of course you have. You're both part of the ship's complement on this sailing, aren't you? Probably sat across from each other many times."

Penny's mouth turned into a hard line. "What do you mean? Have you been following us, too?" Her hands clenched into fists. "You won't get away with it, Miss Nosey-Parker."

Carly raised her eyebrows. "I don't know what you're talking about, I'm sure. I just thought you probably had staff briefings, meetings. Eating in the staff dining room. That sort of thing. I meant nothing by it, I'm sure. Please forgive me if I offended you."

Penny leaned closer, the wrinkles around her eyes and mouth deep craters, as though every ounce of youth drained from her. "You knew exactly what you were doing. And got what you wanted. Now get out of my way."

The singer shouldered Carly to the side and strode out of the room, once again tugging her sleeve down over her forearm.

Carly turned to the purser, who smirked at the woman's retreating back. "Well, I never."

He faced her. "Oh, yes you did. And you know it." He lowered his voice. "Keep out of my way. And leave her alone. An angry woman is like a mama bear. Don't cross her."

"You sound like you know her very well."

"As well as I want to. And even I'm a little scared of her. As you should be, too."

$ $ $

Ten minutes later, when Carly slid into her chair next to Mike in the auditorium, the purser's—and the singer's—words still rang in her ears. In fact, they ran through her blood like driftwood down a river, threatening to catch and pierce something along the way.

In her career as a forensic accountant, she faced guilty parties all the time in trials when she testified as to what they were up to in trying to conceal or undervalue assets. Some threatened her. Some tried to make good on their threats.

But never had she witnessed such hatred and pain mixed together into a curious cocktail of desperation as she saw in Penny Goodnight. A woman who walked and talked and dressed like she had the world at her fingertips, while inside was slowly dying.

So what was her secret?

Despite her words to the woman, she didn't really know anything except there was tension between her and the purser, and there was some form of collusion with her and the rest of the gang, as Carly had taken to calling the other characters.

Interesting how Teddy reacted when she made her comments. And Monica. Paling like she'd seen a ghost.

Or heard a truth she didn't want revealed.

And what about Miss Dawson? Trying to cut her off in mid-story.

How could one man—Neil Williams—create so much animosity amongst these different people? Even with Bill and Belle, Dave and Dewey, who separately seemed to have no connection to each other, any of the other characters in their mini onboard play, or the purser.

After all, what were the odds all these people had a past and should meet now in the present?

The real question was, though, would they all have a future?

Or would one of them end up terminated?

And if so, why?

There seemed no end of reasons. A relationship gone bad. Poor investment advice. Complications from a terminated pregnancy. Blackmail.

Neil Williams walked a slender tightrope. One that could disappear from beneath his feet at any second.

Mike pressed his arm against hers. "How was the talk?"

She shrugged. "Same as usual. How was the movie?"

"Oh, it was great. There was this one scene—"

The lights dimmed and Hamish, the cruise director, and a tall, lanky man in a white uniform and white hair and beard but a youthful step came onto the raised stage. Several more people took their seats, and the room quieted as Hamish and the captain sat on chairs arranged in a cozy tête-a-tête fashion.

The cruise director began. "Thank you, ladies and gentlemen, for joining us tonight. Captain Lycas will talk about the cruise line, this ship in particular, and then will have a few minutes to answer questions." He nodded to the man beside him. "Captain, I turn it over to you."

For the next twenty minutes or so, Captain Lycas regaled the audience with information about company policy, ship's systems, navigation, speed, distances, and then he shared stories from several of his cruises. He'd captained this particular ship for almost twenty years, been head man for a total of thirty-five, having sailed ever since he joined the British navy fresh out of school.

Carly found the detail infinitely interesting, but Mike snoozed in his chair after the first five minutes. She nudged him a couple of times, but he promptly fell asleep again.

Oh, well. As long as he doesn't snore.

When the captain concluded his presentation, including a slide show of the bridge, the engine room, and behind the scenes in the kitchens, he opened the floor for questions.

To the far right of the room, a woman stood.

Belle. Of Bill and Belle. "Captain, has there ever been a death on a ship you captained?"

"Well, yes. Sometimes an elderly passenger finds the excitement too much. Sometimes they come on a last cruise knowing they don't have long to live. I've heard that cruising is cheaper than hospice or a nursing home."

A ripple of laughter ran through the room, but Carly shifted in her seat. She suspected the words rang closer to the truth than many realized.

"Next question?"

But Belle remained on her feet. "Any suspicious deaths?"

The captain's mouth pursed as he considered the question. "Not that I recall." He glanced at the audience. "And I think I'd remember that."

Another round of laughter.

"Next?"

Still she persisted. "What would happen if somebody was murdered while we were at sea?"

"I'm not sure what you're asking. We would move the body into an area of the ship away from passengers. A cool place, preferably. Our ship's surgeon would do a preliminary but basic examination of the body to determine mode of death and to preserve any potential evidence on the body. Our highly-trained security team would cordon off the scene of death, again to preserve evidence."

"Would you call in local or federal authorities?"

"Depends on where we are. Weather conditions. Time until next port."

"So if we were at sea, in a storm, unable to communicate, what would happen?"

He bestowed a condescending smile on the woman. "Then I should thank my lucky stars to have a world-renowned mystery author on board like Miss Barbara Ann Dawson who could help me solve the crime before the murderer was able to escape the ship." He scanned the crowd again. "After all, isn't that what Jessica Fletcher would do in the same situation?"

This time, an outbreak of raucous laughter and applause signaled the end of the persistent—and slightly obnoxious—woman's questioning, and the end of the presentation.

The cruise director thanked the captain and the audience for participating, and dismissed them with a short summary of the evening's remaining offerings, including the piano bar, the Wave Bar where a string ensemble would play, as well as a late-night replay of the afternoon's movie.

Mike perked up at that, but Carly declined his offer. "Let's stop at the piano bar for a quick coffee then head back to the stateroom."

He waggled his eyebrows at her.

She sighed. "One thing never changes."

"And what's that?"

"Your one-track mind is no mystery to me."

Chapter 16

The next morning dawned with a light mist in the distance which cast a soft glow on the view over the bow of the ship where Carly huddled next to Mike and a couple of hundred of their closest friends. The wind was bitter, and her ears were cold. She clapped her hands to keep them warm and wished she thought to don a cap.

But she had a great spot right along the railing, and there was no way she was giving that up.

In the distance, out to sea, a pod of whales frolicked, blowing up huge spouts of water. Several people standing near her left their spot to get a closer look, but Mike remained where he was like his feet were glued to the deck.

Or frozen.

Carly peered ahead through eyeballs as cold as marbles. At least, that's how they felt. She was afraid if she didn't blink once in a while, her eyelids would stick in place forever. Then again, if she did blink, might they freeze shut?

According to the captain, in just a few minutes the ship would begin making its turn into Hubbard Bay, where the glacier called home. At first, she'd had no plans to stand on deck for three hours in hopes of catching sight of a calving, as the fall of ice from a glacier was called, but Mike wanted her there to see it firsthand.

She could be inside reading her latest mystery novel or catching up on the most recent White Paper for a forensic accounting report, but instead she agreed to join him. Spending time together was important to him, and she liked to make him happy.

That, and the promise of traditional Dutch pea soup served on the bow in about an hour, were enough to bring her out into the cold.

The nose of the ship turned and headed up a wide passageway, and within minutes, the engine went silent as they coasted the final half mile or so to the face of the glacier.

Well, not exactly the face.

The ship, although smaller than most and so able to get in closer, was still large enough to stay about a half mile from the glacier. Already the air turned colder even while the wind died down within the protection of the harbor.

Hamish, the cruise director, came over the loudspeaker. "Ladies and gentlemen, welcome to Hubbard Bay. This is as close as we will get to the glacier because, as you have probably heard, more than eighty percent of a glacier is under water. And we don't want to run into it, as you can appreciate."

A man standing near Carly nodded. "Yeah, we don't wanna pull a Titanic, do we?"

Titanic, Poseidon Adventure, and other shipwreck jokes abounded, it seemed, on cruise ships. Carly tossed him a half smile as Hamish continued.

"We'll maintain this position for about an hour, then slowly turn to starboard and about an hour after that, we'll turn to port. That way we don't have to rush to one side or the other, and can enjoy the entire vista from our staterooms, lounge chairs, seats in the restaurants or viewing areas, or from the bow. Just remember that in about an hour we'll serve hot pea soup on the bow. You don't want to miss that. Now please welcome Joan, our naturalist, who'll give you a few tips on what to watch for."

A woman's voice came over the speakers. "Hi. I'm Joan, and I'm your ship's naturalist. This is an exciting day for us all. Off to the starboard side a few minutes ago was a pod of humpback whales heading north. This morning, around breakfast, we spotted several lone male grey whales. Join me tomorrow morning around six and maybe we'll see some seals as we near our next port."

Six a.m. on cruise ships should be banned.

"But today you want to know about the glacier. It's actually an ice field that formed in the mountains and is flowing downhill like a giant river of ice at about the rate of two feet per year. The wall ahead of you is more than two hundred feet high, although the distance can make it look much smaller. If you look to the port side, you'll see a helicopter landing on the ice. See how small it is in comparison to the glacier."

Carly squinted against the sun's glare on the water and ice as the mist burned off, revealing more of the harbor. Sure enough, about halfway down the glacier, a red whirlybird landed. People the size of ants jumped out, and soon cell phones were snapping selfies of people doing goofy poses.

"Listen to the sounds the glacier makes. The deep rumbles you hear, much like the far-off roar of jets, is actually the ice moving, scraping against the rock, heaving and buckling under the surface. If you hear a loud crack, like a board being snapped in two, that means a piece of ice is getting ready to fall. Get your cameras ready. If you hear the splash as the ice hits the water, you're too late. At this distance, about two seconds after it hits is when you hear the BOOM!

"Generally speaking, the glacier will calve in several places that are close together. So if you see one—or even if you miss it—keep your camera trained on that area, panning back and forth about a hundred feet in either direction. You are more likely to catch another calving in that area.

"And if you see chunks of ice falling over the edge into the water, watch there especially. Today is a really good day. There should be lots of activity, because the air has been warming over the past few days."

Joan had a few more instructions, but Carly tuned her out. Mike had the camera. He'd get the shots. She could spend some time people watching. Take, for instance, that couple over there. Young, in love, he showing off for her, she trying to re-enact the famous scene in the *Titanic* movie of a few years ago, standing on the steel cables around the edge of the bow, face into the wind, arms spread wide.

If she ended up in the water, she'd get a huge surprise.

Carly wandered over to the railing on the starboard side and watched mini-icebergs float past. While at first it felt like the ship stood still, in actuality there was a small wake at the bow indicating minimal movement. A particularly large berg went past, several seagulls quarreling over a bit of something. A large greyish one snatched the morsel and flew off with it, the others in close pursuit, reminding her of that fish story her grandkids loved so much. Mine. Mine. Mine.

When she grew tired of standing, she went back to where Mike stood. "Anything interesting?"

He shook his head, never taking his eyes off his viewfinder. "Not yet. A few small ones. I took some shots. Got some video."

"I'm going inside to warm up. Are you okay?"

"Uh-huh."

She headed back to the passageway that led to the interior of the ship. Just a few minutes, long enough for her nose to thaw out, and she'd be good again. She glanced at her watch. Half an hour until soup was served. She didn't want to miss that, for sure.

The path she chose led her into a small, open area with a few armchairs scattered around. She chose one in a corner, unbuttoned her jacket, and slipped off her gloves. She closed her eyes—just to let her eyeballs thaw, too—when a familiar voice met her ears.

Belle.

She feigned sleep, hoping if they saw her, they'd think she couldn't hear them.

Footsteps neared.

"I'm so glad I told you the truth, Bill."

"He can't hold anything over you unless you try to keep it a secret. I could just kill that man, though, for the pain he's put you through."

"He's not worth it. I wish I'd had the strength to stand up to him before."

"Well, you got me, babe, as the old song goes. Nobody will ever hurt you again."

"Just promise me you won't do anything."

"I can't promise, babe. He's a dirty, rotten scoundrel, and somebody needs to stop him."

Their voices trailed off as they continued down the passageway away from Carly. She peeked through a slitted lid but saw nobody, then stood and stuck her nose around the corner.

Empty.

Had she dreamt the whole thing?

$ $ $

Two hours later, her tummy full of pea soup and her nose and fingers warming again in the comfort of their stateroom, Carly smiled at her husband while he tried to find the footage of the best calving of the day.

An award winner, to hear him speak.

It came while she had her back to the railing, slurping on the bowl of pea soup she managed to get from the server. The one she intended on giving to Mike. But he refused, saying he was sure there would be a huge event any second now, and he didn't want to risk missing it.

And sure enough, at the far end of the glacier, about a mile away, a tower of ice over two hundred feet high and likely a hundred feet around collapsed like a high-rise implosion into the ocean. The *oohs* and *aahs* of viewers caught her attention, but by the time she maneuvered her way to the railing, the ice was nothing more than a massive pile of debris at the base of the ice field.

But Mike caught it on video.

So he said.

He looked up. "I know I got it. And some neat pictures as we were turning. And some of you sipping soup." He sighed. "Although most of those were from behind since that's the way you were facing."

"The wind was cold, and I didn't want my soup to be lukewarm by the time I got to the bottom of the bowl." She patted her tummy. "It was really good. All three bowls."

He glanced at her from his perch on the corner of the bed. "Thanks for getting the one for me."

"Well, I had two for you, but you wouldn't eat it. So I did. For you."

"Thanks for your sacrificial spirit."

She lay on the bed and closed her eyes as he muttered and mumbled his way through the frames. "How many pictures did you take today?"

"Only about five hundred. And maybe fifty videos. But most of them are short. I thought something was going to happen, so I focused in on that spot, and when nothing did, I stopped it. But the one I'm looking for was so—oh, here it is."

She scooted to the edge of the bed and looked over his shoulder as he pressed the PLAY button. Sure enough, the camera trained in on the far end of the glacier, where the sunlight shone through the ice, creating a deep blue-green hue. About five seconds in, a flurry of ice and snow tumbled off the top edge, then a small piece—about the size of a car—slid off like icing melting on a cake. Within seconds, the pillar separated from the main body of the ice field, leaned precariously out to sea as though checking its landing spot, then toppled, in slow motion, into the water below, setting up a wave about three feet high that rippled outwards.

The crowd reacted as expected, pointing, exclaiming, some cussing politely, and then about four seconds later, the anticipated BOOM! of the sound wave like somebody beat on a huge drum.

Mike beamed at her. "Was that great? Or what?"

"It was. Thanks for sticking in and getting that great video. What else do you have?"

He scrolled through his shots, pausing to show her one of great interest—at least to him. "Here's one of you eating your soup."

"Or maybe it was your soup. When did you take that one?"

"Let me check the timestamp. Ten-forty. Maybe it was mine."

She studied the shot which highlighted her in the center, her back to the camera, steam rising from her soup. Subsequent photos showed her from slightly different angles as both she and Mike moved in response to the ship's roll as it headed back to sea.

What was that?

"Go back a second."

"Where?"

"A couple of shots back."

He complied. "This one?"

"No, the next, I think. There. Can you get in closer on that lifeboat there?"

He zoomed in and peered at the picture. "Who is it?"

"Got any more of that particular shot?"

He fiddled with the zoom again, returning it to normal before scrolling on. "Should have. I tend to take two or three at a time in case one doesn't come out. There."

"Zoom in, please."

Yes, it was exactly as she thought.

Neil Williams and Penny Goodnight. Arguing. The tendons in Neil's neck stood out, and Penny beat on his chest with her fists.

So what would two people who practically ignored each other just yesterday at the lecture series find to argue about?

$ $ $

When Carly entered the lecture room after lunch—her tummy now considerably fuller than it previously felt after consuming the pea soup—she checked to see if either the purser or the singer were in attendance.

They were not.

Teddy turned as she came in, and based on his earlier response to her questions, she expected him to glare at her. However, he surprised her by bounding from his seat and meeting her halfway.

He gripped her hands. "I'm so glad you came back. We treated you so awfully yesterday, didn't we? I just know that Miss Dawson is so-so-so sorry for that. She'll be so-so-so happy to see you. And go ahead and ask questions. It keeps the talk interesting."

Carly doubted very much that was true—at least as it pertained to the author—but was glad Teddy made an effort to be nice to her. Attendance seemed down for this class, and whether that was due to the topic—Reader Expectations—or to the heightened tension in the room over the past few lectures, she wasn't certain.

She pasted on a smile. "Thanks, Teddy. That means a lot to me. I'll try not to make a pest of myself today."

He giggled—sounding suspiciously like a high school girl—then released her hands. "Good. Now we're friends again. Come sit by me."

She'd sat in the front row during the first lecture, and wasn't certain she wanted to go through that again, but for his sake, she did as he asked. If nothing else, maybe he'd see that Miss Dawson's sense of contrition wasn't as inflated as his own.

Then again, if Monica's reaction to Carly sitting between her and Teddy was any indication, maybe ruffled feathers were being smoothed over. Monica smiled and nodded in her direction, then actually included her in a question, however awkwardly worded it was.

"Are you two enjoying your cruise?"

Carly cringed inside. The form of the question made it sound like she and Teddy were together, which they definitely were not. She smiled back. "I don't know about him, but I most certainly am. My husband got some great video of the calving earlier today at the glacier. Did you have a chance to get out on deck?"

Monica shook her head. "I was working on my novel in my stateroom."

"And I was updating the membership list for Miss Dawson's fan club. You wouldn't believe how many new members have joined as a result of the cruise and her gracious appearance at these lectures."

Carly scanned the room. Attendance started at about fifty, increased to maybe as much as a hundred for a couple of lectures, but had now dwindled to around forty. Seemed like what remained were the diehard core of readers on the cruise. Then again, forty names might be more than were previously on the list.

She turned to Teddy. "Does the gift shop carry her books?"

He beamed. "Oh, yes. All of them. And they're on sale, too." His smile dropped. "Although I can't fathom why. She is such a great author. Her books are in great demand."

Maybe. "Perhaps it's because there is a smaller market on the ship than there would be at a bookstore in a mall. Of the two thousand or so passengers, what percentage are fans? And how many of them already have her books?"

Teddy sniffed. "Then, of course, there are those readers who never buy a book, preferring to read library copies."

So much for mending fences. Carly chose to ignore the snide remark. "So, Monica, tell me about the book you're working on."

Monica's eyes widened as though she'd stepped on a tack. "Oh, I never share my work in process with anybody. They might steal my story."

Teddy giggled again. "She's so afraid somebody might steal her story and publish it under their own name, she never shows her stuff to anybody. Not even me."

"So you've not been published?"

"Not yet."

"How many books have you written?"

Although Carly would not have said it was anatomically possible, Monica's eyes opened further. This time, though, a red flush ran up her neck and into her face. "Twelve."

The woman's answer surprised Carly. "Wow. I'm impressed. Seems a shame you won't let somebody else read them. Like a publisher, for example."

"Oh, no, they might—"

Teddy reached across Carly and patted Monica's hand. "We know. Steal them." He sat back and rolled his eyes, making a circular motion with his forefinger on the far side of his head—where Monica wouldn't see. "Judging by the couple of times she's opened up and told me a little about the books, I think she's writing the same book using different names and cities. And it sounds suspiciously like Miss Dawson's first release."

Which, if Carly recalled, was not one of the author's better stories. Poor Monica, if she was making a hackneyed attempt to emulate her heroine, there was no telling how bad the story would be.

She was probably better off not showing it to anybody.

Miss Dawson appeared through a side door and approached the lectern, cleared her throat, went through her welcome and introduction, then launched directly into her talk. "Readers have a pre-set expectation based on the author, the genre, the cover, and the back cover write-up before they ever begin reading page one."

She then explained the differences between various genres and the unwritten rules about these types of stories. "So you see, in a romantic mystery, for example, the reader expects the romance to be about half of the story, and the mystery the other half. If that's out of balance, it's not truly a romantic mystery. It's either a romance, or a mystery. Doesn't mean a romance can't have some mystery, or a mystery can't have romance."

Carly raised a hand, and Miss Dawson's mouth worked its way into a smile. "I was wondering if it's more difficult to write a blended book, one that could fit into two genres, such as a romantic mystery, or if it's more difficult to stick with one genre."

"That depends on the author. As we get more experienced, we find ourselves growing bored with a label and want to expand into new territory, as it were."

When nobody else had a question, Carly stepped up again. "Can you give us an example of a true romance, a true mystery, and a hybrid of the two?"

"Well, among my books, *Love in Bloom* is a true romance, where boy meets girl, they fall in love, they encounter some difficulties, then they marry."

Yes, Carly recalled that particular one. The girl acted like a two-year-old, throwing temper tantrum after temper tantrum until she got her way, and the boy cowered beneath her blistering gaze throughout the story. She could only imagine what kind of a marriage they'd have.

"And I did write a pure mystery. *The Case of the Cuckolded Husband.* No romance there, I'm afraid."

Yes, another memorable book. Carly guessed the wife killed him before the murder actually happened, which didn't come until halfway through the book, after a long and convoluted narrative about setting and backstory.

"And a hybrid, as you so eloquently put it, would be *Somebody's Daughter.* A police detective and the female coroner fall in love while they investigate a young girl's disappearance."

Ah, yes. A good premise badly mucked up by poor writing and inconsistent facts.

The author continued with her presentation, actually mentioning a few other books—probably because she didn't write any fantasy, supernatural, thriller, or westerns herself, although she tried to imply that the mere mention of a horse or a steer in a story could constitute a cross-over theme.

Carly was fairly certain that wasn't true.

However, by the end of the lecture, she knew what kind of books to avoid. Anything with a picture of a woman in a low-cut bodice, a man without a shirt, or a sports car were likely to be something she wouldn't want to read.

And, of course, anything with Barbara Ann Dawson's name on the cover.

As she headed down her passageway on the way to her stateroom to meet up with Mike and get ready for their final Gala Night, she lost her balance and collided with the wall of the passageway. Gripping the rail running the length of the hall, she steadied herself, only to find herself careening toward the other wall.

What that—

Sam stuck his head out of a room and smiled. "Seas getting little rough. Hold on."

"Are we in for bad weather?"

"Captain say we're fine. Maybe higher winds and slightly rough seas. Nothing to spoil your evening, though. Enjoy your dinner. Maybe I see you there. In restaurant?"

"Yes, we have reservations at The Captain's Table at five."

"I work there this evening. I look for you."

When he returned to his work, she continued down the hall to their room. High winds and rough seas did not the perfect conditions for eating a heavy meal make. At least, not in her book.

And speaking of books, what was it with Monica and her fear of somebody stealing her stuff? If she was using Miss Dawson as her model, she had no worries about that.

Personally, Carly wouldn't steal Barbara Ann Dawson's writing if it floated past her on a barge.

$ $ $

Carly sipped her coffee. Dinner proved a delicious affair, as usual, and Sam as good as his word, stopping at their table to say hello even though he was working another section. The young man certainly dressed up nice, in his white shirt, black tie, gloves, and waist-cut jacket and black pants.

She scanned the room, looking for other familiar faces. Bill and Belle sat across the room, but when she waved—although she was certain Bill looked directly at her—he didn't acknowledge her. Oh well, once they disembarked in Seattle on Sunday, she'd never see either of them again.

Which, judging by their recent attitude, was fine by her.

Dave and Dewey, on the other hand, stopped by and said hello. Dewey looked worried about something. Money?

Or something else?

The two couples seated at their table were friends and golf aficionados, and pretty much ignored her and Mike after the initial introductions were made. Which was fine with her. She'd had about enough of people and their problems. She looked forward to spending the next day at sea as they steamed homeward. Maybe she could finally get some reading time.

At one point, she excused herself to go powder her nose. As she passed the host's desk, she overheard Tomas, their favorite dining room supervisor, on the telephone. His agitated expression and furtive manner begged her to slow so she could learn what upset him.

"Yes, I understand. No, nobody's seen him since breakfast. He's supposed to be here on the host desk in The Captain's Table. No, I already checked the other restaurants. He's not there. And he's not in his cabin. I sent somebody to the bar in case he was there. Yes, you know how he can be. Most likely he ingratiated himself into some woman's arms—and her stateroom—and won't be in any shape to serve tonight. No, that's fine, Captain. I'll let you speak with him. And discipline him appropriately. We should not allow this kind of behavior to go on. Yes, I did check with the infirmary. He's not there either. Thank you, Sir." He disconnected the call and caught her gaze. "Mrs. Turnquist. Can I help you?"

"No. I'm sorry. I overheard you saying that Mr. Williams is missing?"

Tomas smiled. "Not missing. MIA. There's a difference."

Carly gripped the host desk when a particularly hard roll of the ship threatened to throw her off balance. Good thing she chose not to drink.

Wouldn't want to go around looking like she was tipsy. "Hopefully he didn't go overboard in this weather."

"Very unlikely. He'd have no reason to be topside. He is supposed to be here."

While Tomas probably believed what he said, he likely didn't know about the times she'd seen him on deck and arguing with one passenger or the other. Perhaps she should apprise him. Then again, if she said anything, she'd have to name names, and she didn't want to get anybody in trouble over nothing more than the lecherous purser's romantic life.

She'd stay quiet.

For now.

After she returned to the table, and feeling a little green around the gills because of the rocking and rolling of the ship, she gathered her shawl around her shoulders and picked up her evening bag. Without waiting for their tablemates to pause in their discussion of round-the-world golf tours, she nodded to each in turn. "Good night, and thank you for a most pleasant evening."

The older gentleman smiled. "Hopefully we didn't bore you to death."

"Not at all." She turned to loop her arm through Mike's. "I think I can honestly say I learned more tonight about golf than I thought possible."

Mike walked her toward the elevators, steadying her following another roll of the ship. "You are terrible, Carly. I heard the sarcasm in your voice back there."

She chuckled. "When somebody is passionate about a particular topic, there is no offending them. They took what I said as a compliment." She paused while they waited for the car. "You know what, let's get off at the Promenade Deck and walk down the steps to our room."

"It's freezing out there."

"I'd like to see just how big the waves really are."

He shrugged. "Fine." He led the way into the elevator and the brass doors swished shut. "What took you so long in the bathroom?"

"Nothing."

"You seemed to be gone a long time."

"I stopped to talk to Tomas at the host desk." She gripped his forearm.

"Seems the purser is on the missing list. But they think he's holed up somewhere with a woman." She wrinkled her nose. "I guess I thought maybe they left that kind of stuff onshore."

Mike chuckled. "A cruise ship isn't some kind of paradise, you know. People are people wherever you go."

That certainly seemed the case. Even Miss Dawson didn't go out of her way to be nice to people she would spend a week with. Strange, that.

They exited the elevator on Deck Three and turned down the passageway toward the double door leading outside. As the barrier closed behind them, a blast of wind raced along the deck, slamming into them, almost knocking them off their feet. Mike held onto her, and she gripped the railing, peering over the side, as they battled their way forward.

Whitecaps rolled as far as the eye could see, illuminated by the full moon near the horizon. Waves slapped against the hull, and seagulls rode the currents in a crazy out-of-control ballet. Salt spray reached up and tickled her lips, reminding her they were floating on water hundreds of feet deep. She peered at the black ocean, wondering where the playful whales of this morning took shelter in a storm.

Mike wrapped his arm around her shoulders. "This is crazy. Let's go inside."

Her hair, wet with salt water, whipped around her face and into her eyes, stinging like needles but creating an interesting taste sensation. She shook her head. "It's just about twenty feet along to the bow where we'll be under shelter, then another twenty feet to the doors on the other side. Maybe the wind isn't so strong over there."

He ducked his head, and together they hurried along to the covered portion of the deck. Overhead, the lifeboats rocked in time with the waves, creating a mesmerizing, almost hypnotic, effect. Carly focused on the wet wood under her feet, splashed with the spray. No way did she want to fall.

They rounded the corner and slowed. Carly, glad to be out of the deluge, shook her head like a dog, sending water in all directions.

Mike gasped and brushed the glistening drops from his jacket. "Stop that. You're soaking me."

"More than you already were?" She stepped closer and shook her head again. "Take that."

He laughed and pulled her close. "Keep that up, and I'll toss you over my shoulder and take you back to our stateroom. And you'll never see the light of day again. Or at least not until we hit landfall in Seattle."

She wriggled out of his grasp. "Oh, no you don't." She turned to escape his clutching hands then stopped. "That's interesting."

He stood beside her. "What?"

She pointed. "Over there. The footprints on the dry part of the deck."

"Why should that interest you? A crew member walked through the water, just like we did, and tracked water onto the dry part of the deck." He stomped his feet a couple of times. "Just like that."

"But the sign on the door says LOUNGERS. Why would somebody be taking out or putting in lounge chairs? At night?"

He threw up his hands. "I give up. Why would they?"

"Unless they weren't."

"That doesn't make sense. Wait. Where are you going?"

She headed for the door where the footsteps ended and tried the handle.

Mike followed close behind. "It's no use. It's locked."

But the latch turned easily, and the door swung open on well-oiled hinges.

A light switch on the inside wall beckoned to her, and she clicked it on.

Neil Williams lay splayed across a stack of lounge chairs.

But he wasn't taking a nap.

His open, staring eyes bored into her, and the red matting of blood on the side of his head glistened in the light.

He was dead.

And not for long, judging by the deep color of the blood.

She stepped back. "Mike, you'd better get Security. I'll wait here and make sure nobody touches the crime scene."

"I knew it. I just knew it."

She turned to peer at him. "You knew he was here? Dead?"

"No. I knew we couldn't just take a cruise. You had to get involved." He stared at her. "Did you really just find him, or did you suspect he was here?"

His question surprised her. "I didn't know he was dead. But I thought it was a possibility."

"Why?"

"So many people hated him, it seemed a foregone conclusion."

$ $ $

Back in their stateroom two hours later, Carly was still fuming.

Not about Neil Williams being dead. No, he pretty much deserved that. Well, okay, nobody deserved to be murdered and dumped in a storage closet like a bag of trash, but Neil Williams deserved something bad. He'd hurt so many innocent people over the years, including Belle, Dave and Dewey, Penny, Monica, and even Miss Dawson.

Okay, not all his victims were nice, and maybe none of them were really innocent, but still—she couldn't get the image of his face out of her mind.

But that wasn't what really upset her.

When Mike returned with the security officer, he also brought the captain. A gale had blown in by that time, and the ship struggled to remain stable. Captain Lycas explained he was heading out to open sea in hopes of finding calmer sailing, and that they were on their own for now. Neither the FBI nor the Coast Guard could get to them in the midst of the storm.

A crowd gathered once Security cordoned off the area using crime scene tape, drawn into the relative calm of the bow section, perhaps, from their evening walk. Although why anybody would choose to walk in a storm was beyond her.

Something she couldn't explain, either. Not to Mike. Not to the captain. Not to the security officer.

Not even to herself.

Should she tell them she had a hunch? No, that was too strong a word.

She was as surprised as Mike to find the body there.

Not that it was the purser.

Just that it was where it was.

And then who came along but Miss Barbara Ann Dawson. Offering her services as an expert in crime. Like she was a regular LEO. Which she wasn't. Why, she probably had never taken even one criminal forensic course in her life.

The only mystery she was involved in was how she got to be such a big name author.

Carly gritted her teeth as the captain latched onto the author like a lifesaver. There was no doubt his chief of security was in over his head, particularly when the man brought three more reports of missing jewelry and the possibility that perhaps the purser tried to stop the thief and was rewarded with a blow to the head.

Because that, apparently, was the cause of death, according to the ship's doctor's preliminary report. He promised to do a more extensive examination of the body once it was moved to the infirmary, but would refrain from performing an actual autopsy. Not his area of expertise, and he didn't want to muck it up.

No, what really got Carly's goat was how Miss Dawson became the captain's pet and how she was shooed aside, despite her protests that she was the one who found the body. However, after she caught the chief of security eyeing her like he thought she might turn into a serial killer in front of him, she backed down.

No point getting on the suspect list.

Because if there were two things she knew for certain, they were that the killer was one of the people Neil Williams had a run-in with on this ship.

That, and the fact she knew for certain that neither she nor Mike had killed the purser.

Well, she for sure was innocent.

Mike? Well. . . she was pretty sure he was, too.

Chapter 17

Saturday morning—their second-to-last day aboard—dawned overcast and still stormy. The seas pitched and rolled in cadence with a song only they could hear, while the clouds hugged the horizon, blotting out the sun's attempts to brighten the day. The temperature seemed intent on hanging just above freezing, which was a good thing. At least there was little danger of ice forming on the railings and lifeboats, creating a near-invisible but concrete-like weight that could imperil the ship.

Still, the decks and steps were slick, and most passengers took advantage of the opportunity—and the rationale—to stay inside.

But not Carly.

Slipping out of bed before Mike awoke, getting dressed in the dark, and sneaking out the door before he figured out she was gone took some doing. A couple of times his breathing changed, and once, he turned over, flinging his arm into the void where she had lain. At that time in particular, her heart clamored like a bell rung by a drunken monk.

Still, he settled down and soon was snoring again, and she made her escape, pulling the hood of her jacket up around her ears and jamming her hands into her pockets.

She had work to do. No matter what Miss Barbara Ann Dawson said.

Down the passageway, out the doors, battling against the wind, she made her way to the steps leading to the Promenade Deck and the scene of the crime. Surely nobody in their right mind—barring present company, of course—was out here at this time of—whoosh! The persistent but rude walker brushed past her in the dim light and sea spray, this time going in the opposite direction.

"Excuse me." The wind snatched Carly's words off, tossing them to the four winds. "But you're going the wrong way." She pointed to a sign on the bulkhead that instructed walkers, joggers, and runners to head toward the bow, going in a counter-clockwise direction. "Or maybe you can't read?"

The man ignored her and continued on his way, head down, arms and legs pumping in a ridiculous pantomime. Carly shrugged and turned to go in the other direction—the right direction.

Except before she got to her destination, an accordion-type folding barrier barred her way.

"Well, of all the—"

She moved to the outside rail to get a better view of whatever was going on around the corner. Right in front of the storage locker where she found the body. Didn't seem fair that the one person with on-the-scene knowledge shouldn't be permitted to assist in the investigation.

Voices carried on the same wind, but she caught only snatches. Something about expertise. Prior knowledge. Received any threats. Disliked the man.

Carly stifled a snort. If they were asking who might want Neil Williams dead, she had an entire list. Including the fox in the hen house, as it were. Miss Barbara Ann Dawson. Arguing with the purser about money. A partnership. Broken deal. Bad terms. Something like that.

Carly could still remember the evil eye the author tossed at the man in the buffet restaurant, threatening to kill him.

No, that wasn't quite true. She sighed and leaned against the railing. The woman said she *could* kill him right then. And wished he'd drop dead. Not exactly solid evidence. But her words—and her anger—might speak to intent.

She straightened. She had to find out what was going on. What if she went around the other side? Would there be a barrier there? She glanced around for the nearest cross-passageway when the irate walker rounded the stern again, heading for her.

Oh-oh. She had enough trouble without dealing with a man who could probably lift her over the railing and toss her overboard like a candy wrapper if he wanted to. He looked pretty strong. Chugging along like a steam engine. Jowls wagging like a rabid bulldog.

Boy, some people's children.

She gripped the barrier. If he planned to throw her over, she'd put up a fight.

But the man wheeled about not ten feet from her and started back the other way, muttering something about what was the deal with blocking off half the Promenade Deck and how were people to get their exercise and now he'd have to do twice as many laps to make up the same distance.

Which meant there was a barrier on the other side of the ship, too. No point in going over there—something clicked between her fingers, and she turned around. What was this?

She'd managed to unhook the fastener from the railing.

Without even trying.

She cast her eyes heavenward. "Thank you, God."

She slipped through the opening then paused. Is that really the kind of stuff God would be interested in? She shrugged. Must be if He opened the way for her. A hazy recollection of a Bible verse quoted by her granddaughter filtered into her memory.

Oh, well, didn't matter now. She was in.

Sticking her hands back in her pockets, a square object met her fingertips. She pulled it out—last evening's chocolate that she neglected to eat in all the excitement. She tucked it back in. Might come in handy if she needed sustenance to keep her going until breakfast.

She peeked around the corner. Sure enough, Miss Dawson stood, notebook in hand, pen poised, beside the chief of security, who shook his head at something the woman said.

The author beamed up at him. "But Chief, the Captain said I was to help in the investigation. I'm here to assist in any way I can."

"Thank you, madam, but I believe we have it under control. He slipped and fell in the storage locker, and unfortunately, he died."

"Well, that's too bad. I was all set for a murder investigation."

The man's eyes widened. "Oh, no, madam, that would never do. We have never had a murder on our ship."

"I thought this situation reminded me of *Lost in Paradise*, my first mystery. Except that one took place on an island, not on a ship. And the victim was a woman, not a man. Killed by her husband. But otherwise, exactly like this."

"Her body was found in a storage locker?"

"Well, no. Buried in the sand, actually. She was in love with the pool boy, and she wanted to run away with him, and—"

Carly could stand no more of this inane chatter. She stepped around the corner and checked the deck outside the storage locker. Dry, now. But she knew what she saw last night. "Chief, did you take pictures of the scene last night?"

Miss Dawson eyed her up and down like she was a cheap knock-off hanging in a consignment shop window. "What are you doing here?"

"Since I was the person who found the body, thought I might help."

"We don't need your help." The author turned to the chief. "Do we, Chief?"

"I have the investigation well in hand. Thank you."

But Carly was not to be deterred. "Did you compare the shoe prints on the deck with the purser's?"

The security officer dropped his gaze. "No, madam."

"Well, they weren't his. He wears smooth-soled shoes like the rest of the officers. The prints were more like a hiking boot. And I noticed that the regular crew doesn't wear that kind of shoe, either. So the prints likely belong to the killer."

He squinted his eyes at her. "You think the killer carried him to the locker?"

She shook her head. "No, I think the killer dragged him. You'll see in your pictures that there was a wet spot here." She pointed to the location. "Then the footprints came from there and stopped at another wet spot here." She moved a foot or so to the right. "The killer kept dragging him bit by bit until they were close enough to stuff him in the lounger locker."

Miss Dawson raised an eyebrow. "You surmise much from so little evidence."

Carly ignored the jibe and addressed the security chief. "Have you interviewed the passengers and crew yet?"

"Yes." He shook his head. "Nobody knew him. Nobody had a reason to kill him."

Carly stared directly at the author, who licked her lips, smearing lipstick on her teeth. "I have talked with at least six people on this ship who knew him from before, and all had reason to want to hurt him."

The author gasped. "That's not true. What a wicked thing to say."

Carly allowed a tiny smile to tease her lips. "And one of them was you." She turned to the chief of security. "Do you really think she's the best person to help with your investigation?"

"Actually, I was trying to tell her just that." He faced Miss Dawson. "Madam, the captain was trying to be polite, but after he and I talked, he decided that perhaps I could call on you if I needed your expertise."

Miss Dawson's eyes narrowed and her lips formed a straight line. Well, almost straight, given that her lipstick looked applied with a shaky hand. She took a step back and might have fallen if Carly hadn't reached out to steady her.

The chief of security helped her to sit on a nearby bench. "Are you all right, madam?"

She brushed his hand from her shoulder. "Fine. Leave me be."

Carly recalled the square of chocolate, and held it out. "Eat this. When I get hungry, sometimes I find myself lightheaded."

But the author shook her head. "No, thanks. I'm diabetic."

The chief's brow pulled down. "Should I call the Infirmary? Perhaps you need food? Or insulin?"

"I'll be fine. I've just received a shock, that's all." She pulled a tissue from her purse. "Practically being accused of murder would send anybody off the rails."

Miss Dawson straightened her shoulders, gathered her coat around herself, and stood on shaky legs before heading around the corner.

The security officer turned to Carly. "The captain made a few inquiries about you last night."

Her breath caught in her throat. "Oh?"

"Yes. Apparently when he woke the police chief in your town and told him what happened, the man said he wasn't surprised. Dead bodies seem to find you, or something like that."

"He likes to joke around."

"Perhaps. But he did say he didn't know anybody else with a nose for a mystery and a head for solving them like you. Outside law enforcement, that is. A regular Jessica Fletcher."

Chief Donovan said that about her? What a compliment. "Actually Jessica Fletcher is—"

"I know. He said. Your hero."

"Right up there with Agatha Christie."

The chief peered at Carly then quirked his head in the direction Miss Dawson had taken. "Were you serious when you said she had a reason to want Williams dead?"

"I overheard them argue. But I don't think she's our killer."

"Oh? Why not?"

"Well, first of all, I can't see her carrying a strapping younger man anywhere, can you? Or wearing hiking boots."

He grinned. "True. So that narrows down the field some."

"Right. Doesn't mean she isn't involved in some way. But the fact she's a diabetic does answer one question. They argued about a deal they made where apparently the terms weren't clear to both parties. Or not as clear as they should have been. I have some ideas about that, but I'll talk to her later. Neil made a comment about her always having to be in control. I thought he was referring to their deal. Now I see it's about how much sugar she planned to eat that day. She had a plate piled high with desserts."

He didn't look as sure as she felt. "O-Okay. So where does that leave us?"

"I'm not sure. But despite what she says, the other suspects did know each other. I saw them in the restaurant, eating together like old friends."

"So who are these other suspects?"

"I'd rather not say right now. Can you give me a few hours to ask questions and hopefully rule out two or three? It will be a lot easier to work with fewer suspects."

"Very well. The storm is supposed to continue through tonight. If you don't have some answers by Sunday morning, before we dock, we'll have to detain the entire complement of passengers and crew, making for some very unhappy folks."

She nodded. "I'll work as quickly as I can."

"And keep me informed."

She tossed him a mock salute. "I feel like I've been deputized. How exciting."

"That will wear off as soon as folks know what you're up to. You might regret getting involved."

Somehow she doubted it. Jessica would never let the killer get away.

And neither would she.

$ $ $

On her way from the crime scene to the Lanai Buffet, Carly stepped off the elevator on Deck 5 instead of 6, her mind trying to wrap itself around the murder and the suspects. She sighed. Well, she could walk up through the shopping area—which should be fairly quiet this time of the morning—and go up the forward stairway to the restaurant for breakfast. But first, a quick call to their stateroom to let Mike know where she was.

A white courtesy phone rested on a table beside a comfy armchair, and she sank into the soft plushness, reveling in the warmth while her toes thawed out. She dialed their number and listened to the rings—three. Four. Five.

Just as she was about to hang up, her husband's breathless voice reached through the wire. "Hello?"

"Mike, it's me."

A pause. Then, "Where are you?"

"Out for a walk."

"I thought you were still in bed. Sorry, I was in the shower."

"I'm heading for breakfast."

"Okay. I'll be there in about ten minutes."

"No rush. I'll have coffee while I wait. Watch the storm a bit."

"Okay. See you then."

She rang off, glad he hadn't worried about her. But seriously, the bed wasn't so big there was any chance of her getting lost in it. Then again, maybe he thought she wanted to sleep in a little.

She headed toward the front of the ship, passing the still-closed jewelry, leather goods, and shoe stores, holding onto the handrails to keep her balance. No doubt about it—the rolling sea was a challenge to this landlubber. Thankfully, no seasickness yet. Maybe she'd best eat light until the storm eased some.

Then again—maybe not.

As she passed the Faberge display nook, she paused. A light shone through a crack in the closed curtains. Strange. When she came past here last night, not even the display cases were illuminated. She checked the sign indicating the display's hours. Not open for another ninety minutes.

She tapped on the wall. "Hello? Anybody in there?"

Kalim's olive-skinned face met hers from the other side of the curtain and metal security grating separating them. "We're not open."

"I know. I saw the lights on." She stood on tiptoe to look over his shoulder. One of the display case doors stood open. "What going on?"

He sighed then stepped back. "Come in. Please be quiet. I don't want to raise the alarm."

He slid back the steel grate and held the curtain for her to slip in, then replaced the curtain and latched the gate again. He gestured to the display case. "It was like this when I passed by this morning."

"Why did you even notice it?" She studied the small key latch in the glass, scratched and bent like someone forced their way in. "Why didn't the alarm sound?"

"The curtain was open just as you found it." He sighed again. "And the alarm was set last night when I left. But this morning, it was not."

"Could it have malfunctioned?"

He shook his head.

"And you're certain you set it last night?"

"Positive. Last thing before I left. I always do it that way."

"Anybody else know the code to turn it off?"

"I didn't think so. But obviously someone did."

She eyed the other cases. "What was taken?"

He groaned and sank into a chair, burying his face in his hands. "Nothing except the Tenth Anniversary Egg. The most valuable in our collection." He looked up at her. "The one that you—"

"That I almost dropped?"

He nodded. "The same."

"Do you have a telephone?"

He gestured to one hanging on the wall. She hurried across the room and dialed her stateroom, asking Mike to bring his camera to breakfast. "I don't have time to answer questions right now, but I'll fill you in when I see you."

Now it was her husband's turn to groan. "What are you involved in?"

"Nothing. Just bring the camera." She turned to Kalim. "So the egg and the base are missing?"

"Yes. Thousands of dollars of precious metal in the base alone. Diamonds, rubies, gold. I will lose my job over this."

"Not if I can help it."

"You know who took it?"

"Not yet. For sure. But I will. You can count on me."

She hurried from the room, feeling a little like the Lone Ranger riding off to find the bad guy.

The question was: would Mike be willing to ride alongside her as her Tonto?

$ $ $

Sure enough, she found the answer to her question in the pictures on the camera, sitting across a very civilized table from her husband over breakfast. The images of the eggs on display brought back happy memories of a time when Neil Williams was still very much alive. Before she knew some of the things she now knew about her friends. When she had no suspicions about one of them being a killer.

Before the base was used to crack Neil Williams over the head, snuffing out his life.

Because she was fairly certain that was what happened.

Just the idea of a priceless piece of history being used in such a brutal manner was almost unimaginable. Was it really only Tuesday—four days ago—that she knocked over the table and ended up with the egg in her lap?

At least it wasn't on her face.

After breakfast, armed with her evidence, she hurried down the steps to Deck Five where the Infirmary resided. A quick call to the doctor before breakfast assured her he'd be there for at least an hour. Mike followed close behind as though afraid to let her out of his sight.

Which, once she filled him in over salmon crepes and hot coffee, were his exact words to her. That any thoughts she had of a moment's peace without him for the few remaining hours of their dream cruise were gone.

In fact, he shook his head as though expressing great disappointment.

It was at that point she defended herself. "I didn't go looking for this investigation. I stumbled on it. You were with me when I found the body."

"I was. I saw you. But you have to admit you were determined to go that particular direction on that significant night, right? Like a bloodhound on the scent trail. Or a shark following the blood. Or a—"

"All right. Enough with the animal analogies."

Now, as they neared their destination, he pulled her to a halt. "Promise me you won't push your way into this any more than is necessary."

"Promise."

He rolled his eyes. "Let me reword that. Any more period."

"I can't just walk away and hope they figure out who killed the man."

"From what you said, he was a dirty rotten scoundrel who was going to buy it sooner or later."

Her brow drew down. "If you asked him, he probably would have chosen later."

"I just don't want you to get hurt. We get that note, our towel monkey is wrecked, our chocolate is eaten—"

"And we are almost killed in that rock fall."

He glared at her. "You think that was deliberate?"

"I saw who did it."

"You didn't tell me."

"I didn't want to worry you."

He gripped her by the forearms and stared into her eyes. As usual, those dark chocolate orbs melted her heart—and her resolve. Her vision misted, and he pressed her close to his chest. They stood that way a long moment, and she almost decided to drop the whole thing and let the authorities take over finding the killer.

Then she remembered the missing egg, and the two thousand or so passengers and crew who would be forced to stay on board—themselves included—while the Seattle police did their jobs. Thousands of innocent people. All because of the one guilty.

She pulled away. "With you by my side, nobody can hurt me. Right?"

He straightened and puffed out his chest. "They'll have to get through me to get to you, that's for sure."

"Then let's carry on together. Let's identify the guilty so the innocent can get on with their lives."

He hesitated, and for a moment she feared he'd deny her the opportunity to solve this murder. Then his shoulders relaxed, and he offered her his arm. "Deal."

Deal. That reminded her of something else Miss Dawson and the purser argued about. That her deal with fifty-fifty, and his was seventy-thirty.

How could she prove what that was all about?

A doorway opened and the doctor nodded to them. "Just in time. My last patient just left. Seasickness is rampant onboard right now, with passengers and crew alike." He stepped aside to let them pass. "What do you have for me?"

Carly stepped into a small office much like any doctor's office on the mainland and sat in the nearest chair. "I just talked to Kalim at the Faberge Egg display." Quickly she filled the doctor and Mike in on what Kalim discovered that morning. Both men expressed their irritation at the theft. "I have pictures of the base of the egg. Kalim said it was several pounds of gold and precious stones. I'm thinking maybe it's the murder weapon."

The doctor nodded. "That would be a novel tool to be sure."

"Well, I think it would prove that the murder wasn't premeditated, which would be good for the killer. Maybe they could get off with manslaughter, depending on the circumstances."

"True." The doctor crossed his office and pulled a file from a cabinet drawer. "I have x-rays here." He flipped a switch on the wall, turning on a film viewer, and jammed the black-and-white sheet into the holder. "Let's see."

Carly handed over Mike's camera, and the doctor scrolled back several images then forward again before holding it up to the film. "Yep. Of course, I can't be a hundred percent sure until I have the actual base, but it sure looks close enough to be a match. If not that one, then one much like it. See the rounded edge, and the knob-like protrusions on the wound?" He lowered the camera. "We will likely find blood, tissue, and hair on the weapon, no matter how well the killed tried to clean it off."

"I'll—" She glanced at Mike. "We'll keep looking for it."

They turned to leave but stopped when the doctor spoke again. "There was one other thing."

"What was that?"

"A preliminary examination raised some questions for me. I looked up his primary care provider and contacted him. Apparently his doc is out of the country for a few days, so I left a message for him to contact me on his return."

"What kind of questions?"

"I don't have confirmation yet, of course, so this is still unofficial. But I'd say if Neil Williams hadn't been murdered, he didn't have long to live anyway."

Chapter 18

Armed with this information, Carly returned to her stateroom and made a list of suspects and motives, leaving plenty of space for alibis. So far she had Monica, Penny Goodnight, Barbara Ann Dawson, Belle and hence Bill, and Dave and Dewey. Their motives ranged from an unspecified past wrong for Monica, to Miss Dawson's allegation of a deal gone awry, to Belle's past relationship and resulting sterility, to Bill's defense of the woman he loved, all the way to Dave and Dewey's financial downturn, although the purser alleged he'd advised against the investment.

But could—or indeed should—she believe anything he said?

She very much doubted it.

After she completed the list, she called the doctor to confirm time of death. Four to five hours before she found the body. Having gone for a walk with Mike around nine, that made it four to five that evening. Right as they were getting ready to go to the Gala Night.

She shivered. How bizarre to think that at about the same time she was thinking ahead to shrimp cocktail and dessert, Neil Williams might have been breathing his last.

Life was so short. Snuffed out in a heartbeat.

Unless she subscribed to her daughter's faith, which said that people live forever. And they live their time on earth to choose where that forever will be. Heaven. Or the other place.

She closed her eyes. Had Neil Williams had the opportunity to make that choice? If living a good life was any indication, he appeared destined for the other place. If the perceptions of one's acquaintances had any say in the matter, he definitely was going to hell in a handcart.

But if, as Denise contended, it was a personal choice made between each individual and God, then Neil had a chance.

She opened her eyes and studied her list. She needed to find out where her suspects were during the critical hours, then double-check their alibis to be sure they were telling her the truth. Because, really, why should they? She wasn't the police. She couldn't threaten to arrest them, haul them down to the station for questioning.

In fact, with the storm still raging outside, she couldn't take them anywhere.

But maybe she could get them to lower their guard enough to tell her something that filled in a blank or answered a question. Corroborated somebody else's story, perhaps.

She'd start with the one person who she most wanted to be guilty: Miss Barbara Ann Dawson. She looked and acted the guiltiest of the bunch, although Carly was fairly certain she didn't act alone. Still, Teddy or another man could have helped her move the body once she did the dastardly deed.

Although, Miss Dawson struck her as singularly independent, unwilling or unable to acknowledge that she needed another's help.

In fact, this particular character trait might well prove her innocent.

Then again—maybe not.

After explaining to Mike exactly what her plan of attack was—have lunch first then ask questions until she found what she needed to prove who was the guilty party—and assuring him she was perfectly safe on board—after all, nobody had actually approached her or tried to harm her—he finally agreed that she could go seek out a particular young change room attendant while he went back to the spa to ask their masseuse couple questions about the rumor mill on the ship.

She was fairly certain he wouldn't learn much—that was how rumors tended to work. Folks never remembered who told them what, or how the story got started. Still, he was a smart man. He might just find out something.

When he left her sitting at their table in the Lanai Buffet, she went over the questions she wanted to ask, should she be so lucky as to find the same young woman Miss Dawson spoke with in the change room. And hopefully she'd recognize the young woman—what was her name? Tanya? No. Teresa? No. Something like that. Talia. That was it. From Malaysia. Loved working for the cruise line. That information should help her when—and if—she located the woman.

Armed with a plan, she headed for the bow of the ship, walking through the Lanai Poolside Taco Bar, tempted to grab a snack as she did. But no, she just had lunch, and dessert was reserved for—rats, she'd eaten her last dessert on the cruise the previous evening. Oh, for thin thighs and more willpower.

Through the swimming pool area, past the loungers, she made a beeline for the women's changing room. Pushing in through the swinging door, she paused to survey the room. Tidy, with fresh pool towels piled atop the counter near the door. Stacks of folded hand towels waited use beside each sink, which sparkled from frequent polishing.

Her heart dipped. Maybe Talia had already done her work and gone for the day. She turned to leave, then paused when a door marked EMPLOYEES ONLY opened and a four-wheeled cart pushed through.

Talia swiped at her bangs and smiled at Carly. "Hello, Madam. I didn't mean to startle you."

"You didn't. In fact, you're just the person I was looking for."

"Me, Madam?"

"Yes. I was here the other day when you were talking with Miss Barbara Ann Dawson."

"The mystery writer? She is rude."

"Yes, I got that impression. I wonder if you might tell me a little about your conversation with her."

"She said she was doing research for a book that would be set on a cruise ship. A love story. So she wanted to talk to young women who work on ships. For background, she said." Talia peered at her. "Are you a friend of hers? I don't want to get into trouble."

"Not a friend." At least, Carly was fairly certain the author would claim no such relationship with her. "I've attended several of her lectures."

Talia grinned. "Are they as terrible as the staff says?"

"I don't know. What are the staff saying?"

"That she doesn't really know what she talks about. Especially the mystery stuff. That she sells trash book with no good stories. That—" Talia clapped a hand over her mouth. "I say too much. Excuse me. I must work."

Carly stepped aside and let the woman push the cart forward. "I kind of heard the part where she was asking you if you had ever been, you know, molested on a ship."

"Yes. She said she read some accounts of bad things happening on ships. I said I don't know anything about that, but she didn't believe me." She ran a hand down her arm. "If not white, all lie."

The injustice—but the truth, at least in some quarters—of the girl's statement tugged at Carly's heart. "I don't believe that. I noticed that when you tried to say nothing happened, she kept asking questions."

"Yes. She said she knew security on ship is bad. I tell her because we don't want passengers bothered by seeing police everywhere. She said she heard about missing money and jewels. I tell her I know nothing." Talia straightened a stack of hand towels. "Again, she not believe me. Try to describe things that happen, bad things, say that happen to me." She shook her head. "Never. I love my job, but if I even think that might happen, I leave right away. I have man in Malaysia who want to marry me, but if I am not pure, he will not."

Carly was well aware of the double standards for chastity in many countries that usually punished the woman but not the man. And the circumstances surrounding the incident made little difference. Rape, incest, or consensual, always the woman paid the ultimate price with their reputation, their family shunning them, and sometimes even imprisonment or death.

"Is there anything else you can tell me?"

Talia shook her head. "She not nice woman, but I don't think she is bad. Does that make sense?"

"Perfectly. Thank you for your time."

Carly left the change room, glad she was lucky enough to find the young girl, and headed for her next destination: the captain.

Having checked in with the bridge earlier, she knew he was spending a couple of off-hours in the employee lounge on the Exploration Deck. Following his directions, she wound her way through the various offices, meeting rooms, and the casino before reaching the lounge near the aft or stern. She knocked then stepped inside.

Several semi-familiar faces looked up then dismissed her and went back to what they were doing when she arrived: reading, playing cards, or staring out the windows at the stormy sea mere feet beyond. Looking down at the waves from this vantage point was disconcerting, as there was no deck visible below them. The contour shape of the ship hid the Promenade Deck under cover at this point, and the lower decks were completely out of sight. Whitecaps dotted the waves, and the rain beat against the plate glass windows separating them from the elements beyond.

Carly spotted the captain in a wingback chair beside a fireplace, his legs crossed at the knee. She lifted a hand in greeting before making her way across the room, threading between conversation pits, a piano standing quiet for lack of someone to play, and several games tables awaiting competitors.

She sat in the matching chair across from him and held her hands toward the gas-fired flames. "This is nice. Especially on a cold and dreary day like today."

He looked out the window as though noticing the weather for the first time. His rich baritone voice, executed in a perfect British accent, resonated off the walls, the furniture, and penetrated her chest like a bass speaker at a rock concert. Without the ear-splitting volume. "Oh, this is nothing. You've not seen a real storm until you round Cape Horn. Or Cape of Good Hope in Africa. Now those are real gushers."

She smiled. "This is my first cruise, and I don't like boats much, so I figured I'm doing well to still be on my feet."

He nodded. "Drink lots of water. Don't eat much at one sitting. And if you find your tummy rising, paste your focus on the horizon. The feeling should pass fairly quickly."

"Thanks. Wish I'd known that the time I ferried from Cape Cod to Nantucket. Sick the whole way there, the entire weekend, and then I still had to get back to the mainland. I dreaded it."

"Some of those smaller boats heave more even in a small gale. Not to mention the diesel fumes."

"I guess that's what did it."

He uncrossed his legs and sat up. "You wanted to talk to me about something, but before we do, I have two little pieces of information I thought you might be interested in."

"Go ahead."

"First, a certain famous author sent a transmission to her agent while we were still close enough to accomplish that. Something about "STOP MYSTERY LINE. NO MORE STORIES. BACK TO STRAIGHT ROMANCE. PROFITS BE DAMNED.""

Interesting. "When was that?"

"About fifteen-hundred hours yesterday."

Three p.m. At least an hour before Neil Williams was murdered.

She opened her mouth to speak but he held up a hand to silence her. She complied. Mike would have been proud.

"The second thing is, I want to let you know I talked with Chief Donovan in Bear Cove about you."

"Your chief of security told me."

"He speaks highly of you."

"I wish he'd say some of those nice things to my face."

"Professional pride, no doubt. He said you have a good nose for solving mysteries, and I should trust your intuition."

"You didn't get that in writing by any chance, did you?"

"No, sorry." He sat back and crossed his arms over his chest. "Let me preface what I will ask you next with this. I trust you understand the extreme circumstances we find ourselves in. A dead body. Forced into international waters because of the storm which, by the way, is whipping up twenty-foot waves closer to shore. I don't know if the ship could have handled a storm that bad, so although our change of course has put us outside the accessibility of law enforcement, as a whole, I believe the ship is safer. Unless there's a serial murderer on board?"

She smiled, hoping to defray his concerns. "I don't believe there is a serial killer. I think the purser's murder is an isolated event, although we can never be certain. However, based on some evidence I've managed to uncover and confirm with the ship's doctor, I am certain this was a crime of opportunity."

"He mentioned you brought him pictures of the missing egg and base. Do you think he was killed because he came upon the robbery and the thief struck out in desperation? Or do you think he was lightened of his booty, to use an old pirate phrase?"

"I think the latter. Did he have the code to turn off the security system in the Faberge display room?"

Captain Lycas nodded. "The purser is much like the chief financial officer of a land-based corporation. He had access to the code, to be certain. Without raising any questions or suspicions. As do I." He studied her. "Does that make me a suspect, too?"

"No. Not unless I've really missed something."

"So how can I help you?"

This time she grinned. "I thought you'd never ask." She handed him a second list with just the names penned on it. "Can you get records from the cruise line that will tell us the prior sailings of these people?"

"Good heavens, that's a substantial list. Suspects?"

"Let's just call them persons of interest for now."

"Very well." He stood. "It may take several hours. Sometimes the storm plays havoc with our communications."

"No worries, as long as I have the information before debarkation tomorrow."

He smiled. "My dear lady, if we don't have a suspect in the brig by that time tomorrow, none of us will be going ashore anytime soon."

Yes, that was exactly what she was trying to avoid. Because as much as she was enjoying herself, she didn't want to spend more time on board with a killer than was absolutely necessary.

Chapter 19

Carly went in search of the next name on her list—Monica. As she passed a white courtesy phone, she caught sight of a familiar face.

Or rather, back.

Penny Goodnight. Talking, with her back to the passageway, one shoulder hitched as though trying to shield her words.

Carly slowed then stooped to tie and retie her shoe lace, hoping to buy a few extra minutes of listening time.

". . . snooping around. I heard it from some of the crew. Never mind who. But she's on to us. I just know it." A long pause. "I told you to stay out of sight. But no, you had to get off the ship. That was a stupid thing to do. What were you thinking?" Another pause as the singer listened. "Well, if you don't stay put, I'll hear about it. I got eyes and ears everywhere on this ship."

Carly stood as Penny listened some more, changing the phone to her other ear and using her shoulder to hold the handset in place.

"No. No. I'm not listening any more to you. Maybe you need to find yourself somewhere else to stay. Then fine. Be quiet."

Oh-oh. Looked like the conversation was about to end. She'd best beat a hasty retreat.

Which she did, just as the receiver slammed back into its cradle.

That was close.

She peeked back around the corner, but the singer was gone from sight, nothing remaining of her presence except the dangling coiled phone cord.

Well, that was interesting.

Probably the same person Penny was arguing with in her cabin when she tried to say she was watching television. An old movie, indeed! So who was this person?

As she headed toward the Explorers Lounge—where Sam said Monica spent most afternoons—she considered what she knew about mysterious people on the ship.

Or on land.

The image of the young man on top of the rocks, pushing boulders down on her and Mike as callously as guests at a wedding tossing rice at the happy couple, flashed across her memory. Dark eyes and dark moustache. Could Penny and that pickpocket be related in some way? He seemed much too young to be a love interest, but perhaps a brother. Or cousin.

If so, how did he end up on the ship? The last time she saw him before the glacier incident he was being hauled away by the police. In handcuffs. Did Penny bail him out? Then stow him away? How did she accomplish that? And who else was in cahoots with her? Because surely somebody must be.

Carly shrugged. She'd figure that out later.

Right now, Monica. Number two Barbara Ann Dawson fan to question.

And sure enough, there was her quarry sitting in a corner, her nose in a book. Carly crossed the room and sat in a comfy armchair across from the woman then waited until she looked up.

"Oh, hello." Monica laid her paperback in her lap. "Nice day." The ship took a particularly hard roll, and Monica grabbed at her coffee cup to keep it on the side table near her elbow. "Or not."

"Not a nice day for Neil Williams, to be sure."

Monica's cheeks colored. "I heard rumors. It's terrible."

"Not everybody would agree with you."

"That's a sad epitaph for a man's life, don't you think?"

Time to change the subject.

Carly smiled and rubbed her fingers on the edge of the table. "I think it's interesting that practically every surface on the ship has a small raised edge. Probably for days like this."

Monica's smile didn't quite reach her eyes. "I think I need something more than a half-inch rise to keep me stable. Especially after everything that's happened."

Carly leaned forward, elbows on her knees and hands clasped. "Sometimes sharing a problem cuts it in half."

Monica studied her for a long moment before nodding. "Maybe you're right. It's bound to come out anyway." She leaned forward, too, until their knees almost touched. "But this is all in confidence, right?"

Carly straightened and crossed her heart with a forefinger. "Promise. Apart from my husband, of course. Or if you're going to confess that you killed Neil Williams."

Monica sat back in her seat and chuckled. "No, I'm not going to do that, because I didn't. I might be a liar and a thief, but I'm no murderer."

Carly raised an eyebrow then let it slip back into place. "Someone once told me that if a man—or I guess, a woman—will lie to you, they'll steal from you. And if they steal from you, they'll kill you." She raised a hand. "Not that I'm saying it's always true. Probably just one of those Maine truisms."

"There can be a lot of truth in those sayings, though, can't there? I mean, they must stem from somewhere."

A white-uniformed server hovered at Carly's elbow. "Coffee or tea, madam?"

"No, thanks."

Monica nodded. "But not too full. I'm on edge enough without too much caffeine."

Conversation halted while her cup was topped up and she added cream and sugar then sipped. She closed her eyes. "Oh, that's good." She set the cup on the table again. "So, where were we?"

"The truth. In confidence."

"Right. They say confession is good for the soul. Let's see how I feel after this. So Neil and I knew each other from a long time back."

Carly adopted what she hoped was a compassionate expression. "I thought so."

"I was young and naïve. I thought he loved me. Apparently it's one of his many gifts, making his current conquest feel like she is, has been, and always will be the only one for him."

"Some men—and women—are very good at that particular lie. And we always fall for it, don't we?"

Is this how counseling works? Make it sound like the problem is universal, or at least personal?

"Well, as I said, he was very good. I was about nineteen, fresh out of high school, still living at home with my parents. I had a job at a bank. In the loans department. He came in one day. Right to me, like he was looking for me."

"He probably watched the bank for a while, looking for a likely victim."

Monica nodded. "He was. Told me later. But at the time, I thought he hung the stars and the moon. Hooked me in to spending every penny I had, every cent I made, and every dollar of credit I could rustle up, on him. On us, he said. And when I had no more, he told me how to get more."

This was interesting. "You robbed the bank?"

Monica chuckled. "Goodness, no. I wasn't that stupid. No, he told me how I could contact dormant account holders and get their permission to close out their accounts because it cost the bank money to have the accounts there. If there was much money in the account, I was to lie and say it was just a few cents. Well, this was an old branch with lots of old customers. Pretty soon I conned those people out of tens of thousands of dollars."

"Whew. That's a lot of money."

"Right. Then Neil disappeared, and the cops showed up on my doorstep. He covered his trail well. Never came to the bank more than that one time. Nobody at the bank remembered him. I had no pictures. Said he didn't like having his picture taken. No proof he even existed. Neil Watkins had no driver's license, no bank account, no nothing. Because he didn't exist."

"Then what happened?"

"I went to jail for eighteen months. And I've been working for the past fourteen years paying back what I stole." She leaned forward again. "But here's the good news."

"There's good in all of this?"

"I had a lot of time to think while I was in jail. About what I wanted to do with my life once I got out. If I had another chance. I knew it would be tough because felons don't find jobs easy, unless they get a break. Especially for financial crimes. I met a lady who used to come to the prison every week to talk to us gals in there. About Jesus. And I finally saw I had no hope unless I made some changes. So I started going to chapel, reading the little testament she gave me, and one night I gave my heart—and my life—over to Him."

Carly expected to hear a lot—but it wasn't this. "Wow. That blows my mind. I mean, I know people do that sort of thing, but I never knew you could do it in a prison. I mean, seems like some things are too big to get past, you know?"

Monica chuckled. "I know. Me, too. But I did. And when I got out, that woman hired me to take care of her ailing mother for the last three years of her mama's life. And she gave me a good reference for my next job. So I've been trying to make amends ever since, taking care of folks who are in their last days. Seemed it was the least I could do after stealing money from so many of them."

"So what happened when you saw Neil onboard?"

"You know what's funny? I spent the last years working on forgiving Neil for what he did. I thought I managed to do it, until I saw him. I wanted to punch his lights out. But I didn't. I prayed a lot because I really wanted to be free of that anchor around my neck. I went to his cabin the afternoon he died to tell him that. And do you know what he did?"

"What?"

"He laughed at me then said he had the perfect game for me."

"Game?"

"Yeah, it's what we call it in the con racket. A game. Like it's harmless and nobody gets hurt." Her eyes narrowed. "But it's not. Somebody always loses. And usually in a big way. And in my case, the only winner was Neil Williams. Or Watkins. Or whatever his name really is."

"Then what? Because I overheard you telling Teddy you wanted to get even for something Neil did in the past." Carly glanced around. The room was now empty of other passengers, and even the server wasn't in sight. If this woman got desperate, or violent—well, no telling what she might do. "Not that I think you killed him."

"I didn't. I just felt really sad for him. I mean, I had fifteen years of such joy and peace, until I saw him. And he hadn't changed one bit." Monica sighed. "Don't you think that's sad?"

Yes, it was. Particularly since it seemed the man had so much to make up for. "So when you left him, he was still alive?"

"Of course. When I turned down his offer, he laughed and said it didn't matter. He had a bigger fish on the hook right now, and I needed to scoot along because he had a date. He practically slammed the door in my face."

Carly nodded. "So you left?"

"I did. Went back to my cabin. Spent the evening there. By myself."

"Can you prove you were there?"

"Well, I called my steward and said I didn't want to be disturbed. That was around four-thirty."

Right in the sweet spot of the murder.

Carly stood. "Thanks for your time. I appreciate your candor."

Monica picked up her book again. "Have a blessed day."

A blessed day, indeed. Denise often said that to her.

Well, if being blessed meant finding a killer, she was about to have the biggest blessed day of her life.

$ $ $

The next four people on her list were sitting in the Acoustics Bar in club chairs overlooking the land-side of the ship as it headed south. Somewhere over there, many miles away, shrouded in mist and fog, the mountains along the shore braced against the ocean like sentinels preventing the waves from washing too far inland. In the waning sunlight exaggerated by the low-lying cloud cover, she couldn't make out any details, and hoped the captain—or whoever was driving the ship right now—knew where they were going. To her, it all looked the same. If she was at the wheel, they'd likely end up in Hawaii.

Belle looked up as she neared. "Oh, Carly. Won't you join us?"

Carly ignored the sharp glance from Bill and the roll of the eyes from Dave, and plunked herself into the lone empty chair. "Thanks. How are you guys doing?"

Dave sighed. "Fine. Just fine."

Dewey reached over and stroked the back of his hand. "I'm sad to see the cruise coming to an end. How about you, Carly?"

"Me, too. Although I must admit, it's been exciting."

Bill peered at her. "Exciting. How can you say that? A man is dead. Murdered, we heard. I must say, I don't appreciate your sense of adventure. Next thing you'll tell us you're investigating the crime."

Carly lifted one shoulder in a half-shrug. "Well, actually. . . "

Belle leaned forward. "You are?"

Dave jumped to his feet. "What right do you have? You're not a cop, are you?" He turned to Dewey. "I told you there was something strange about her. And I was right. She lied to us."

Carly counted to five to give the man time to sit, which he finally did. His wife rubbed his hand again, an endearing gesture meant to calm him, no doubt. "I didn't lie to you. Because of the storm, the Coast Guard and FBI can't board the ship. The captain has asked me to help out."

Dave clenched his fists. "Why you?"

"I've had some experience in the past assisting police with investigations."

Bill's lip lifted in a sneer. "Oh, a real Jennifer Fletcher, are you?"

Carly smiled. "Jessica. It's Jessica Fletcher. No. Nothing like that. Seems wherever she goes, either a friend is murdered or is a suspect. That doesn't happen to me. Usually."

Belle's eyes widened. "Usually?"

"Okay, there have been a couple of times but that's not why I'm here."

Dave nodded and glanced at his companions. "I know why you're here. You think one of us killed that purser, don't you?"

"No. Not at all." Oh dear, maybe she should come back later. Or not at all. Dave seemed very agitated. The question was: why? "All right. I confess."

Belle giggled. "Isn't that what we're supposed to do?"

Carly tossed her a grin. "Hopefully not. What I mean is, I don't think you killed him, but there are a couple of things I need to clear up. You don't have to answer my questions, but I think it will be for the best if you do. If you're not honest, it might cast suspicion on an innocent party. Or the guilty person could get away. Not to mention, if the captain doesn't have somebody under arrest by the time we reach Seattle tomorrow morning, nobody gets off this ship."

Dewey patted her husband's hand. "I, for one, have nothing to hide. Not from Dave, anyway. I'll tell you the truth. What do you want to know?"

"Why were you arguing with Neil?"

Dewey's hand flew to her throat and played with a string of beads. "I'm very protective of Dave. Neil really hurt him when he stole our money. And I wanted to let Neil know what I thought of him."

Carly's gaze went to Dave. "And you?"

"I wanted to give Dewey a good retirement. We worked hard and did without so we could travel. Then that scoundrel comes along and fills our head with get-rich-schemes, while he takes his twenty percent off the top, and then we lose it all." He hung his head. "Yes, it was our—my—fault for getting involved. But the stock market had gone down so much. I just saw our savings dwindling away to nothing." He gripped Dewey's hand. "But it really was our choice. Once I had it out with him and he reminded me of how greedy I was, I saw that. So you see, we had no reason to kill him."

Dewey nodded. "He's right. Neil advised us not to make that last investment, the one where we lost everything. If we had listened to him, we would have come out ahead. It was just such a surprise seeing him on the ship. That's all."

Carly fastened her gaze on Belle. "And your argument with him?"

Belle's eyes filled and she turned to Bill, who wrapped an arm around her shoulders. He whispered something in her ear, and she nodded then straightened, brushing the tears from her cheeks. "I had an affair with Neil when I was young. Before I married for the first time." She hiccoughed. "And I got pregnant. Had a back-alley termination. Ended up sterile. My first husband said it didn't matter. We could adopt. But that abortion kept the adoption agencies from giving us a baby. That was a lot of years ago, before terminations were so common. Almost a badge of honor these days. He finally left me and remarried so he could have a family."

"So Neil was blackmailing you?"

Belle nodded. "But I finally told Bill about the whole thing. He said he suspected something like that. And I told Neil that Bill knew and I wasn't going to pay anymore. So I didn't have a reason to kill him."

"And what about you, Bill? Are you her knight in shining armor, coming to her defense?"

He glowered. "I admit I was angry with the scoundrel. And I could have killed him."

Belle gripped his hand. "Bill. Don't say that."

He shook his head. "I mean it. Hurting her that way. Breaking her heart. Forcing her to do that to her body. And then taking money all these years to keep quiet about it. He deserved to die. But I didn't kill him."

"Can you prove it?"

"I don't know. What time did he die?"

"Between four and five yesterday evening."

Bill smiled. "For the first time in my life, I'm glad I got sick."

Carly's brow pulled down. "How's that?"

"I was in sick bay from three-thirty until about five-fifteen, puking my guts up. The doc can vouch for me. And the fellow they called in to clean up the place. Man, the storm and a shrimp cocktail I had with an afternoon drink didn't set well in my gut." He turned to the other three. "And they were there with me. Well, Dewey was. Bill and Belle were sitting outside." He beamed at her. "So I guess all four of us are off the hook."

Carly stood. "Thanks for talking to me. I appreciate you wanting to do the right thing.

Belle offered her hand. "I didn't like Neil, but I'm sorry he's dead."

Dave guffawed. "Well, I'm not. The world is a better place without him."

Carly left the four toasting their good success at escaping the hangman's noose, as Bill so morbidly put it.

But her suspect list was growing shorter by the minute.

Where once there were seven, now there were but two.

One more conversation, and hopefully she'd have the list whittled down to one.

When it came to murderers, one was more than enough.

$ $ $

"Well, I must say, you have a nerve showing your face here." Miss Dawson's flushed face contrasted with the orange-and-white flowered muumuu that billowed around her feet. "I shouldn't help you at all. Let you make a fool of yourself."

Carly nodded then sat in the chair at the table/desk in the author's cabin. "Thank you for agreeing to talk with me. We didn't get off on exactly the right footing, right from the start, did we?"

Miss Dawson sat with her back against the headboard of her bed and tucked the copious material around her. "We did not. I'm not sure why. But you seemed to always pick on me about my writing. In front of fans. Humiliating me."

"That was not my intention." Funny how some folks took questions and interpreted them as calling their credibility into question. "I wanted to know how a good mystery was structured." She leaned forward. "But then again, I should have asked Neil Williams about that, not you? Right?"

The author played with a string of white beads around her neck. "I don't know what you mean."

"I think you do. But let's pretend this is the plot of a book, and you can tell me if I have it right." Carly sat back. "A famous romance writer who, by the way, is very good at what she does, decides to branch out to take advantage of new readers. How am I doing so far?"

"Carry on."

"She decides to write mysteries. Except she's never written them before, and doesn't want to get it wrong. So she hires—or goes into partnership—with a writer. They agree he will get paid to write the mystery part, and she'll write the romance, because her current readers still expect a romance. So far so good?"

Miss Dawson waggled her fingers for her to continue.

"Then the mystery writer sees how well the books are doing, and he wants more money. The romance writer is desperate. If her readers learn she hasn't written the previous books, she might lose their future sales. So she says she'll give him seventy percent of the royalties instead of the fifty percent they previously agreed on. After all, she'd have none of it if he didn't do the writing. And she's still got all the royalties from her straight romance books."

"Sounds a weak motive for murder, though."

"Oh, I disagree." Carly peered at the older woman. "You see, she has her career, her fan clubs, her readers, her pride. And he's threatening to wipe it all out in a flash of anger."

"Why? If she's paying him?"

"That's just it. I think she stopped paying. Book sales were down. Readers complained that the romance felt tacked on in the mysteries, not like the Miss Barbara Ann Dawson they were used to. Costs were going up. Travel, living expenses. If she could just hold him off until income went back up, she'd pull through. And if he revealed who was really writing the mysteries, they would both suffer, so it really wasn't in his best interests to do that. And she knew it."

Miss Dawson picked at a fingernail. "So what happened?"

"The romance writer decided she wanted out of the deal."

"So did she kill the scoundrel who was holding her career ransom?"

"No. She contacted her agent and said she wasn't writing any more mysteries. Back to straight romance only."

The author's shoulders relaxed. "So when the crook is killed, she had no motive, right?"

"Right. Which lets her off the hook."

"Well, thanks for sharing that little story." The woman swung her legs over the side of the bed and stood. "If you don't mind, I have a celebration party to throw. For a party of one." She jabbed her thumb into her chest. "Me."

Carly stood and headed for the door. "If you ever think about writing that particular story, maybe you'll send me a copy."

Miss Barbara Ann Dawson shook her head, her earrings swaying in time. "No, dear, I won't write that book. You already know the ending. Wouldn't be any fun."

Carly headed to her next meeting. The author was correct, of course.

Knowing the ending was rarely fun.

Of a book, or of a murder investigation.

Because even when she was right, she still felt like she lost something in the process.

Chapter 20

Captain Lycas stood when Carly and Mike entered the Explorer's Lounge, now blocked from passenger use. At the far end of the table, Miss Barbara Ann Dawson lounged in an armchair, her lips pursed and eyes narrowed. Despite knowing the truth about the author, Carly requested that she be included in this meeting. Seated around the table like participants in the Mad Hatter's Tea Party, were Dave and Dewey, next to Bill and Belle, while Monica and Penny sat on the opposite side.

Squelching the knot in her stomach, Carly slipped into the first chair opposite the handsome captain, and Mike sat beside her, while the captain resumed his seat.

The captain slid a sheaf of papers across the polished surface. "This is a list of sailings that all of our suspects were on, if any. Bill and Belle, as you know, have never cruised before."

Bill patted his thinning hair. "I won't say we've never cruised. Just not on a ship." He jabbed Mike with an elbow. "Get my meaning?"

Mike nodded.

Carly sorted the stack, setting the pages with the victim and key suspect to one side. "I'm pretty certain I've eliminated most of our suspects.

I haven't checked out all the alibis yet, but I've narrowed the list down."

Miss Dawson tapped a manicured nail on the table. "Captain Lycas, as you know, I've solved dozens of mysteries, and I still think I am far more superior in that regard."

Captain Lycas smiled. "Thank you, Miss Dawson. I appreciate your efforts in this regard. We're sort of sailing in the fog here, as you know."

She blinked and looked out the window. "I would say you need a weather update, Captain. The sun is hovering on the horizon, ready to make an appearance."

Carly stifled a snort. Apparently the author was still in a fog. She turned back to the pages and studied the information, setting aside a couple of pages. "Captain, Penny and Neil sailed together at least seven times in the past eighteen months." She went to another set of reports. "On all seven, valuables, including money, jewelry, and passports, went missing."

Miss Dawson gasped. "Are you saying that Neil was stealing? Why, that scoundrel. I knew he was no good."

The captain cleared his throat softly. "Regardless of his character, he seems not to have been in this on his own."

Carly nodded. "Right." She ran a finger down a column then flipped to another sheet. "I also note here that Neil sailed at least once without Penny, and there were also thefts reported on that sailing. You know what that means, don't you?"

The author nodded. "It means that robbery is common onboard cruise ships." She fanned her face with one hand. "Really. I had no idea. Then again, I do the sensible thing and lock my valuables in the safe in my stateroom."

Carly exhaled. "I think it's more likely that Neil has been freelancing."

The captain brow drew down. "You mean, he was in cahoots with Miss Goodnight, then branched out on his own?"

"I think so." She glanced at Mike, who sat back in his chair, one eyebrow raised. "What do you think?"

"I must say, I'm impressed. I used to think you simply jumped to conclusions without any real sense of logic behind your reasoning, but now I see I was wrong."

She grinned at him. "Can I have that in writing?"

He glanced at the captain. "Better not."

Captain Lycas nodded. "I agree. It might set you off on a whirlwind tour of too much confidence." He sobered. "But I agree. At least on the surface, that's what it looks like."

Miss Dawson slapped the table. "Well, I disagree. I mean, Neil is a thief, no doubt. But why would he freelance? Seemed he had a good thing going with this bar singer." She sniffed. "Although why he'd take up with the likes of her is beyond my understanding."

Carly agreed she had a point. "Some people don't know when they're better off. Then again, he managed to lead another woman into a disastrous situation that impacted her entire life, and he convinced another to steal for him. She went to prison. So maybe you should count yourself lucky he didn't get you involved in something like that."

This seemed to appease the author, as her shoulders relaxed and she stopped tapping her fingers on the table. Instead, she sat back and folded her hands in her lap. "So, what do we do next?"

Carly grunted. What was this "we"? Funny how some people liked to appropriate the work of others. She turned back to the captain. "Have you searched Neil's cabin?"

"No." He stood and pulled a key from a pocket. "Let's do that now."

Carly turned to Mike. "How about you keep Miss Dawson and the others company? I'm sure she'd love to share some tidbits from her next novel with potential fans." She faced the author. "The staff cabins are really small and claustrophobic. Hardly room for one, let alone two. Can you keep Mike entertained? He's a computer programmer and doesn't get out much."

Miss Dawson looked from Mike to her and back again, apparently deciding that if she couldn't run the investigation, at least she could entertain a good-looking man.

Carly reconsidered. Then again, maybe she shouldn't leave them alone together. . .

Mike stood, tossed her a look that she couldn't quite interpret, then held out his arm to the author. "Better yet, how about I treat you to a gourmet beverage at the java bar?"

Carly giggled. No worries. Mike was a perfect gentleman.

Miss Dawson smiled. "I'd like that." She waggled several fingers over her shoulder as Mike led her from the room. "See you later." She snuggled into his arm. "We are going to have so much fun."

Another look from Mike, and he was gone, swathed in a cloud of hairspray and chiffon.

The captain exhaled. "Good sense of tact there, Carly. I was trying to figure out how to keep her occupied." He smiled. "She is a nice woman. Genuine, beneath those layers of false eyelashes and hair extensions. And I know her readers love her."

"That's a nice thing to say, Captain. You are a true gentleman."

After instructing the remaining people in the room to stay put for a few minutes, he led the way to the elevators then down to Deck One, turning to the aft of the ship, along the same corridor where Carly overheard the argument with Penny and the young man from the Space Needle.

Because any doubts she had as to that young man's identity were completely dispelled now.

She might not know his name, but she was certain the murderer and the pick-pocket were connected.

Neil's cabin was further along the passageway, almost to the end of the hallway. The captain unlocked the door, standing aside to let her enter before closing the door behind them. The room, about half the size of Carly's compact stateroom, was neat and tidy, the bed made, towels hanging at the ready beside the sink. None of the niceties of the passenger rooms were in evidence such as towel animals, chocolate on the pillow, or beveled glass mirrors. Instead, the sink stood outside the cramped water closet, fixtures were faded chrome rather than shiny brass, indoor-outdoor carpet replaced plush pile, and a folding camp-style canvas-and-wood contraption took the place of the ergonomic desk her stateroom sported.

Captain Lycas glanced into the bathroom. "I'll start here. Do we know what we're looking for?"

She shook her head then opened a drawer in the dresser. "Something that confirms our suspicions. Jewels, money, maybe a ledger. If he and Penny were in cahoots, perhaps he'd keep a tally."

Carly picked through socks and boxer briefs, disturbing the contents as little as possible. Just because the man was dead didn't mean she needed to disrespect him. Even a dirty, rotten scoundrel like Neil Williams likely had family—or somebody—that cared about him and would take possession of his belongings. "When you sent a security officer to fetch Miss Goodnight, did he mention seeing or hearing somebody else in her cabin?"

The captain quirked an eyebrow. "No. You mean she's entertaining a man?"

"What I overheard didn't sound like entertaining. Rather, I think she's hiding somebody. A young man I ran into in Seattle. Tried to pick a man's pocket and steal an old lady's purse. Got arrested. Might be interesting to know their connection."

He straightened. "And how she got him onboard."

"That too. Likely a loophole you'll want to close off."

"Absolutely. We can't have stowaways. Not only is it against national and international law, but it can pose a safety issue for crew and for passengers."

In the second drawer, Carly felt around through t-shirts and souvenirs. Her fingers touched a hard, square object about the size of—she clutched it and held it closer for inspection.

A diary.

She perched on the end of the bed and opened the small leather-bound book. The first date, about two years before, began with a description of a visit to his doctor.

An oncologist.

Neil Williams had liver cancer, brought on by alcohol consumption over the years.

Eighteen to twenty-four months prognosis.

She thumbed to the dates covered by the cruise. His entries included everything she already suspected.

And more.

"Captain, we have our evidence. Let's go confront our suspect."

$ $ $

Ten minutes later, the Explorer's Lounge felt claustrophobic. It was as though the mere act of waiting had resulted in every person in the room doubling the volume they occupied. The captain had sent the chief of security and two armed officers to Miss Goodnight's cabin, and they returned with the surly young man who said his name was Steven.

Or perhaps the feeling stemmed from the presence of not just the one additional person, but also the chief and his two officers. Mike and Carly resumed their former seats around the table, while the rest of the players in this impromptu drama—or tragedy?—sat in various stages of irritation, suspicion, or agitation. Bill kept clenching his hands into white-knuckled fists while Belle clung to his forearm. Dave folded and unfolded his arms in a restless dance, while Dewey dabbed at her nose, and Monica toyed with an earring.

Only Miss Dawson was conspicuous by her absence.

For which Carly was eternally grateful. Apparently the still-roiling seas and too many Irish coffees combined to upset the woman's tummy. She was recovering in her stateroom after a quick visit to the ship's infirmary for a seltzer.

Mike presence beside her was comforting, given the circumstances. Despite what others might think, this was Carly's least favorite part of solving a mystery: the revelation of the killer.

The captain stood and acknowledged each in turn with a glance. "Thank you for joining us today."

Steven grunted. "Didn't seem we had much choice."

Bill nodded. "Right. Summoned here like being called to the principal's office. Told to stay while you traipsed off somewhere."

Captain Lycas smiled. "Sorry about that. But as you can appreciate, we have a serious matter aboard ship."

Dewey giggled. "I don't know why we're here. I'm sure we don't know anything."

Penny tossed her a sneer. "I'm sure you don't."

Dewey tilted her head in question before leaning close to her husband.

"What is she talking about?"

Penny exhaled sharply. "See what I mean?"

The captain rapped the table with his knuckles. "As you all know, there's been a murder on this ship."

Bill shifted in his chair. "Couldn't have happened to a nicer guy."

"You might think that, sir, but it was on my watch, so I take it personally." He glanced at his notes then turned to Carly. "I asked Carly Turnquist here to assist our security chief in the preliminary investigation into Mr. Williams's murder. Turns out she has quite the nose for a mystery."

Dave's lips pursed. "She sure has no problem sticking it in where it's not wanted."

The captain acknowledged the man's comments with a brisk nod. "I'm going to turn this meeting over to her now."

Heat rushed to Carly's cheeks as she stood, all eyes on her.

Except for Steven's.

Which was just as well.

The last couple of times the man looked at her, she saw nothing but contempt and loathing.

That she didn't need.

She referenced her notes. "Thank you, Captain Lycas. So, Neil Williams. Who was he? What was he up to? And why would anybody want to kill him?"

She paused for effect, glancing at each of the suspects gathered around the table. Bill wouldn't look at her, while Belle stared, bottom lip trembling, as though ready to break into tears at any moment. Dave glared, while Dewey nibbled at a broken nail. Monica returned her gaze, high spots of color dotting her cheeks. Was she concerned Carly might reveal a confidence?

Carly continued. "First of all, I want to assure you that anything revealed to me in confidence that has no bearing on the murder, I won't bring up."

Monica's shoulders relaxed, as did Belle's.

"I'd like to tell you a story about Neil Williams." She tossed Dave a half-smile. "And you're right. He wasn't very nice."

Penny crossed her arms over her chest and huffed.

"Neil Williams lived a life of petty crime, cons, and burglary under several different names. He used people until they wised up, and then he moved on to the next pretty face or the next desperate victim." She paused to let her words sink in. "So you see, none of you are alone. You were all his victims. In one way or another."

Penny straightened. "Well, this is a nice story, but I'm nobody's victim."

"Yes, you are. You believed him when he told you he loved you. That you were the only one who understood him. You were his soul mate." She glanced around the room. Belle's eyes welled with tears, and Monica stared at her hands clasped in her lap. "As women, we've all fallen for a guy like that at some point in our lives."

Bill chuckled. "And what about us guys? You're not going to say we fell for him, are you?"

"No. In your case, your involvement was because of your desire to protect Belle." She turned to Dave. "But Neil was right about you, Dave. You were duped by him because of your desire to reap a greater investment than you could do legally. But you already know that."

Penny sneered. "Well, I had no reason to get involved with him."

"Oh, but you did. Love. The greatest reason of all." Carly paused. "Usually when a crime occurs, there really is a simple reason. Money. Or love. And in your case, both. Neil came to you with a sure-fire proposition. Make the rounds of the cruise ships. Take a little here, a little there. Not enough to launch a full-scale investigation. Just enough for victims and management to attribute to crooked room stewards or carelessness."

The singer quirked her chin toward Monica. "And what about that little butter-wouldn't-melt-in-her-mouth over there? She went to prison, you know."

Carly nodded. "I know. She told me all about it."

A sneer marred the otherwise-beautiful woman's face. "Her side."

"Enough. But she wasn't involved with Neil recently. You were."

"And how do you know that?"

Carly lifted the dead man's diary. "He told us. Right here. In the pages of his journal." She opened the book and read. "Penny is always good for a few laughs. Hooked up with her again, and put forward my business plan."

The singer shrugged. "So we were going into business."

"According to his entries, you had an agreement. Fifty-fifty split. At first. And then he changed the plan. Wanted more."

"So what? I was just going along for the kicks."

"No, you were really and truly in love with him."

Belle leaned forward. "Oh, that can't be. I saw how angry she was with him."

"It was an act they put on so they didn't draw attention to their partnership. The cruise line frowns on fraternizing between staff. They wouldn't have a hope of getting assigned to the same ship if management knew they were lovers."

Penny sniffed. "So what if we were? It goes on all the time."

Carly nodded. "And then you found out he was freelancing. Going out on his own. Taking assignments and not including you." She tapped the book. "It's all in here. No point denying it."

The woman's eyes blazed, anger lighting them from within. "So what if he did? Nothing to me."

"It was a great deal to you." Carly opened the diary to the first page. "But this is something you didn't know. Something that could have saved you from a life sentence. Let me read this. 'Doctor tells me I have two years or less to live. Cancer. How ironic. I have everything to live for, and now I get to look forward to dying. Going to work harder so I can live the last few months in the lap of luxury. Hopefully I can ditch the ditzy singer.'" She looked up. "See, the funny thing is, if you had known this, you wouldn't have had to kill him. He was going to die. Probably within a month or so."

Penny jumped to her feet. "You're lying. You just want me to confess."

The door opened and another security officer stepped in, handing a box to the captain, who looked inside before setting the container on the table. "No. We have the proof we need."

He lifted the item from the cardboard box and placed it gingerly on the table.

The base to the Faberge Tenth Anniversary egg.

Carly nodded. "The doctor already confirmed this is the same basic shape as the mortal wound on Neil's skull."

Belle's hand flew to her mouth to stifle a sob. Dave shifted in his seat, and Mike shifted closer to Carly.

Otherwise, the room remained silent as her words sank in.

Captain Lycas lifted the egg from the box and set it on the base. "Thankfully this priceless artifact wasn't damaged." He hefted the base in one hand. "But tell me why this as the weapon?"

Penny shrugged. "It was handy. I caught him trying to hide it in a lifeboat. When I asked about it, he didn't deny he was going out on his own. Didn't need me anymore. We wrestled for the base." She smiled. "I won." Then she glared at Carly. "How did you know it was me?"

"Several things. It had to be somebody strong enough to kill a man with a single blow to the back of the head. Your footprints on the deck. I saw you hiking in Juneau. I knew you were fit enough. Neil's diary filled in the blanks. Neil wanted to retire, but you didn't. He was packing away more and more of what you stole, and when he told you he wanted out, you wouldn't hear of it."

"Did he put that in his precious diary, too?"

"He did. But he didn't tell you why. Because he was already dying."

Penny laughed. "Well, now he finally did. No long, drawn-out sickness for him. I put him out of his misery. And mine."

$ $ $

After the security chief formally arrested Penny Goodnight and escorted her to the makeshift brig until docking, Carly smiled at those gathered around the table. Apart from the captain, everybody else remained as though frozen in a tableau of shock.

Or relief.

While Carly had no grand delusion that most of these folks would become her fast friends, at least they could sit in restrained animosity and watch their cruise draw to a close.

Carly nodded to the hustle and bustle of workers on the dock. "It's no wonder Penny was able to smuggle her cousin aboard. He told the captain that after she bailed Steven out on the petty theft charges, she got him into the cargo hold by carrying in some boxes, then he simply had to make his way up one flight of steps to the deck where her cabin was located. She brought food from the staff kitchen and he was supposed to stay hidden, out of sight."

Mike sighed. "But he slipped out the day we went to the glacier, and when he spotted Carly, his anger got the best of him, so he tried to injure us by rolling rocks down on us."

Dave smiled. "You sure have a lot of people who don't like you."

Dewey exhaled. "Present company excluded, of course." She reached across the table and gripped Carly's hand. "I sure am glad to meet you. Otherwise. . . "

Belle nodded. "Otherwise one of us might have been arrested for a murder we didn't commit."

Bill hugged his wife close. "So, what's next on your agenda?"

Mike shrugged. "Home, I guess."

Sounded good to Carly. "We fly back to Bear Cove tomorrow. I, for one, am looking forward to going back to work. Peace and quiet. Routine. It's why I like numbers."

Monica tilted her head to one side in question. "And why is that?"

"Because numbers never change, but people do. Although, did you hear the joke about the accountant who went for a job interview with a government agency? His potential employer asked him, 'What is two plus two?' And the young man said, 'What do you want it to be?' And the interviewer said, 'You got the job.'" She looked around the table, but not a single person cracked so much as a smile. "Get it? Two and two is always four. That never changes. But working for the government—well—"

Mike hugged her. "Time to go, Carly."

"That's my cue." She shook each one's hand and wished them well before linking hands with Mike to leave. "I really am looking forward to quiet old Bear Cove. I mean, nothing ever happens there."

He groaned. "The last time you said that, a man died."

She grinned up into his handsome face. "Well, that was just the one time."

"Just the one time? Carly, wherever you go, something happens. Why, there was the time. . ."

Yes, she loved this man.

If only he wasn't so melodramatic all the time.

To my readers:

Thanks for joining me and Carly on another adventure. I actually took the cruise described in this book, and much of our onboard and onshore activities are included for you to enjoy throughout the story. And yes, I worried about seasickness, although the storm in the book never happened. But I needed a plot point to keep the local authorities from interfering with Carly's investigation.

For those who know about maritime law, in 2005, when this story was set, there were no federal or international laws concerning cruise ships in the eventuality that a murder or other serious crime occurred while at sea. As nearly as possible, I stated the law as it stood at the time.

Bill and Belle, and Dave and Dewey, are real couples I met onboard. Their names were just too good to pass by, and I have their permission to use them in the story, although none of the other details are real to them. Thanks for the use of your names, guys.

Barbara Ann Dawson is a real person. She won a contest to be a victim, a suspect, or the killer in my next book. She said she definitely didn't want to be a victim, and wouldn't know how to be a culprit, so would settle for being a suspect. I thought that making her a writer doing research for her next mystery novel while also giving presentations to her fan club would be a neat way to bring her into the investigation while getting in Carly's way occasionally. The real Barbara Dawson bears no resemblance to my mystery romance writer/bumbling detective whatsoever. Thanks, Barbara, for the use of your name, too.

Now, stay tuned for a Bonus Section that includes the backbone of Miss Dawson's talks. Hope you enjoy this.

Leeann Betts

Bonus Section
By Miss Barbara Ann Dawson
Mystery romance author

Session 1: Introduction to mystery writing and book clubs
Greetings to all my darling readers. Thanks for coming on this cruise, and especially for taking your valuable time to join our lecture series.

As you know, a good mystery includes plenty of suspects, a killer with a good motive, a victim with a good reason for dying, and always a splash of romance. When developing suspects, we want to be careful not to give away too much too soon. But if there's one thing I hate, it's when the hero or heroine knows something the reader doesn't. So we always want to be upfront with our readers.

When it comes to finding a good motive for the killer, there are really only a few reasons why people kill other people. Love is at the top of the list, including broken hearts, unrequited love, adultery, and rejection. Money is another biggie, either trying to get it, trying to keep it, or trying to prevent somebody else from getting it.

Of course, there are instances of accidental murder, which, in our country, is called manslaughter, where we punch somebody in the nose because they make us angry, and the bone punctures into their brain, for example, killing them. We also have vehicular homicide, where our careless driving results in an accidental killing.

Power is a big motivator, either getting it or keeping it. So if a candidate for a job dies, always look to see who else got the job. We see a lot of this in big corporations and even in small, family-owned businesses.

Grief can be a motivator for murder, but usually that can be linked to love. For example, if a drunk driver kills your spouse, you might kill the driver out of revenge because the police can't nail him for what he did.

Motive is important, but so is the reason for the killing. We all likely have a motive to kill somebody who has harmed us in some way, but few of us actually do. What pushes a person over the edge to actually commit a murder? Most often, it's because they think they're smarter than the police and won't get caught. However, the surprising statistic is that most murders are spur-of-the-moment passion decisions. In this case, murderers who aren't caught never kill again.

There are also lots of different ways to commit the dastardly deed. A killing weapon, of course, like a knife or gun. Something else used in a way it wasn't originally intended, such as a baseball bat, a tire iron, or a screwdriver. Poison, drugs, asphyxiation, strangulation, exsanguination, beheading, and hanging are still common methods of killing another.

And then there's the use of whatever is at hand. A rock, a brick, a lamp. A chair. A vase. A bottle. Almost anything can be turned into a weapon. I once read about somebody who died after being stabbed by an icicle, which, once it melted, left no evidence of what the weapon was.

But enough of murder. On to book clubs. Specifically I'm talking about the kind of club where everybody reads then discusses a particular book. Most of you are likely members of at least one book club. You might meet once a month, once a quarter, or even every week, depending on how much the members like to read and how long the books are.

Book clubs accomplish a couple of goals for readers. You're introduced to authors you've not read before, which expands your reading list. Perhaps you're operating through a library, so that expands the library readership which helps their numbers, meaning they can supply more books, which is good for you and others. Particularly when it comes to a series, if you enjoyed the book, now you can catch up on the rest of the stories.

Book clubs also benefit writers. It means we get to meet our readers personally. Writing is a solitary endeavor, for the most part, and it's nice to interact with our readers, who give us insights into how our stories work—or don't—and what they'd like to see from us next.

I'll take some questions now, and then I hope you'll come back tomorrow for my next session.

Session 2: Developing Characters and Suspects

Welcome back to our second session. If you missed the first, you can find a transcript on the ship's onboard website. You don't need internet access to find that.

So yesterday we talked a little about writing mysteries and about book clubs. We had an interesting question and answer period, however, certain people seemed to hog the limelight, so we'll not have a repeat of that today, will we?

The best characters are believable. People you'd meet at a party, on the street, or in a movie theater. Characters are the backbone of any good story. The trick is to make sure we portray folks as they really are, warts and all. Creating a good suspect involves many aspects, including giving them a reason to be suspected. Without characters, all we have is a geography lesson or a book on interior design. And it doesn't matter if the characters are people, or animals, or the weather, or the setting. But the characters need to move the story forward, they need to impact each other, and they need to be changed in some way by the end of the book.

One of the biggest mistakes new writers make is to have all their characters sound alike and look alike and act alike. They all sit around talking, nodding, smiling, and grinning, but they do little else. They have no backstory, no future story, and don't change one bit.

Boring.

We don't want our characters to look and sound like little gingerbread men. We want them to do something, be something. And I don't mean they go to work, they eat, they fight. I mean, what is the purpose of their life? What are their dreams? Their aspirations? We talk a little about this on Wednesday when we discuss about their motives for what they do.

You see, people are creatures of habit and creatures of comfort. We do what we generally do, and generally we look for the easiest way to do a thing, in a way that benefits us the most. In many ways, we are selfish beasts.

And it's the selfishness that forces us to make choices we wouldn't ordinarily make. In a murder mystery, we choose to kill somebody for our own convenience or benefit. Might not make sense to others, but it makes sense to us.

As for suspects, we have to give them good reasons to act as they do. In any good mystery, the best thing to do is to have most of your characters also be suspects. This limits the number of people cluttering up your story, it gives your characters something to do as they try to prove themselves innocent—or prove another guilty. And it gives you time to reveal their backstory, their motives, and their personalities.

And now, questions?

Session 3: Investigation Techniques
Welcome back, and although yesterday's question and answer session seemed to go better, we still had some struggles. Let's see if we can be a little more sensitive to others in the room, shall we?

Today I'm going to share some of my secrets about how to investigate an actual crime. Well, not an actual crime, but one I've made up. Unlike many of those police shows you see on television, where the cops show up and threaten to take a suspect downtown if they don't tell the truth, most investigations aren't handled that way.

When a crime happens, there is a first-on-scene officer who discovers the body. That officer then calls in the death, tells the dispatcher what is known at the time, and waits for an investigator to take over the crime scene. However, this FOS officer is responsible to make sure neighbors and witnesses don't trample over the crime scene, perhaps obliterating crucial evidence. And this officer separates witnesses and suspects from each other so their stories aren't tainted.

The investigating officer arrives and appoints a crime scene officer to record names of folks going in and out of the scene, times of arrival and departure, and any evidence they find in the course of their search. Officers go through the neighborhood to canvass neighbors, while a family liaison officer sits with family of the victim to ask sensitive questions. The coroner's office shows up to pronounce time of death and to remove the body.

After all of this is done, the real investigation begins. Police officers are trained to ask questions that require more than a yes or no answer. They are also trained to observe body language, to use psychological methods of drawing out more information than perhaps the witness or suspect wants to give, and to ask the same question in several different ways to gauge credibility and forthrightness.

When I'm researching a particular story, I often use investigative techniques to ask questions of people who could contribute to my story. I employ many of the same methods the police use, even though I can't force anybody to talk to me. However, once I tell folks I'm an author and I'm writing a book about XYZ subject, I usually find they are more than willing to tell me what I need to know.

Well, that's it for today. Join us again tomorrow. Today I'll take questions only from somebody who hasn't asked one before.

Session 4: Red Herrings, Suspects, and Motives

So, here we are again. Thanks for sticking with me, and for sharing some wonderful stories yesterday about police investigations you've been involved in.

Today I'll share why it's important to provide red herrings, multiple suspects, and good motives, particularly for a mystery, although the same is true of almost any genre, including a romance or mystery romance. I prefer writing mystery romances because I like to have at least two reasons why my hero and heroine shouldn't get together. Increasing tension between the love interests can get repetitive at times by having them misunderstand each other and argue, then make up and repeat, so by I prefer to introduce a mystery that provides a little diversion, or a reason for them to spend time together, getting to know each other.

Characters, I always say, are like bread dough. You want them to rise during the story so they don't just lay flat on the page. But, people are people everywhere you go. We all have secrets to hide, things we don't want the world to know. And giving your characters a couple of juicy secrets is critical to the success of a novel.

We also want to give them a story. That's the part of their life that happened before the book began. But one thing we don't want to do is regurgitate that story. For example, in a simple love story, we don't want to tell the reader that our heroine is afraid of water because her father threw her in the deep end of the pool when she was three. Instead, we can show her not swimming with the other characters, or not venturing out over her head, or panicking when a boy pulls her under the water. Gradually revealing a secret or a fear builds tension as the reader tries to figure out, along with the other characters, just what is the heroine's problem.

Suspects need secrets and they need fears, too. In fact, they need more than the ordinary person, so we can keep them on the hook as the killer until almost the end of the book. And the killer needs a huge reason why they kill, but a reason that makes sense to them. Most of us will never kill another. A person doesn't set out to be evil, but they make choices along the way that take them down that path. A well-written killer will create the feeling in the reader that they understand why they did that, and given the same circumstances, might have done the same thing.

So that's it for developing characters and suspects. Join us again tomorrow for one of my favorite topic.

Session 5: Writing a series or a stand-alone?

Welcome back. Well, we've had some exciting times on the cruise, and I thank you for sticking with me. Now, settle back as we wrap up our last two sessions.

The decision to write a series or a stand-alone can actually come at any point during the writing of the book. In my first book, I didn't know it would be a series until I got almost to the end. By that time, I loved the main character, and I wanted to spend more time with her, so I left the ending open for that possibility. At the time, I wasn't sure I had another book in me, but I wanted to give it a try.

I've also written several stories where I knew the main character had changed as much as they were going to change, and as I already said in an earlier session, change is important. Unless you're writing literary fiction, of course, when readers don't necessarily expect that. But in commercial fiction, including romance, mystery, thriller, suspense, and fantasy, readers want to see a character improve.

Because, if you think about it, we all want to improve, right? We hope that by next week, next month, next year, we will be in better health, have more money, be kinder to our dog, get a promotion, overcome a fear, or just be a nicer person, because without that, well, life will get boring, and there will be nothing to work toward. I always say, if we didn't have the inbuilt stress of change, we'd all be cats.

Not that I have anything against cats. They just seem to have a great life. Nobody to please. Nothing to do but sit around, sleep, play, tussle with each other, eat, and lick.

But back to whether to write a series or a stand-alone. It really comes down to how big a story do you want to tell? And I'm not talking about number of words or pages here. I really mean how slowly will your character change, and how long can you draw that change out while still keeping readers interested?

With a series, your main character should probably have several areas of their life they want to change. Get over an abusive marriage. Raise children. Learn to follow a budget. Control their temper. These are all long-term, time-intensive processes.

On the other hand, losing weight to win a beauty contest is a short-term goal and process. However, maybe the weight isn't the real issue. Losing weight to develop self-confidence to enter a beauty contest—now, that's a longer deal. So look at what your character really wants to accomplish.

You'll also want to look at your main character and decide if you want to spend more time with this person. If you don't, your readers probably won't want to, either.

Stand-alones can also serve as a sweet treat for a reader, one that employs a character from a series but in a peripheral way. Already there is a sense of familiarity, but then the excitement of reading about new characters, too.

So, do we have any questions about any of this, or any of the lectures we've had this week?

Session 6: Reader Expectations

First of all, let me say once again how much I appreciate my readers. Without you, there would be no reason to write these stories. As I sit to write, I try to visualize each of you sitting there, holding my story, laughing or crying at the appropriate places. And when you contact me, I am thrilled beyond belief. One of my favorite phrases is: I couldn't put it down. You kept me up all night.

Readers have a pre-set expectation based on the author, the genre, the cover, and the back cover write-up before they ever begin reading page one. In a romantic mystery, for example, the reader expects the romance to be about half of the story, and the mystery the other half. If that's out of balance, it's not truly a romantic mystery. It's either a romance, or a mystery. Doesn't mean a romance can't have some mystery, or a mystery can't have romance.

I am careful to write what my readers expect without boring them. I am super-careful when choosing titles and book covers, because I believe that is the first step in setting up a new reader's expectations. When they pick up one of my mysteries, I want them to know this is a murder mystery with a little tongue-in-cheek self-deprecation. I want readers to know my heroine doesn't take herself too seriously because nobody else does, either. When they choose a romance, they expect a sweet story, with a little zing on the side, with a good guy and a good girl who will be together at the end. We all love happily-ever-afters, right?

And then in the writing, I want to be sure to meet existing reader expectations. I write in an Agatha Christie style because she's my favorite author. I enjoy the fact that Dame Christie didn't hide the facts, didn't try to trick me. Like her, I get a kick out of it when readers tell me they figured out whodunit right along with my heroine. To me, that's a great compliment. And in my romances, I like to use some old-fashioned words readers might not be accustomed to, defining them within the context of the story. Never too old to learn a new word, I like to say.

Some authors say that if they do what readers expect, their readers will get bored. I say, "Wrong." Readers never get bored with a good story, great characters, and a satisfying outcome. Am I right about that? I thought so.

When I keep you, my readers, in mind as I write my stories, I show that I respect you. I want to deliver what was promised by my last book, by my title, my cover, and the write-up on the back cover. From the get-go, I don't want to deviate from that promise.

However, keeping a promise doesn't mean I can't deviate from how my character might ordinarily act. Because none of us are consistent in what we say and do in all circumstances. By throwing situations at my character, I test their resolve, their moral fiber, and their steadfastness, and I force them to make choices anew. In some cases, bad choices. Because we all do, from time to time.

Thank you for your time and your interest, and I hope to see you all at another book event, or maybe even on another cruise. For sure, within the pages of my next books.

About the Author

Leeann Betts writes contemporary suspense, while her real-life persona, Donna Schlachter, pens historical suspense. This is her ninth title in her cozy mystery series. In addition, Leeann has written a devotional for accountants, bookkeepers, and financial folk, *Counting the Days,* and, with her real-life persona, Donna Schlachter, has published two books on writing, *Nuggets of Writing Gold* and *More Nuggets of Writing Gold,* a compilation of essays, articles, and exercises on the craft, as well as a contemporary suspense, *In Search of Christmas Past.*
All books are available on Amazon.com in digital and print,
and at Smashwords.com in digital format.

She publishes a free quarterly newsletter that includes a book review and articles on writing and books of interest to readers and writers. You can subscribe at www.LeeannBetts.com or follow Leeann at
www.AllBettsAreOff.wordpress.com

Website: www.LeeannBetts.com Receive a free ebook just for signing up for our quarterly newsletter.

Blog: www.AllBettsAreOff.wordpress.com
Facebook: http://bit.ly/1pQSOqV
Twitter: http://bit.ly/1qmqvB6
Books: Amazon http://amzn.to/2dHfgCE and Smashwords:
http://bit.ly/2z5ecP8

Other Books By Leeann Betts:
Counting the Days: a 31-day devotional
In Search of Christmas Past – a novel
Available at Amazon.com in print & digital, & at Smashwords.com in digital

By the Numbers **series featuring Carly Turnquist, forensic accountant**
No Accounting for Murder
There Was a Crooked Man
Unbalanced
Five and Twenty Blackbirds
Broke, Busted, and Disgusted
Hidden Assets
Petty Cash
A Deadly Dissolution
Silent Partner
Available at Amazon.com in print & digital, &
at Smashwords.com in digital

By Leeann and Donna:
Nuggets of Writing Gold -- articles and essays on writing.
More Nuggets of Writing Gold – more articles and essays on writing
Available at Amazon.com in print & digital, &
at Smashwords.com in digital

Follow us:
Donna: www.HiStoryThruTheAges.wordpress.com
Leeann: www.AllBettsAreOff.wordpress.com
We are also active on Facebook and Twitter